Dark Hollow

Published by Hesperus Press Limited
28 Mortimer Street, London W1W 7RD
www.hesperuspress.com

Dark Hollow first published 1914
First published by Hesperus Press Limited, 2014

Designed and typeset by Fraser Muggeridge studio
Printed in Great Britain by CPI Group (UK) Ltd, Croydon, CR0 4YY

ISBN: 978-1-84391-490-7

Dark Hollow

Anna Katharine Green

Book I

The Woman in Purple

Where is Bela?

A high and narrow gate of carefully joined boards, standing ajar in a fence of the same construction! What is there in this to rouse a whole neighbourhood and collect before it a group of eager, anxious, hesitating people?

I will tell you.

This fence is no ordinary fence, and this gate no ordinary gate; nor is the fact of the latter standing a trifle open, one to be lightly regarded or taken an inconsiderate advantage of. For this is Judge Ostrander's place, and anyone who knows Shelby or the gossip of its suburbs, knows that this house of his has not opened its doors to any outsider, man or woman, for over a dozen years; nor have his gates – in saying which, I include the great one in front – been seen in all that time to gape at anyone's instance or to stand unclosed to public intrusion, no, not for a moment. The seclusion sought was absolute. The men and women who passed and repassed this corner many times a day were as ignorant as the townspeople in general of what lay behind the grey, monotonous exterior of the weather-beaten boards they so frequently brushed against. The house was there, of course, – they all knew the house, or did once – but there were rumours (no one ever knew how they originated) of another fence, a second barrier, standing a few feet inside the first and similar to it in all respects, even to the gates which corresponded exactly with these outer and visible ones and probably were just as fully provided with bolts and bars.

To be sure, these were reports rather than acknowledged facts, but the possibility of their truth roused endless wonder and gave to the eccentricities of this well-known man a mysterious significance which lost little or nothing in the slow passage of years.

And now! in the freshness of this summer morning, without warning or any seeming reason for the change, the strict habit of years has been broken into and this gate of gates is not only standing unlocked before their eyes, but a woman – a stranger to the town as her very act shows – has been seen to enter there! – to enter, but not come out; which means that she must still be inside, and possibly in the very presence of the judge.

Where is Bela? Why does he allow his errands... But it was Bela, or so they have been told, who left this gate ajar... he, the awe and terror of the town, the enormous, redoubtable, close-mouthed negro, trusted as man is seldom trusted, and faithful to his trust, yes, up to this very hour, as all must acknowledge, in spite of every temptation (and they had been many and alluring) to disclose the secret of this home of which he was not the least interesting factor. What has made him thus suddenly careless, he who has never been careless before? Money? A bribe from the woman who had entered there?

Impossible to believe, his virtue has always been so impeccable, his devotion to his strange and dominating master so sturdy and so seemingly unaffected by time and chance!

Yet, what else was there to believe? There stood the gate with the pebble holding it away from the post; and here stood half the neighbourhood, staring at that pebble and at the all but invisible crack it made where an opening had never been seen before, in a fascination which had for its motif, not so much the knowledge that these forbidden precincts had been invaded by a stranger, as that they were open to any intruding foot – that they, themselves, if they had courage enough, might go in, just as this woman had gone in, and see – why, what she is seeing now – the unknown, unguessed reason for all these mysteries; the hidden treasure or the hidden sorrow which would explain why he, their first citizen, the respected, even revered judge of their highest court, should make use of such precautions and show such unvarying determination to bar out all comers from the place he called his home.

It had not always been so. Within the memory of many there it had been an abode of cheer and good fellowship. Not a few of the men and women now hesitating before its portals could boast of meals taken at the judge's ample board, and of evenings spent in animated conversation in the great room where he kept his books and did his writing.

But that was before his son left him in so unaccountable a manner; before – yes, all were agreed on this point – before that other bitter ordeal of his middle age, the trial and condemnation of the man who had waylaid and murdered his best friend.

Though the effect of these combined sorrows had not seemed to be immediate (one month had seen both); though a half-year had elapsed before all sociability was lost in extreme self-absorption, and a full one before he took down the picket-fence which had hitherto been considered a sufficient protection to his simple grounds, and put up these boards which had so completely isolated him from the rest of the world, it was evident enough to the friends who recalled his look and step as he walked the streets with Algernon Etheridge on one side and his brilliant, ever-successful son on the other, that the change now observable in him was due to the violent sundering of these two ties. Affections so centred wreck the lives from which they are torn; and Time, which reconciles most men to their losses, had failed to reconcile him to his. Grief slowly settled into confirmed melancholy, and melancholy into the eccentricities of which I have spoken and upon which I must now enlarge a trifle further, in order that the curiosity and subsequent action of the small group of people in whom we are interested may be fully understood and, possibly, in some degree pardoned.

Judge Ostrander was, as I have certainly made you see, a recluse of the most uncompromising type; but he was such for only half his time. From ten in the morning till five in the afternoon, he came and went like any other citizen, fulfilling his judicial duties with the same scrupulous care as formerly and with more affability. Indeed, he showed at times, and often when it was least expected, a mellowness of temper quite foreign to him in his early days. The admiration awakened by his fine appearance on the bench was never marred now by those quick and rasping tones of an easily disturbed temper which had given edge to his invective when he stood as pleader in the very court where he now presided as judge. But away from the bench, once quit of the courthouse and the town, the man who attempted to accost him on his way to his carriage or sought to waylay him at his own gate, had need of all his courage to sustain the rebuff his presumption incurred.

One more detail and I will proceed with my story.

The son, a man of great ability who was making his way as a journalist in another city, had no explanation to give of his father's peculiarities. Though he never came to Shelby – the rupture between the two, if rupture it were, seeming to be complete – there were many who had visited him in his own place of business and put such questions concerning the judge and his eccentric manner of living as must have provoked response had the young man had any response to give. But he appeared to have none. Either he was as ignorant as themselves of the causes which had led to his father's habit of extreme isolation, or he showed powers of dissimulation hardly in accordance with the other traits of his admirable character.

All of which closed inquiry in this direction, but left the maw of curiosity unsatisfied.

And unsatisfied it had remained up to this hour, when through accident – or was it treachery – the barrier to knowledge was down and the question of years seemed at last upon the point of being answered.

Was he living? – Was he dead?

Meantime, a fussy, talkative man was endeavouring to impress the rapidly collecting crowd with the advisability of their entering all together and approaching the judge in a body.

'We can say that we felt it to be our dooty to follow this woman in,' he argued. 'We don't know who she is, or what her errand is. She may mean harm; I've heard of such things, and are we goin' to see the judge in danger and do nothin'?'

'Oh, the woman's all right,' spoke up another voice. 'She has a child with her. Didn't you say she had a child with her, Miss Weeks?'

'Yes, and –'

'Tell us the whole story, Miss Weeks. Some of us haven't heard it. Then if it seems our duty as his neighbours and well-wishers to go in, we'll just go in.'

The little woman towards whom this appeal – or shall I say command – was directed, flushed a fine colour under so many eyes, but immediately began her ingenuous tale. She had already related it a half dozen times into as many sympathising ears, but she was not one to shirk publicity, for all her retiring manners and meekness of disposition.

It was to this effect:

She was sitting in her front window sewing. (Everybody knew that this window faced the end of the lane in which they were then standing.) The blinds were drawn but not quite, being held in just the desired position by a string. Naturally, she could see out without being very plainly seen herself; and quite naturally, too, since she had watched the same proceeding for years, she had her eyes on this gate when Bela, prompt to the minute as he always was, issued forth on his morning walk to town for the day's supplies.

Always exact, always in a hurry – knowing as he did that the judge would not leave for court till his return – he had never, in all the eight years she had been sitting in that window making button-holes, shown any hesitation in his methodical relocking of the gate and subsequent quick departure.

But this morning he had neither borne himself with his usual spirit nor moved with his usual promptitude. Instead of stepping at once into the lane, he had lingered in the gateway peering to right and left and pushing the gravel aside with his foot in a way so unlike himself that the moment he was out of sight, she could not help running down the lane to see if her suspicions were correct.

And they were. Not only had he left the gate unlocked, but he had done so purposely. The movement he had made with his foot had been done for the purpose of pushing into place a small pebble, which, as all could see, lay where it would best prevent the gate from closing.

What could such treachery mean, and what was her neighbourly duty under circumstances so unparalleled? Should she go away, or stop and take one peep just to see that there really was another and similar fence inside of this one? She had about decided that it was only proper for her to enter and make sure that all was right with the judge, when she experienced that peculiar sense of being watched with which all of us are familiar, and turning quickly round, saw a woman looking at her from the road – a woman all in purple even to the veil which hid her features. A little child was with her, and the two must have stepped into the road from behind some of the bushes, as neither of them were anywhere in sight when she herself came running down from the corner.

It was enough to startle anyone, especially as the woman did not speak but just stood silent and watchful till Miss Weeks in her embarrassment began to edge away towards home in the hope that the other would follow her example and so leave the place free for her to return and take the little peep she had promised herself.

But before she had gone far, she realised that the other was not following her, but was still standing in the same spot, watching her through a veil the like of which is not to be found in Shelby, and which in itself was enough to rouse a decent woman's suspicions.

She was so amazed at this that she stepped back and attempted to address the stranger. But before she had got much further than a timid and hesitating 'Madam', the woman, roused into action possibly by her interference, made a quick gesture suggestive of impatience if not rebuke, and moving resolutely towards the gate Miss Weeks had so indiscreetly left unguarded, pushed it open and disappeared within, dragging the little child after her.

The audacity of this act, perpetrated without apology before Miss Weeks' very eyes, was too much for that lady's equanimity. She stopped stock-still, and, as she did so, beheld the gate swing heavily to and stop an inch from the post, hindered as we know by the intervening pebble. She had scarcely got over the shock of this when plainly from the space beyond she heard a second creaking noise, then the swinging to of another gate, followed, after a breathless moment of intense listening, by a series of more distant sounds, which could only be explained by the supposition that the house door had been reached, opened and passed.

'And you didn't follow?'

'I didn't dare.'

'And she's in there still?'

'I haven't seen her come out.'

'Then what's the matter with you?' called out a burly, high-strung woman, stepping hastily from the group and laying her hand upon the gate still standing temptingly ajar. 'It's no time for nonsense,' she announced, as she pushed it open and stepped promptly in, followed by the motley group of men and women who, if they lacked courage to lead, certainly showed willingness enough to follow.

One glance and they felt their courage rewarded.

Rumour, which so often deceives, proved itself correct in this case. A second gate confronted them exactly like the first even to the point of being held open by a pebble placed against the post. And a second fence also! built upon the same pattern as the one they had just passed through; the two forming a double barrier as mysterious to contemplate in fact as it had ever been in fancy. In gazing at these fences and the canyon-like walk stretching between them, the band of curious invaders forgot their prime errand. Many were for entering this path whose terminus they could not see for the sharp turns it took in rounding either corner. Among them was a couple of girls who had but one thought, as was evinced by their hurried whispers. 'If it looks like this in the daytime, what must it be at night!' To which came the quick retort: 'I've heard that the judge walks here. Imagine it under the moon!'

But whatever the mysteries of the place, a greater one awaited them beyond, and presently realising this, they burst with one accord through the second gate into the mass of greenery, which, either from neglect or intention, masked this side of the Ostrander homestead.

Never before had they beheld so lawless a growth or a house so completely lost amid vines and shrubbery. So unchecked had been the spread of verdure from base to chimney, that the impression made by the indistinguishable mass was one of studied secrecy and concealment. Not a window remained in view, and had it not been for some chance glimmers here and there where some small, unguarded portion of the enshrouded panes caught and reflected the sunbeams, they could not have told where they were located in these once well-known walls.

Two solemn fir trees, which were all that remained of an old-time and famous group, kept guard over the untended lawn, adding their suggestion of age and brooding melancholy to the air of desolation infecting the whole place. One might be approaching a tomb for all token that appeared of human presence. Even sound was lacking. It was like a painted scene – a dream of human extinction.

Instinctively the women faltered and the men drew back; then the very silence caused a sudden reaction, and with one simultaneous rush, they made for the only entrance they saw and burst without further ceremony into the house.

A common hall and common furnishings confronted them. They had entered at the side and were evidently close upon the kitchen. More they could not gather; for blocked as the doorway was by their crowding figures, the little light which sifted in over their heads was not enough to show up details.

But it was even darker in the room towards which their determined leader now piloted them. Here there was no light at all; or if some stray glimmer forced its way through the network of leaves swathing the outer walls, it was of too faint a character to reach the corners or even to make the furniture about them distinguishable.

Halting with one accord in what seemed to be the middle of the uncarpeted floor, they waited for some indication of a clear passageway to the great room where the judge would undoubtedly be found in conversation with his strange guest, unless, forewarned by their noisy entrance, he should have risen already to meet them. In that case they might expect at any minute to see his tall form emerging in anger upon them through some door at present unseen.

This possibility, new to some but recognised from the first by others, fluttered the breasts of such as were not quite impervious to a sense of their own presumption, and as they stood in a close group, swaying from side to side in a vain endeavour to see their way through the gloom before them, the whimper of a child and the muttered ejaculations of the men testified that the general feeling was one of discontent which might very easily end in an outburst of vociferous expression.

But the demon of curiosity holds fast and as soon as their eyes had become sufficiently used to the darkness to notice the faint line of light marking the sill of a door directly in front of them, they all plunged forward in spite of the fear I have mentioned.

The woman of the harsh voice and self-satisfied demeanour, who had started them upon this adventure, was still ahead; but even she quailed when, upon laying her hand upon the panel of the door she was the first to reach, she felt it to be cold and knew it to be made not of wood but of iron. How great must be the treasure or terrible the secret to make necessary such extraordinary precautions! Was it for her to push open this door, and so come upon discoveries which –

But here her doubts were cut short by finding herself face to face with a heavy curtain instead of a yielding door. The pressure of the crowd behind had precipitated her past the latter into a small vestibule which acted as an antechamber to the very room they were in search of.

The shock restored her self-possession. Bracing herself, she held her place for a moment, while she looked back, with a finger laid on her lip. The light was much better here and they could all see both the move she made and the expression which accompanied it.

'Look at this!' she whispered, pushing the curtain inward with a quick movement.

Her hand had encountered no resistance. There was nothing between them and the room beyond but a bit of drapery.

'Now hark, all of you,' fell almost soundlessly from her lips, as she laid her own ear against the curtain.

And they hearkened.

Not a murmur came from within, not so much as the faintest rustle of clothing or the flutter of a withheld breath. All was perfectly still – too still. As the full force of this fact impressed itself upon them, a blankness settled over their features. The significance of this undisturbed quiet was making itself felt. If the two were there, or if he were there alone, they would certainly hear some movement, voluntary or involuntary – and they could hear nothing. Was the woman gone? Had she found her way out front while they approached from the rear? And the judge! Was he gone also? – this man of inalterable habits – gone before Bela's return – a thing he had not been known to do in the last twelve years? No, no, this could not be. Yet even this supposition was not so incredible as that he should still be here and silent. Men like him do not hold their peace under a provocation so great as the intrusion of a mob of strangers into a spot where he never anticipated seeing anybody, nor had seen anybody but his man Bela for years. Soon they would hear his voice. It was not in nature for him to be as quiet as this in face of such audacity.

Yet who could count upon the actions of an Ostrander, or reckon with the imperious whims of a man mysterious beyond all precedent? He may be there but silent, or –

A single glance would settle all.

The woman drew the curtain.

Sunshine! A stream of it, dazzling them almost to blindness and sending them, one and all, pellmell back upon each other! However dismal the approach, here all was in brilliant light with every evidence before them of busy life.

The room was not only filled, but crammed, with furniture. This was the first thing they noticed; then, as their blinking eyes became accustomed to the glare and to the unexpected confusion of tables and chairs and screens and standing receptacles for books and pamphlets and boxes labelled and padlocked, they beheld something else; something, which once seen, held the eye from further wandering and made the apprehensions from which they had suffered sink into insignificance before a real and only too present terror.

The judge was there! but in what a condition.

From the end of the forty foot room, his seated figure confronted them, silent, staring and unmoving. With clenched fingers gripping the arms of his great chair, and head held forward, he looked like one frozen at the moment of doom, such the expression of features usually so noble, and now almost unrecognisable were it not for the snow of his locks and his unmistakable brow.

Frozen! Not an eyelash quivered, nor was there any perceptible movement in his sturdy chest. His eyes were on their eyes, but he saw no one; and down upon his head and over his whole form the sunshine poured from a large window let into the ceiling directly above him, lighting up the strained and unnatural aspect of his remarkable countenance and bringing into sharp prominence the commonplace objects cluttering the table at his elbow; such as his hat and gloves, and the bundle of papers he had doubtless made ready for court.

Was he living? Was he dead? – stricken by the sight of so many faces in a doorway considered sacred from all intrusion? No! the emotion capable of thus transforming the features of so strong a man must have a deeper source than that. The woman was to blame for this – the audacious, the unknown, the mysteriously clad woman. Let her be found. Let her be made to explain herself and the condition into which she had thrown this good man.

Indignation burst into words, and pity was beginning to voice itself in inarticulate murmurs which swelled and ebbed, now louder, now more faintly as the crowd surged forward or drew back, appalled by that moveless, breathless, awe-compelling figure. Indignation and pity were at their height when the strain which held them all in one common leash was loosed by the movement of a little child.

Attracted possibly by what it did not understand, or simply made fearless because of its non-comprehension of the mystery before him, a curly-haired boy suddenly escaped its mother's clutch, and, toddling up by a pathway of his own to the awesome form in the great chair, laid his little hand on the judge's rigid arm and, looking up into his face, babbled out:

'Why don't you get up, man? I like oo better up.'

A breathless moment; then the horrified murmur rose here, there and everywhere: 'He's dead! He's dead!' and the mother, with a rush, caught the child back, and confusion began its reign, when quietly and convincingly a bluff and masculine voice spoke from the doorway behind them and they heard:

'You needn't be frightened. In an hour or a half-hour he will be the same as ever. My aunt has such attacks. They call it catalepsy.'

Bela the Redoubtable

Catalepsy!

A dread word to the ignorant.

Imperceptibly the crowd dwindled; the most discreet among them quite content to leave the house; others, with their curiosity inflamed anew, to poke about and peer into corners and curtained recesses while the opportunity remained theirs and the man of whom they stood in fear sat lapsed in helpless unconsciousness. A few, and these the most thoughtful, devoted all their energies to a serious quest for the woman and child whom they continued to believe to be in hiding somewhere inside the walls she had so audaciously entered.

Among these was Miss Weeks whose importance none felt more than herself, and it was at her insistence and under her advice (for she only, of all who remained, had ever had a previous acquaintance with the house) that the small party decided to start their search by a hasty inspection of the front hall. As this could not be reached from the room where its owner's motionless figure sat at its grim watch, they were sidling hastily out, with eyes still turned back in awful fascination upon those other eyes which seemed to follow all their movements and yet gave no token of life, when a shout and scramble in the passages beyond cut short their intent and held them panting and eager, each to his place.

'They've seen her! They've found her!' ran in quick, whispered suggestion from lip to lip, and some were for rushing to see.

But Miss Weeks' trim and precise figure blocked the doorway, and she did not move.

'Hark!' she murmured in quick admonishment; 'what is that other sound? Something is happening – something dreadful. What is it? It does not seem to be near here yet, but it is coming – coming.'

Frightened in spite of themselves, both by her manner and tone, they drew their gaze from the rigid figure in the chair, and, with bated breaths and rapidly paling cheeks, listened to the distant murmur on the far-off road, plainly to be heard pulsing through the nearer sounds of rushing feet and chattering voices in the rooms about.

What was it? They could not guess, and it was with unbounded relief they pressed forward to greet the shadowy form of a young girl hurrying towards them from the rear, with news in her face. She spoke quickly and before Miss Weeks could frame her question.

'The woman is gone. Harry Doane saw her sliding out behind us just after we came in. She was hiding in some of the corners here, and slipped out by the kitchen-way when we were not looking. He has gone to see –'

But interesting as this was, the wonder of the now rapidly increasing hubbub was more so. A mob was at the gates! Men, women and children shouting, panting and making loud calls.

Breathlessly Miss Weeks cut the girl's story short; breathlessly she rushed to the nearest window, and, helped by willing hands, succeeded in forcing it up and tearing a hole in the vines, through which they one and all looked out in eager excitement.

A motley throng of people were crowding in through the double gateway. Someone was in their grasp. Was it the woman? No; it was Bela! Bela, the giant! Bela, the terror of the town, but no longer a terror now but a struggling, half-fainting figure, fighting to free itself and get in advance, despite some awful hurt which blanched his coal-black features into an indescribable hue and made his great limbs falter and his gasping mouth writhe in anguish while still keeping his own and making his way, by sheer force of will, up the path and the two steps of entrance – his body alternately sinking back or plunging forward as those in the rear or those in front got the upper hand.

It was an awful and a terrifying sight to little Miss Weeks and, screaming loudly, she left her window and ran, scattering her small party before her like sheep, not into the near refuge of the front hall and its quiet parlours, but into the very spot towards which this mob seemed headed – the great library pulsing with its own terror, in the shape of the yet speechless and unconscious man to whom the loudest noise and the most utter silence were yet as one, and the worst struggle of human passion a blank lost in unmeaning chaos.

Why this instinctive move? She could not tell. Impulse prevailed, and without a thought she flew into Judge Ostrander's presence, and, gazing wildly about, wormed her way towards a heavily carved screen guarding a distant corner, and cowered down behind it.

What awaited her?

What awaited the judge?

As the little woman shook with terror in her secret hiding-place she felt that she had played him false; that she had no right to save herself by the violation of a privacy she should have held in awe. She was paying for her temerity now, paying for it with every terrible moment that her suspense endured. The gasping, struggling men, the frantic negro, were in the next room now – she could catch the sound of the latter's panting breath rising above the clamour of strange entreaties and excited cries with which the air was full; then a quick, hoarse shout of 'Judge! Judge!' rose in the doorway, and she became conscious of the presence of a headlong, rushing force struck midway into silence as the frozen figure of his master flashed upon the negro's eyes; then a growl of concentrated emotion, uttered almost in her ear, and the screen which had been her refuge was violently thrust away from before her, and in its place she beheld a terrible being standing over her, in whose eyes, dilating under this fresh surprise, she beheld her doom, even while recognising that if she must suffer it would be simply as an obstacle to some goal at her back which he must reach – now – before he fell in his blood and died.

What was this goal? As she felt herself lifted, nay, almost hurled aside, she turned to see and found it to be a door before which the devoted Bela had now thrown himself, guarding it with every inch of his powerful but rapidly sinking body, and chattering defiance with his bloodless, quivering lips – a figure terrible in anger, sublime in purpose, and piteous in its failing energies.

'Back! all of you!' he cried, and stopped, clutching at the door-casing on either side to hold himself erect. 'You cannot come in here. This is the judge's –'

Not even his iron resolve or once unequalled physique could stand the sapping of the terrible gash which disfigured his forehead. He had been run over by an automobile in a moment of blind abstraction, and his hurt was mortal. But though his tongue refused to finish, his eye still possessed its power to awe and restrain. Though the crowd had followed him almost into the centre of the room, they felt themselves held back by the spirit of this man, who as long as he lived and breathed would hold himself a determined barrier between them and what he had been set to guard.

As long as he lived and breathed. Alas! that would be but a little while now. Already his head, held erect by the passion of his purpose, was sinking on his breast; already his glazing eye was losing its power of concentration, when with a final rally of his decaying strength, he started erect again and cried out in terrible appeal:

'I have disobeyed the judge, and, as you see, it has killed him. Do not make me guilty of giving away his secret. Swear that you will leave this door unpassed; swear that no one but his son shall ever turn this lock; or I will haunt you, I, Bela, man by man, till you sink in terror to your graves. Swear! sw–'

The last adjuration ended in a moan. His head fell forward again and in that intense moment of complete silence they could hear the splash of his life-blood as it dropped from his forehead on to the polished boards beneath; then he threw up his arms and fell in a heap to the floor.

They had not been driven to answer. Wherever that great soul had gone, his ears were no longer open to mortal promise, nor would any oath from the lip of man avail to smooth his way into the shadowy unknown.

'Dead!' broke from little Miss Weeks as she flung herself down in reckless abandonment at his side. She had never known an agitation beyond some fluttering woman's hope she had stifled as soon as born, and now she knelt in blood. 'Dead!' she again repeated. And there was no one this time to cry: 'You need not be frightened; in a few minutes he will be himself again.' The master might reawaken to life, but never more the man.

A solemn hush, then a mighty sigh of accumulated emotion swept from lip to lip, and the crowd of later invaders, already abashed if not terrified by the unexpected spectacle of suspended animation which confronted them from the judge's chair, shrank tumultuously back as little Miss Weeks advanced upon them, holding out her meagre arms in late defence of the secret to save which she had just seen a man die.

'Let us do as he wished,' she prayed. 'I feel myself much to blame. What right had we to come in here?'

'The fellow was hurt. We were just bringing him home,' spoke up a voice, rough with the surprise of unaccustomed feeling. 'If he had let us carry him, he might have been alive this minute; but he would run and struggle to keep us back. He says he killed his master. If so, his death is a retribution. Don't you say so, fellows? The judge was a good man –'

'Hush! hush! the judge is all right,' admonished one of the party; 'he'll be waking up soon'; and then, as every eye flew in fresh wonder towards the chair and its impassive occupant, the low whisper was heard – no one ever could tell from whose lips it fell – 'If we are ever to know this wonderful secret, now is the time, before he wakes and turns us out of the house.'

No one in authority was present; no one representing the law, not even a doctor; only haphazard persons from the street and a few neighbours who had not been on social terms with the judge for years and never expected to be so again. His secret! – always a source of wonder to every inhabitant of Shelby, but lifted now into a matter of vital importance by the events of the day and the tragic death of the negro! Were they to miss its solution, when only a door lay between it and them – a door which they might not even have to unlock? If the judge should rouse, if from a source of superstitious terror he became an active one, how pat their excuse might be. They were but seeking a proper place – a couch – a bed – on which to lay the dead man. They had been witness to his hurt; they had been witness to his death, and were they to leave him lying in his blood, to shock the eyes of his master when he came out of his long swoon? No tongue spoke these words, but the cunning visible in many an eye and the slight start made by more than one eager foot in the direction of the forbidden door gave Miss Weeks sufficient warning of what she might expect in another moment. Making the most of her diminutive figure – such a startling contrast to the one which had just dominated there! – she was about to utter an impassioned appeal to their honour, when the current of her and their thoughts, as well as the direction of all looks, was changed by a sudden sense common to all, of some strange new influence at work in the room, and turning, they beheld the judge upon his feet, his mind awakened, but his eyes still fixed – an awesome figure; some thought more awesome than before; for the terror which still held him removed from all about, was no longer passive but active and had to do with what no man there could understand or alleviate. Death was present with them – he saw it not. Strangers were making havoc with his solitude – he was as oblivious of their presence as he had been unconscious of it before. His faculties and all his attention were absorbed by the thought which had filled his brain when the cogs of that subtle mechanism had slipped and his faculties paused inert.

This was shown by his first question:

'Where is the woman?'

It was a cry of fear; not of mastery.

'And where was I when all this happened?'

The intensity of the question, the compelling, self-forgetful passion of the man, had a startling effect upon the crowd of people huddled before him. With one accord, and without stopping to pick their way, they made for the open doorway, knocking the smaller pieces of furniture about and creating havoc generally. Some fled the house; others stopped to peer in again from behind the folds of the curtain which had been only partially torn from its fastenings. Miss Weeks was the only one to stand her ground.

When the room was quite cleared and the noise abated (it was a frightful experience to see how little the judge had been affected by all this hubbub of combined movement and sound), she stepped within the line of his vision and lifted her feeble and ineffectual hand in an effort to attract his attention to herself.

But he did not notice her, any more than he had noticed the others. Still looking in the one direction, he cried aloud in troubled tones:

'She stood there! the woman stood there and I saw her! Where is she now?'

'She is no longer in the house,' came in gentle reply from the only one in or out of the room courageous enough to speak. 'She went out when she saw us coming. We knew that she had no right to be here. That is why we intruded ourselves, sir. We did not like the looks of her, and so followed her in to prevent mischief.'

'Ah!'

The expletive fell unconsciously. He seemed to be trying to adjust himself to some mental experience he could neither share with others nor explain to himself.

'She was here, then? – a woman with a little child? It wasn't an illusion, a –' Memory was coming back and with it a realisation of his position. Stopping short, he gazed down from his great height upon the trembling little body of whose identity he had but a vague idea, and thundered out in great indignation:

'How dared you! How dared she!' Then as his mind regained its full poise, 'And how, even if you had the temerity to venture an entrance here, did you manage to pass my gates? They are never open. Bela sees to that.'

Bela!

He may have observed the pallor which blanched her small, tense features as this name fell so naturally from his lips, or some instinct of his own may have led him to suspect tragedy where all was so abnormally still, for, as she watched, she saw his eyes, fixed up to now upon her face, leave it and pass furtively and with many hesitations from object to object, towards that spot behind him, where lay the source of her great terror, if not of his. So lingeringly and with such dread was this done, that she could barely hold back her weak woman's scream in the intensity of her suspense. She knew just where his glances fell without following them with her own. She saw them pass the door where so many faces yet peered in (he saw them not), and creep along the wall beyond, inch by inch, breathlessly and with dread, till finally, with fatal precision, they reached the point where the screen had stood, and not finding it, flew in open terror to the door it was set there to conceal – when that something else, huddled in oozing blood, on the floor beneath, drew them unto itself with the irresistibleness of grim reality, and he forgot all else in the horror of a sight for which his fears, however great, had failed to prepare him.

Dead! Bela! Dead! and lying in his blood! The rest may have been no dream, but this was surely one, or his eyes, used to inner visions, were playing him false.

Grasping the table at his side to steady his failing limbs, he pulled himself along by its curving edge till he came almost abreast of the helpless figure which for so many years had been the embodiment of faithful and unwearied service.

Then and then only, did the truth of his great misfortune burst upon his bewildered soul; and with a cry which tore the ears of all hearers and was never forgotten by anyone there, he flung himself down beside the dead negro, and, turning him hastily over, gazed in his face.

Was that a sob? Yes; thus much the heart gave; but next moment the piteous fact of loss was swallowed up in the recognition of its manner, and, bounding to his feet with the cry, 'Killed! Killed at his post!' he confronted the one witness of his anguish of whose presence he was aware, and fiercely demanded: 'Where are the wretches who have done this? No single arm could have knocked down Bela. He has been set upon – beaten with clubs, and –' Here his thought was caught up by another, and that one so fearsome and unsettling that bewilderment again followed rage, and with the look of a haunted spirit, he demanded in a voice made low by awe and dread of its own sound, 'And where was I, when all this happened?'

'You? You were seated there,' murmured the little woman, pointing at the great chair. 'You were not – quite – quite yourself,' she softly explained, wondering at her own composure. Then quickly, as she saw his thoughts revert to the dead friend at his feet, 'Bela was not hurt here. He was downtown when it happened; but he managed to struggle home and gain this place, which he tried to hold against the men who followed him. He thought you were dead, you sat there so rigid and so white, and, before he quite gave up, he asked us all to promise not to let anyone enter this room till your son Oliver came.'

Understanding partly, but not yet quite clear in his mind, the judge sighed, and stooping again, straightened the faithful negro's limbs. Then, with a sidelong look in her direction, he felt in one of the pockets of the dead negro's coat, and drawing out a small key, held it in one hand while he fumbled in his own for another, which found, he became on the instant his own man again.

Miss Weeks, seeing the difference in him, and seeing too, that the doorway was now clear of the wondering, awestruck group which had previously blocked it, bowed her slight body and proceeded to withdraw; but the judge, staying her by a gesture, she waited patiently near one of the book-racks against which she had stumbled, to hear what he had to say.

'I must have had an attack of some kind,' he calmly remarked. 'Will you be good enough to explain exactly what occurred here that I may more fully comprehend my own misfortune and the death of this faithful friend?'

Then she saw that his faculties were now fully restored, and came a step forward. But before she could begin her story, he added this searching question:

'Was it he who let you in – you and others – I think you said others? Was it he who unlocked my gates?'

Miss Weeks sighed and betrayed fluster. It was not easy to relate her story; besides it was woefully incomplete. She knew nothing of what had happened downtown, she could only tell what had passed before her eyes. But there was one thing she could make clear, to him, and that was how the seemingly impassable gates had been made ready for the woman's entrance and afterwards taken such advantage of by herself and others. A pebble had done it all, a pebble placed in the gateway by Bela's hands.

As she described this, and insisted upon the fact in face of the judge's almost frenzied disclaimer, she thought she saw the hair move on his forehead. Bela a traitor, and in the interests of the woman who had fronted him from the other end of the room at the moment consciousness had left him! Evidently this intrusive little body did not know Bela or his story, or –

Why should interruption come then? Why was he stopped, when in the passion of the moment, he might have let fall some word of enlightenment which would have eased the agitated curiosity of the whole town! Miss Weeks often asked herself this question, and bewailed the sudden access of sounds in the rooms without, which proclaimed the entrance of the police and put a new strain upon the judge's faculty of self-control and attention to the one matter in hand.

The commonplaces of an official inquiry were about to supersede the play of a startled spirit struggling with a problem of whose complexities he had received but a glimpse.

'She wore purple'

The library again! but how changed! Evening light now instead of blazing sunshine; and evening light so shaded that the corners seemed far and the many articles of furniture, cumbering the spaces between, larger for the shadows in which they stood hidden. Perhaps the man who sat there in company with the judge regretted this. Perhaps, he would have preferred to see more perfectly that portion of the room where Bela had taken his stand and finally fallen. It would have been interesting to note whether the screen had been replaced before the mysterious door which this most devoted of servants had protected to his last gasp. Curiosity is admissible, even in a man, when the cause is really great.

But from the place where he sat there was no getting any possible view of that part of the wall or of anything connected with it; and so, with every appearance of satisfaction at being allowed in the room at all, Sergeant Doolittle from headquarters, drank the judge's wine and listened for the judge's commands.

These were slow in coming, and they were unexpected when they came.

'Sergeant, I have lost a faithful servant under circumstances which have called an unfortunate attention to my house. I should like to have this place guarded – carefully guarded, you understand – from any and all intrusion till I can look about me and secure protection of my own. May I rely upon the police to do this, beginning tonight at an early hour? There are loiterers already at the corner and in front of the two gates. I am not accustomed to these attentions, and ask to have my fence cleared.'

'Two men are already detailed for the job, your honour. I heard the order given just as I left headquarters.'

The judge showed small satisfaction. Indeed, in his silence there was the hint of something like displeasure. This surprised

Sergeant Doolittle and led him to attempt to read its cause in his host's countenance. But the shade of the lamp intervened too completely, and he had to be content to wait till the judge chose to speak, which he presently did, though not in the exact tones the Sergeant expected.

'Two men! Couldn't I have three? One for each gate and one to patrol the fence separating these grounds from the adjoining lot?'

The sergeant hesitated; he felt an emotion of wonder – a sense of something more nearly approaching the uncanny than was usual to his matter-of-fact mind. He had heard, often enough, what store the judge set on his privacy and of the extraordinary measures he had taken to insure it, but that a man, even if he aped the hermit, should consider three men necessary to hold the public away from a two hundred and fifty foot lot argued apprehensions of a character verging on the ridiculous. But he refrained from expressing his surprise and replied, after a minute of thought:

'If two men are not enough to ensure you a quiet sleep, you shall have three or four or even more, Judge Ostrander. Do you want one of them to stay inside? That might do the business better than a dozen out.'

'No. While Bela lies above ground, we want no third here. When he is buried, I may call upon you for a special to watch my room door. But it's of outside protection we're talking now. Only, who is to protect me against your men?'

'What do you mean by that, your honour?'

'They are human, are they not? They have instincts of curiosity like the rest of us. How can I be made sure that they won't yield to the temptation of their position and climb the fences they are detailed to guard?'

'And would this be so fatal to your peace, judge?' A smile tempered the suggestion.

'It would be a breach of trust which would greatly disturb me. I want nobody on my grounds, nobody at all. Has not my long life of solitude within these walls sufficiently proved this? I want to feel that these men of yours would no more climb my fence than they would burst into my house without a warrant.'

'Judge, I will be one of the men. You can trust me.'

'Thank you, sergeant; I appreciate the favour. I shall rest now as quietly as any man can who has met with a great loss. The coroner's inquiry has decided that the injuries which Bela received in the street were of a fatal character and would have killed him within an hour, even if he had not exhausted his strength in the effort he made to return to his home and die in my presence. But I shall always suffer from regret that I was not in a condition to receive his last sigh. He was a man in a thousand. One seldom sees his like among white or black.'

'He was a very powerfully built man. It took a sixty horsepower racing machine, going at a high rate of speed, to kill him.'

A spasm of grief or unavailing regret crossed the judge's face as his head sank back again against the high back of his chair.

'Enough,' said he; 'tread softly when you go by the sofa on which he lies. Will you fill your glass again, sergeant?'

The sergeant declined.

'Not if my watch is to be effective tonight,' he smiled, and rose to depart.

The judge, grown suddenly thoughtful, rapped with his fingertips on the table-edge. He had not yet risen to show his visitor out.

'I should like to ask a question,' he finally observed, motioning the other to re-seat himself. 'You were not at the inquiry this afternoon, and may not know that just as Bela and the crowd about him turned this corner, they ran into a woman leading a small child, who stopped the whole throng in order to address him. No one heard what she said; and no one could give any information as to who she was or in what direction she vanished. But I saw that woman myself, earlier. She was in this house. She was in this room. She came as far as that open space just inside the doorway. I can describe her, and will, if you will consent to look for her. It is to be a money transaction, sergeant, and if she is found and no stir made and no talk started among the Force, I will pay all that you think it right to demand.'

'Let me hear her description, your honour.' The judge, who had withdrawn into the shadow, considered for a moment, then said:

'I cannot describe her features, for she was heavily veiled; neither can I describe her figure except to say that she is tall and slender. But her dress I remember to the last detail, though I am not usually so observant. She wore purple; not an old woman's purple, but a soft shade which did not take from her youth. There was something floating round her shoulders of the same colour, and on her arms were long gloves such as you see our young ladies wear. The child did not seem to belong to her, though she held her tightly by the hand. I mean by that, that its clothes were of a coarser material than hers and perhaps were a little soiled. If the child wore a hat, I do not remember it. In age it appeared to be about six – or that was the impression I received before –'

The sergeant, who had been watching the speaker very closely, leaned forward with a hasty, inquiring glance expressive of something like consternation. Was the judge falling again into unconsciousness? Was he destined to witness in this solitary meeting a return of the phenomenon which had so startled the intruding populace that morning?

No, or if he had been witness to something of the kind, it was for a moment only; for the eyes which had gone blank had turned his way again, and only a disconnected expression which fell from the judge's lips, showed that his mind had been wandering.

'It's not the same but another one; that's all.'

Inconsequent words, but the sergeant meant to remember them, for with their utterance, a change passed over the judge; and his manner, which had been constrained and hurried during his attempted description, became at once more natural, and therefore more courteous.

'Do you think you can find her with such insufficient data? A woman dressed in purple, leading a little child without any hat?'

'Judge, I not only feel sure that I can find her, but I think she is found already. Do you remember the old tavern on the Rushville road? I believe they call it an inn now, or some such fancy name.'

The judge sat quiet, but the sergeant who dared not peer too closely, noticed a sudden constriction in the fingers of the hand with which his host fingered a paper-cutter lying on the table between them.

'The one where –'

'I respect your hesitation, judge. Yes, the one run by the man you sentenced –'

A gesture had stopped him. He waited respectfully for the judge's next words.

They came quickly and with stern and solemn emphasis.

'For a hideous and wholly unprovoked crime. Why do you mention it and – and his tavern?'

'Because of something I have lately heard in its connection. You know that the old house has been all made over since that time and run as a place of resort for automobilists in search of light refreshments. The proprietor's name is Yardley. We have nothing against him; the place is highly respectable. But it harbours a boarder, a permanent one, I believe, who has occasioned no little comment. No one has ever seen her face; unless it is the landlord's wife. She has all her meals served in her room, and when she goes out she wears the purple dress and purple veil you've been talking about. Perhaps she's your visitor of today. Hadn't I better find out?'

'Has she a child? Is she a mother?'

'I haven't heard of any child, but Mrs Yardley has seven.'

The judge's hand withdrew from the table and for an instant the room was so quiet that you could hear some far-off clock ticking out the minutes. Then Judge Ostrander rose and in a peremptory tone said:

'Tomorrow. After you hear from me again. Make no move tonight. Let me feel that all your energies are devoted to securing my privacy.'

The sergeant, who had sprung to his feet at the same instant as the judge, cast a last look about him, curiosity burning in his heart and a sort of desperate desire to get all he could out of his present opportunity. For he felt absolutely sure that he would never be allowed to enter this room again.

But the arrangement of light was such as to hold in shadow all but the central portion of the room; and this central portion held nothing out of the common – nothing to explain the mysteries of the dwelling or the apprehensions of its suspicious owner. With a sigh, the sergeant dropped his eyes from the walls he could barely distinguish, and following Judge Ostrander's lead, passed with him under the torn folds of the curtain and through the narrow vestibule whose door was made of iron, into the room, where, in a stronger blaze of light than they had left, lay the body of the dead negro awaiting the last rites.

Would the judge pass this body, or turn away from it towards a door leading front? The sergeant had come in at the rear, but he greatly desired to go out front, as this would give him so much additional knowledge of the house. Unexpectedly to himself, the judge's intentions were in the direction of his own wishes. He was led front; and, entering an old-fashioned hall dimly lighted, passed a staircase and two closed doors, both of which gave him the impression of having been shut upon a past it had pleasured no one to revive in many years.

Beyond them was the great front door of Colonial style and workmanship, a fine specimen once, but greatly disfigured now by the bolts and bars which had been added to it in satisfaction of the judge's ideas of security.

Many years had passed since Judge Ostrander had played the host; but he had not lost a sense of its obligations. It was for him to shoot the bolts and lift the bars; but he went about it so clumsily and with such evident aversion to the task, that the sergeant instinctively sprang to help him.

'I shall miss Bela at every turn,' remarked the judge, turning with a sad smile as he finally pulled the door open. 'This is an unaccustomed effort for me. Excuse my awkwardness.'

Something in his attitude, something in the way he lifted his hand to push back a fallen lock from his forehead, impressed itself upon the sergeant's mind so vividly that he always remembered the judge as he appeared to him at that minute. Certainly there were but few men like him in the country, and none in his own town. Of a commanding personality by reason of his height, his features were of a cast to express his mental attributes and enforce attention, and the incongruity between his dominating figure and the apprehensions which he displayed in these multiplied and extraordinary arrangements for personal security was forcible enough to arouse any man's interest.

The sergeant was so occupied by the mystery of the man and the mystery of the house that they had passed the first gate (which the judge had unlocked without much difficulty) before he realised that there still remained something of interest for him to see and to talk about later. The two dark openings on either side, raised questions which the most unimaginative mind would feel glad to hear explained. Ere the second gate swung open and he found himself again in the street, he had built up more than one theory in explanation of this freak of parallel fences with the strip of gloom between.

Would he have felt the suggestion of the spot still more deeply, had it been given him to see the anxious and hesitating figure which, immediately upon his departure entered this dark maze, and with feeling hands and cautious step, wound its way from corner to corner – now stopping abruptly to listen, now shrinking from some imaginary presence – a shadow among shadows – till it stood again between the gates from which it had started.

Possibly; even the hardiest of men respond to the unusual, and prove themselves not ungifted with imagination when brought face to face with that for which their experience furnishes no precedent.

Across the Bridge

It was ten o'clock, not later, when the judge re-entered his front door. He was alone, absolutely alone, as he had never been since that night of long ago, when with the inner fence completed and the gates all locked, he turned to the great negro at his side and quietly said:

'We are done with the world, Bela. Are you satisfied to share this solitude with me?' And Bela had replied: 'Night and day, your honour. And when you are not here, when you are at court, to bear it alone.'

And now this faithful friend was dead, and it was he who must bear it alone – alone! How could he face it! He sought for no answer, nor did he allow himself to dwell for one minute on the thought. There was something else he must do first – do this very night, if possible.

Taking down his hat from the rack he turned and went out again, this time carefully locking the door behind him, also the first gate. But he stopped to listen before lifting his hand to the second one.

A sound of steady breathing, accompanied by a few impatient movements, came from the other side. A man was posted there within a foot of the gate. Noiselessly the judge recoiled, and made his way around to the other set of gates. Here all was quiet enough, and sliding quickly out, he cast a hasty glance up and down the lane, and seeing nothing more alarming than the back of a second officer lounging at the corner, pulled the gate quietly to, and locked it.

He was well down the road towards the ravine, before the officer turned.

The time has now come for giving you a clearer idea of this especial neighbourhood. Judge Ostrander's house, situated as you all know at the juncture of an unimportant road with the main highway, had in its rear three small houses, two of them let and one still unrented. Further on, but on the opposite side of the way, stood a very old dwelling in which there lived and presumably worked, a solitary woman, the sole and final survivor of a large family. Beyond was the ravine, cutting across the road and terminating it. This ravine merits some description.

It was a picturesque addition to the town through which it cut at the point of greatest activity. With the various bridges connecting the residence portion with the lower business streets we have nothing to do. But there was a nearer one of which the demands of my story necessitate a clear presentation.

This bridge was called Long, and spanned the ravine and its shallow stream of water not a quarter of a mile below the short road or lane we have just seen Judge Ostrander enter. Between it and this lane, a narrow path ran amid the trees and bushes bordering the ravine. This path was seldom used, but when it was, it acted as a shortcut to a certain part of the town mostly given over to factories. Indeed the road of which this bridge formed a part was called Factory on this account. Starting from the main highway a half mile or so below Ostrander Lane, it ran diagonally back to the bridge, where it received a turn which sent it south and east again towards the lower town. A high bluff rose at this point, which made the further side of the ravine much more imposing than the one on the near side where the slope was gradual.

This path, and even the bridge itself, were almost wholly unlighted. They were seldom used at night – seldom used at any time. But it was by this route the judge elected to go into town; not for the pleasure of the walk, as was very apparent from the extreme depression of his manner, but from some inward necessity which drove him on, against his wishes, possibly against his secret misgivings.

He had met no one in his short walk down the lane, but for all that, he paused before entering the path just mentioned, to glance back and see if he were being watched or followed.

When satisfied that he was not, he looked up, from the solitary waste where he stood, to the cheerless heavens and sighed; then forward into the mass of impenetrable shadow that he must yet traverse and shuddered as many another had shuddered ere beginning this walk. For it was near the end of this path, in full sight of the bridge he must cross, that his friend, Algernon Etheridge, had been set upon and murdered so many years before; and the shadow of this ancient crime still lingered over the spot, deepening its natural gloom even for minds much less sympathetic and responsive to spiritual influences than Judge Ostrander.

But this shudder, whether premonitory or just the involuntary tribute of friend to friend, did not prevent his entering the path or following its line of shadow as it rose and dipped in its course down the gorge.

I have spoken of the cheerlessness of the heavens. It was one of those nights when the sky, piled thick with hurrying clouds, hangs above one like a pall. But the moon, hidden behind these rushing masses, was at its full, and the judge soon found that he could see his way better than he had anticipated – better than was desirable, perhaps. He had been on the descent of the path for some little time now, and could not be far from the more level ground which marked the approach to Long Bridge. Determined not to stop or to cast one faltering look to right or left, he hurried on with his eyes fixed upon the ground and every nerve braced to resist the influence of the place and its undying memories. But with the striking of his foot against the boards of the bridge, nature was too much for him, and his resolve vanished. Instead of hastening on, he stopped; and, having stopped, paused long enough to take in all the features of the scene, and any changes which time might have wrought. He even forced his shrinking eyes to turn and gaze upon the exact spot where his beloved Algernon had been found, with his sightless eyes turned to the sky.

This latter place, singular in that it lay open to the opposite bank without the mask of bush or tree to hide it, was in immediate proximity to the end of the bridge he had attempted to cross. It bore the name of Dark Hollow, and hollow and dark it looked in the universal gloom. But the power of its associations was upon him, and before he knew it, he was retracing his steps as though drawn by a magnetism he could not resist, till he stood within this hollow and possibly on the very foot of ground from the mere memory of which he had recoiled for years.

A moment of contemplation – a sigh, such as only escapes the bursting heart in moments of extreme grief or desolation – and he tore his eyes from the ground to raise them slowly but with deep meaning to where the high line of trees on the opposite side of the ravine met the grey vault of the sky. Darkness piled itself against darkness, but with a difference to one who knew all the undulations of this bluff and just where it ended in the sheer fall which gave a turn to the road at the further end of the bridge.

But it was not upon the mass of undistinguishable tree-tops or the line they made against the sky that his gaze lingered. It was on something more material; something which rose from the brow of the hill in stark and curious outline not explainable in itself, but clear enough to one who had seen its shape by daylight. Judge Ostrander had thus seen it many times in the past, and knew just where to look for the one remaining chimney and solitary gable of a house struck many years before by lightning and left a grinning shell to mock the eye of all who walked this path or crossed this bridge.

Black amid blackness, with just the contrast of its straight lines to the curve of natural objects about it, it commanded the bluff, summoning up memories of an evil race cut short in a moment by an outraged Providence, and Judge Ostrander marking it, found himself muttering aloud as he dragged himself slowly away: 'Why should Time, so destructive elsewhere, leave one stone upon another of this accursed ruin?'

Alas! Heaven has no answer for such questions.

When he had reached the middle of the bridge, he stopped short to look back at Dark Hollow and utter in a smothered groan, which would not be repressed, a name which by all the rights of the spot should have been Algernon's, but was not.

The utterance of this name seemed to startle him, for, with a shuddering look around, he hastily traversed the rest of the bridge, and took the turn about the hill to where Factory Road branched off towards the town. Here he stopped again and for the first time revealed the true nature of his destination. For when he moved on again it was to take the road along the bluff, and not the one leading directly into town.

This meant a speedy passing by the lightning-struck house. He knew this of course, and evidently shrunk from the ordeal, for once up the hill and on the level stretch above, he resolutely forbore to cast a glance at its dilapidated fence and decayed gateposts. Had he not done this – had his eyes followed the long line of the path leading from these toppling posts to the face of the ruin, he would have been witness to a strange sight. For gleaming through the demolished heart of it – between the chimney on the one side and the broken line of the gable on the other – could be seen the half circle of the moon suddenly released from the clouds which had hitherto enshrouded it. A weird sight, to be seen only when all conditions favoured. It was to be seen here tonight; but the judge's eye was bent another way, and he passed on, unnoting.

The ground was high along this bluff; almost fifty feet above the level of the city upon, which he had just turned his back. Of stony formation and much exposed to the elements, it had been considered an undesirable site by builders, and not a house was to be seen between the broken shell of the one he had just left, and the long, low, brilliantly illuminated structure ahead, for which he was evidently making. The sight of these lights and of the trees by which the house was surrounded, suggested festival and caused a qualm of indecision to momentarily disturb him in his purpose. But this purpose was too strong, and the circumstances too urgent for him to be deterred by anything less potent than a stroke of lightning. He rather increased his pace than slackened it and was rewarded by seeing lamp after lamp go out as he approached.

The pant of a dozen motors, the shouting of various farewells and then the sudden rushing forth of a long line of automobiles, proclaimed that the fete of the day was about over and that peace and order would soon prevail again in Claymore Inn.

Without waiting for the final one to pass, the judge slid around to the rear and peered in at the kitchen door. If Mrs Yardley were the woman he supposed her to be from the sergeant's description, she would be just then in the thick of the dish-washing. And it was Mrs Yardley he wished to see.

Three women were at work in this busiest of scenes, and, deciding at a glance which was the able mistress of the house, he approached the large, pleasant and commanding figure piling plates at the further end of the room and courteously remarked:

'Mrs Yardley, I believe?'

The answer came quickly, and not without a curious smile of constraint:

'Oh, no. Mrs Yardley is in the entry behind.'

Bowing his thanks, he stepped in the direction named, just as the three women's heads came simultaneously together. There was reason for their whispers. His figure, his head, his face, were all unusual, and at that moment highly expressive, and coming as he did out of the darkness, his presence had an uncanny effect upon their simple minds. They had been laughing before; they ceased to laugh now. Why?

Meanwhile, Judge Ostrander was looking about him for Mrs Yardley. The quiet figure of a squat little body blocked up a certain doorway.

'I am looking for Mrs Yardley,' he ventured.

The little figure turned; he was conscious of two very piercing eyes being raised to his, and heard in shaking accents, which yet were not the accents of weakness, the surprised ejaculation:

'Judge Ostrander!'

Next minute they were together in a small room, with the door shut behind them. The energy and decision of this mite of a woman were surprising.

'I was going – to you – in the morning –' she panted in her excitement. 'To apologise,' she respectfully finished.

'Then,' said he, 'it was your child who visited my house today?'

She nodded. Her large head was somewhat disproportioned to her short and stocky body. But her glance and manner were not unpleasing. There was a moment of silence which she hastened to break.

'Peggy is very young; it was not her fault. She is so young she doesn't even know where she went. She was found loitering around the bridge – a dangerous place for a child, but we've been very busy all day – and she was found there and taken along by – by the other person. I hope that you will excuse it, sir.'

Was she giving the judge an opportunity to recover from his embarrassment, or was she simply making good her own cause? Whichever impulse animated her, the result was favourable to both. Judge Ostrander lost something of his strained look, and it was no longer difficult for her to meet his eye.

Nevertheless, what he had to say came with a decided abruptness.

'Who is the woman, Mrs Yardley? That's what I have come to learn, and not to complain of your child.'

The answer struck him very strangely, though he saw nothing to lead him to distrust her candour.

'I don't know, Judge Ostrander. She calls herself Averill, but that doesn't make me sure of her. You wonder that I should keep a lodger about whom I have any doubts, but there are times when Mr Yardley uses his own judgement, and this is one of the times. The woman pays well and promptly,' she added in a lower tone.

'Her status? Is she maid, wife or widow?'

'Oh, she says she is a widow, and I see every reason to believe her.'

A slight grimness in her manner, the smallest possible edge to her voice, led the judge to remark:

'She's good-looking, I suppose.'

A laugh, short and unmusical but not without a biting humour, broke unexpectedly from the landlady's lips.

'If she is, he don't know it. He hasn't seen her.'

'Not seen her?'

'No. Her veil was very thick the night she came and she did not lift it as long as he was by. If she had –'

'Well, what?'

'I'm afraid that he wouldn't have exacted as much from her as he did. She's one of those women –'

'Don't hesitate, Mrs Yardley.'

'I'm thinking how to put it. Who has her will of your sex, I might say. Now I'm not.'

'Pretty?'

'Not like a girl, sir. She's old enough to show fade; but I don't believe that a man would mind that. She has a look – a way, that even women feel. You may judge, sir, if we, old stagers at the business, have been willing to take her in and keep her, at any price, a woman who won't show her face except to me, and who will not leave her room without her veil and then only for walks in places where no one else wants to go – she must have some queer sort of charm to overcome all scruples. But she's gone too far today. She shall leave the inn tomorrow. I promise you that, sir, whatever Samuel says. But sit down; sit down; you look tired, judge. Is there anything you would like? Shall I call Samuel?'

'No. I'm not much used to walking. Besides, I have had a great loss today. My man, Bela –' Then with his former abruptness: 'Have you no idea who this Mrs Averill is, or why she broke into my house?'

'There's but one explanation, sir. I've been thinking about it ever since I got wind of where she took my Peggy. The woman is not responsible. She has some sort of mania. Why else should she go into a strange gate just because she saw it open?'

'She hasn't confided in you?'

'No, sir. I haven't seen her since she brought Peggy back. We've had this big automobile party, and I thought my reckoning with her would keep. I heard about what had happened at your place from the man who brought us fruit.'

'Mrs Yardley, you've seen this woman's face?'

'Yes, I've seen her.'

'Describe it more particularly.'

'I can't. She has brown hair, brown eyes and a skin as white as milk; but that don't describe her. Lots of women have all that.'

'No, it doesn't describe her.' His manner seemed to pray for further details, but she stared back, unresponsive. In fact, she felt quite helpless. With a sigh of impatience, he resorted again to question.

'You speak of her as a stranger. Are you quite sure that she is a stranger to Shelby? You have not been so very many years here, and her constant wearing of a veil indoors and out is very suspicious.'

'So I'm beginning to think. And there is something else, judge, which makes me suspect you may be quite correct about her not being an entire stranger here. She knows this house too well.'

The judge started. The strength of his self-control had relaxed a bit, and he showed in the look he cast about him what it had cost him to enter these doors.

'It is not the same, of course,' continued Mrs Yardley, affected in a peculiar way by the glimpse she had caught of the other's emotion unnatural and incomprehensible as it appeared to her. 'The place has been greatly changed, but there is a certain portion of the old house left which only a person who knew it as it originally was would be apt to find; and yesterday, on going into one of these remote rooms I came upon her sitting in one of the windows looking out. How she got there or why she went, I cannot tell you. She didn't choose to tell me, and I didn't ask. But I've not felt real easy about her since.'

'Excuse me, Mrs Yardley, it may be a matter of no moment, but do you mind telling me where this room is?'

'It's on the top floor, sir; and it looks out over the ravine. Perhaps she was spying out the path to your house.'

The judge's face hardened. He felt baffled and greatly disturbed; but he spoke kindly enough when he again addressed Mrs Yardley:

'I am as ignorant as you of this woman's personality and of her reasons for intruding into my presence this morning. But there is something so peculiar about this presumptuous attempt of hers at an interview, that I feel impelled to inquire into it more fully, even if I have to approach the only source of information capable of giving me what I want – that is, herself. Mrs Yardley, will you procure me an immediate interview with this woman? I am sure that you can be relied upon to do this and to do it with caution. You have the countenance of a woman unusually discreet.'

The subtle flattery did its work. She was not blind to the fact that he had introduced it for that very purpose, but it was not in her nature to withstand any appeal from so exalted a source however made. Lifting her eyes fearlessly to his, she responded earnestly:

'I am proud to serve you. I will see what I can do. Will you wait here for just a few minutes?'

He bowed quietly enough; but he was very restless when once he found himself alone. Those few minutes of waiting seemed interminable to him. Would the woman come? Was she as anxious to see him now as she had been in the early morning? Much depended on her mood, but more on the nature of the errand which had taken her into his house. If that errand was a vital one, he would soon hear her steps; indeed, he was hearing her steps now – he was sure of it. Those of Mrs Yardley were quicker, shorter, more businesslike. These, now advancing through the corridor, lingered as if held back by dread or a fateful indecision.

He would fain hasten them, but discretion forbade.

They faltered, turned, then, in an instant, all hesitation was lost in purpose and they again advanced this time to the threshold. Judge Ostrander had just time to brace himself to meet the unknown, when the door fell back and the woman of the morning appeared in the opening.

With Her Veil Down

On the instant he recognised that no common interview lay before him. She was still the mysterious stranger, and she still wore her veil – a fact all the more impressive that it was no longer the accompaniment of a hat, but flung freely over her bare head. He frowned as he met her eyes through this disguising gauze. This attempt at an incognito for which there seemed to be no adequate reason, had a theatrical look wholly out of keeping with the situation. But he made no allusion to it, nor was the bow with which he acknowledged her presence and ushered her into the room, other than courteous. Nevertheless, she was the first to speak.

'This is very good of you, Judge Ostrander,' she remarked, in a voice both cultured and pleasant. 'I could hardly have hoped for this honour. After what happened this morning at your house, I feared that my wish for an interview would not only be disregarded by you, but that you would utterly refuse me the privilege of seeing you. I own to feeling greatly relieved. Such consideration shown to a stranger, argues a spirit of unusual kindliness.'

A tirade. He simply bowed.

'Or perhaps I am mistaken in my supposition,' she suggested, advancing a step, but no more. 'Perhaps I am no stranger to you? Perhaps you know my name?'

'Averill? No.'

She paused, showing her disappointment quite openly. Then drawing up a chair, she leaned heavily on its back, saying in low, monotonous tones from which the former eager thrill had departed:

'I see that the intended marriage of your son has made very little impression upon you.'

Aghast for the moment, this was such a different topic from the one he expected, the judge regarded her in silence before remarking:

'I have known nothing of it. My son's concerns are no longer mine. If you have broken into my course of life for no other purpose than to discuss the affairs of Oliver Ostrander, I must beg you to excuse me. I have nothing to say in his connection to you or to anyone.'

'Is the breach between you so deep as that!'

This she said in a low tone and more as if to herself than to him. Then, with a renewal of courage indicated by the steadying of her form and a spirited uplift of her head, she observed with a touch of command in her voice:

'There are some things which must be discussed whatever our wishes or preconceived resolves. The separation between you and Mr Oliver Ostrander cannot be so absolute (since whatever your cause of complaint you are still his father and he your son) that you will allow his whole life's happiness to be destroyed for the lack of a few words between yourself and me.'

He had made his bow, and he now proceeded to depart, severity in his face and an implacable resolution in his eye. But some impulse made him stop; some secret call from deeply hidden, possibly unrecognised, affections gave him the will to say:

'A plea uttered through a veil is like an unsigned message. It partakes too much of the indefinite. Will you lift your veil, madam?'

'In a minute,' she assured him. 'The voice can convey truth as certainly as the features. I will not deny you a glimpse of the latter after you have heard my story. Will you hear it, judge? Issues of no common importance hang upon your decision. I entreat – but no, you are a just man; I will rely upon your sense of right. If your son's happiness fails to appeal to you, let that of a young and innocent girl lovely as few are lovely either in body or mind.'

'Yourself, madam?'

'No, my daughter! Oliver Ostrander has done us that honour, sir. He had every wish and had made every preparation to marry my child, when – shall I go on?'

'You may.'

It was shortly said, but a burden seemed to fall from her shoulders at its utterance. Her whole graceful form relaxed swiftly into its natural curves, and an atmosphere of charm from this moment enveloped her, which justified the description of Mrs Yardley, even without a sight of the features she still kept hidden.

'I am a widow, sir.' Thus she began with studied simplicity. 'With my one child I have been living in Detroit these many years, – ever since my husband's death, in fact. We are not unliked there, nor have we lacked respect. When some six months ago, your son, who stands high in everyone's regard, as befits his parentage and his varied talents, met my daughter and fell seriously in love with her, no one, so far as I know, criticised his taste or found fault with his choice. I was happy, after many years of anxiety; for I idolised my child and I had suffered from many apprehensions as to her future. Not that I had the right to be happy; I see that now. A woman with a secret – and my heart held a woeful and desperate one – should never feel that that secret lacks power to destroy her because it has long lain quiescent. I thought my child safe, and rejoiced as any woman might rejoice, and as I would rejoice now, if Fate were to obliterate that secret and emancipate us all from the horror of it.'

She paused, waiting for some acknowledgment of his interest, but not getting it, went on bitterly enough, for his stolidity was a very great mystery to her:

'And she was safe, to all appearance, up to the very morning of her marriage – the marriage of which you say you had received no intimation though Oliver seems a very dutiful son.'

'Madam!' – the hoarseness of his tone possibly increased its peremptory character – 'I really must ask you to lay aside your veil.'

It was a rebuke and she felt it to be so; but though she blushed behind her veil, she did not remove it.

'Pardon me,' she begged and very humbly, 'but I cannot yet. You will see why later. Let me reveal my secret first. I am coming to it, Judge Ostrander; I cannot keep it back much longer.'

He was too much of a gentleman to insist upon his wishes, but she saw by the gloom of his eye and a certain nervous twitching of his hands that it was not from mere impassiveness that his features had acquired their rigidity. Smitten with compunction, she altered her tone into one more deprecatory:

'My story will be best told,' she now said, 'if I keep all personal element out of it. You must imagine Reuther, dressed in her wedding finery, waiting for her bridegroom to take her to church. We were sitting, she and I, in our little parlour, watching the clock – for it was very near the hour. At times, her face turned towards me for a brief moment, and I felt all the pang of motherhood again, for her loveliness was not of this earth but of a land where there is no sin, no – there! the memory was a little too much for me, sir; but I'll not transgress again; the future holds too many possibilities of suffering for me to dwell upon the past. She was lovely and her loveliness sprang from a pure hope. We will let that suffice, and what I dreaded was not what happened, inexcusable as such blindness and presumption may appear in a woman who has had her troubles and seen the desperate side of life.

'A carriage had driven up; and we heard his step; but it was not the step of a bridegroom, Judge Ostrander, nor was the gentleman he left behind him at the kerb, the friend who was to stand up with him. To Reuther, innocent of all deception, this occasioned only surprise, but to me it meant the end of Reuther's marriage and of my own hopes. I shrank from the ordeal and stood with my back half turned when, dashed by his own emotions, he bounded into our presence.

'One look my way and his question was answered before he put it. Judge Ostrander, the name under which I had lived in

Detroit was not my real one. I had let him court and all but marry my daughter, without warning him in any way of what this deception on my part covered. But others – one other, I have reason now to believe – had detected my identity under the altered circumstances of my new life, and surprised him with the news at this late hour. We are – Judge Ostrander, you know who we are. This is not the first time you and I have seen each other face to face.' And lifting up a hand, trembling with emotion, she put aside her veil.

With Her Veil Lifted

'Mrs –'

'You recognise me?'

'Too well.' The tone was deep with meaning but there was no accusation in it; nor was there any note of relief. It was more as if some hope deeply, and perhaps unconsciously, cherished had suffered a sudden and complete extinction.

The change this made in him was too perceptible for her not to observe it. The shadow lying deep in her eyes now darkened her whole face. She had tried to prepare him for this moment; tried to prepare herself. But who can prepare the soul for the return of old troubles or make other than startling the resurrection of a ghost laid, as men thought, forever?

'You see that it was no fault of my own I was trying to hide,' she finally remarked in her rich and sympathetic voice.

'Put back your veil.'

It was all he said.

Trembling she complied, murmuring as she fumbled with its folds:

'Disgrace to an Ostrander! I know that I was mad to risk it for a moment. Forgive me for the attempt, and listen to my errand. Oliver was willing to marry my child, even after he knew the shame it would entail. But Reuther would not accept the sacrifice. When she learned, as she was obliged to now, that her father had not only been sentenced to death for the worst crime in the calendar, but had suffered the full penalty, leaving only a legacy of eternal disgrace to his wife and innocent child, she showed a spirit becoming a better parentage. In his presence, and in spite of his dissuasions (for he acted with all the nobility one might expect) she took off her veil with her own hands and laid it aside with a look expressive of eternal renunciation. She loves him, sir; and there is no selfishness in her heart and never has been. For all her frail appearance and the mildness of her temper, she is like flint where principle is involved or the welfare of those she loves is at stake. My daughter may die from shock or shame, but she will never cloud your son's prospects with the obloquy which has settled over her own. Judge Ostrander, I am not worthy of such a child, but such she is. If John –'

'We will not speak his name,' broke in Judge Ostrander, assuming a peremptory bearing quite unlike his former one of dignified reserve. 'I should like to hear, instead, your explanation of how my son became inveigled into an engagement of which you, if no one else, knew the preposterous nature.'

'Judge Ostrander, you do right to blame me. I should never have given my consent, never. But I thought our past so completely hidden – our identity so entirely lost under the accepted name of Averill.'

'You thought!' He towered over her in his anger. He looked and acted as in the old days, when witnesses cowered under his eye and voice. 'Say that you knew, madam; that you planned this unholy trap for my son. You had a pretty daughter, and you saw to it that she came under his notice; nay, more, ignoring the claims of decency, you allowed the folly to proceed, if you did not help it on in your misguided ambition to marry your daughter well.'

'Judge Ostrander, I did not plan their meeting, nor did I at first encourage his addresses. Not till I saw the extent of their mutual attachment, did I yield to the event and accept the consequences. But I was wrong, wholly wrong to allow him to visit her a second time; but now that the mischief is done –'

Judge Ostrander was not listening.

'I have a question to put you,' said he, when he realised that she had ceased speaking. 'Oliver was never a fool. When he was told who your daughter was, what did he say of the coincidence which made him the lover of the woman against whose father, his father had uttered a sentence of death? Didn't he marvel and call it extraordinary – the work of the devil?'

'Possibly; but if he did, it was not in any conversation he had with me.'

'Detroit is a large city and must possess hundreds of sweet young girls within its borders. Could he contemplate without wonder the fact that he had been led to the door of the one above all others between whom and himself Fate had set such an insurmountable barrier? He must have been struck deeply by the coincidence; he must have been, madam.'

Astonished at his manner, at the emphasis he placed upon this point which seemed to her so much less serious than many others, she regarded him doubtfully before saying:

'I was if he was not. From the very first I wondered. But I got used to the fact during the five months of his courtship. And I got used to another fact too; that my secret was safe so far as it ran the risk of being endangered by a meeting with yourself. Mr Ostrander made it very plain to us that we need never expect to see you in Detroit.'

'He did? Did he offer any explanation for this lack of – of sympathy between us?'

'Never. It was a topic he forbore to enter into and I think he only said what he did, to prevent any expectations on our part of ever seeing you.'

'And your daughter? Was he as close-mouthed in speaking of me to her as he was to you?'

'I have no doubt of it. Reuther betrays no knowledge of you or of your habits, and has never expressed but one curiosity in your regard. As you can imagine what that is, I will not mention it.'

'You are at liberty to. I have listened to much and can well listen to a little more.'

'Judge, she is of a very affectionate nature and her appreciation of your son's virtues is very great. Though her conception of yourself is naturally a very vague one, it is only to be expected that she should wonder how you could live so long without a visit from Oliver.'

Expectant as he was of this reply, and resolved as he was, to hear it unmoved, he had miscalculated his strength or his power of concealment, for he turned aside immediately upon hearing it, and walked away from her towards the further extremity of the room. Covertly she watched him; first through her veil, and then with it partly removed. She did not understand his mood; and she hardly understood her own. When she entered upon this interview, her mind had been so intent upon one purpose that it seemed to absorb all her faculties and reach every corner of her heart; yet here she was, after the exchange of many words between them, with her purpose uncommunicated and her heart unrelieved, staring at him not in the interest of her own griefs, but in commiseration of his.

Yet when he faced her once more every thought vanished from her mind save the one which had sustained her through the extraordinary measures she had taken to secure herself this opportunity of presenting her lost cause to the judgement of the only man from whom she could expect aid.

But her impulse was stayed and her thoughts sent wandering again by the penetrating look he gave her before she let her veil fall again.

'How long have you been in Detroit?' he asked.

'Ever since –'

'And how old is Reuther?'

'Eighteen, but –'

'Twelve years ago, then.' He paused and glanced about him before adding, 'She was about the age of the child you brought to my house today.'

'Yes, sir, very nearly.'

His lips took a strange twist. There was self-contempt in it, and some other very peculiar and contradictory emotion. But when this semblance of a smile had passed, it was no longer Oliver's father she saw before her, but the county's judge. Even his tone partook of the change as he dryly remarked:

'What you have told me concerning your daughter and my son is very interesting. But it was not for the simple purpose of informing me that this untoward engagement was at an end that you came to Shelby. You have another purpose. What is it? I can remain with you just five minutes longer.'

Five minutes! It only takes one to kill a hope but five are far too few for the reconstruction of one. But she gave no sign of her secret doubts, as she plunged at once into her subject.

'I will be brief,' said she; 'as brief as any mother can be who is pleading for her daughter's life as well as happiness. Reuther has no real ailment, but her constitution is abnormally weak, and she will die of this grief if some miracle does not save her. Strong as her will is, determined as she is to do her duty at all cost, she has very little physical stamina. See! here is her photograph taken but a short time ago. Look at it I beg. See what she was like when life was full of hope; and then imagine her with all hope eliminated.'

'Excuse me. What use? I can do nothing. I am very sorry for the child, but –' His very attitude showed his disinclination to look at the picture.

But she would not be denied. She thrust it upon him and once his eyes had fallen upon it, they clung there though evidently against his will. Ah, she knew that Reuther's exquisite countenance would plead for itself! God seldom grants to such beauty, so lovely a spirit. If the features themselves failed to appeal, certainly he must feel the charm of an expression which had already netted so many hearts. Breathlessly she watched him, and, as she watched, she noted the heavy lines carved in his face by thought and possibly by sorrow, slowly relax and his eyes fill with a wistful tenderness.

In the egotism of her relief, she thought to deepen the impression she had made by one vivid picture of her daughter as she was now. Mistaking his temperament or his story, classing him in with other strong men, the well of whose feeling once roused overflows in sympathetic emotion, she observed very gently but, as she soon saw, unwisely:

'Such delicacy can withstand a blow, but not a steady heart-break. When, on that dreadful night I crept in from my sleepless bed to see how my darling was bearing her long watch, this was what I saw. She had not moved, no, not an inch in the long hours which had passed since I left her. She had not even stirred the hand from which, at her request, I had myself drawn her engagement ring. I doubt even if her lids had shut once over her strained and wide-staring eyes. It was as if she were laid out for her grave –'

'Madam!'

The harsh tone recalled her to herself. She took back the picture he was holding towards her and was hardly surprised when he said:

'Parents must learn to endure bitterness. I have not been exempt myself from such. Your child will not die. You have years of mutual companionship before you, while I have nothing. And now let us end this interview so painful to both. You have said –'

'No,' she broke in with sudden vehemence, all the more startling from the restraint in which she had held herself up to this moment, 'I have not said – I have not begun to say what seethes like a consuming fire in my breast. Judge Ostrander, I do not know what has estranged you from Oliver. It must be something serious; for you are both good men. But whatever it is, of this I am certain: you would not wilfully deliver an innocent child like mine to a wretched fate which a well-directed effort might avert. I spoke of a miracle – will you not listen, judge? I am not wild; I am not unconscious of presumption. I am only in earnest, in deadly earnest. A miracle is possible. The gulf between these two may yet be spanned. I see a way –'

What change was this to which she had suddenly become witness? The face which had not lost all its underlying benignancy even when it looked its coldest, had now become settled and hard. His manner was absolutely repellent as he broke in with the quick disclaimer:

'But there is no way. What miracle could ever make your daughter, lovely as she undoubtedly is, a fitting match for my son! None, madam, absolutely none. Such an alliance would be monstrous; unnatural.'

'Why?' The word came out boldly. If she was intimidated by this unexpected attack from a man accustomed to deference and altogether able to exact it, she did not show it. 'Because her father died the death of a criminal?' she asked.

The answer was equally blunt:

'Yes; a criminal over whose trial his father presided as judge.'

Was she daunted? No. Quick as a flash came the retort.

'A judge, however, who showed him every consideration possible. I was told at the time and I have been assured by many since that you were more than just to him in your rulings. Such a memory creates a bond of gratitude, not hate. Judge Ostrander,' – he had taken a step towards the hall-door; but he paused at this utterance of his name – 'answer me this one question. Why did you do this? As his widow, as the mother of his child, I implore you to tell me why you showed him this leniency? You must have hated him deeply –'

'Yes. I have never hated anyone more.'

'The slayer of your dearest friend; of your inseparable companion; of the one person who stood next to your son in your affections and regard!'

He put up his hand. The gesture, the way he turned his face aside showed that she had touched the raw of a wound still unhealed. Insensibly, the woman in her responded to this evidence of an undying sorrow, and modulating her voice, she went on, with just a touch of the subtle fascination which made her always listened to:

'Your feeling for Mr Etheridge was well known. Then why such magnanimity towards the man who stood on trial for killing him?'

Unaccustomed to be questioned, though living in an atmosphere of continual yes and no, he stared at the veiled features of one who so dared, as if he found it hard to excuse such presumption. But he answered her nevertheless, and with decided emphasis:

'Possibly because his victim was my friend and lifelong companion. A judge fears his own prejudices.'

'Possibly; but you had another reason, judge; a reason which justified you in your own eyes at the time and which justifies you in mine now and always. Am I not right? This is no courtroom; the case is one of the past; it can never be reopened; the prisoner is dead. Answer me then, as one sorrowing mortal replies to another, hadn't you another reason?'

The judge, panoplied though he was or thought he was, against all conceivable attack, winced at this repetition of a question he had hoped to ignore, and in his anxiety to hide this involuntary betrayal of weakness, allowed his anger to have full vent, as he cried out in no measured terms:

'What is the meaning of all this? What are you after? Why are you raking up these bygones which only make the present condition of affairs darker and more hopeless? You say that you know some way of making the match between your daughter and my son feasible and proper. I say that nothing can do this. Fact – the sternest of facts is against it. If you found a way, I shouldn't accept it. Oliver Ostrander, under no circumstances and by means of no sophistries, can ever marry the daughter of John Scoville. I should think you would see that for yourself.'

'But if John should be proved to have suffered wrongfully? If he should be shown to have been innocent?'

'Innocent?'

'Yes. I have always had doubts of his guilt, even when circumstances bore most heavily against him; and now, as I look back upon the trial and remember certain things, I feel sure that you had doubts of it, yourself.'

His rebuke was quick, instant. With a force and earnestness which recalled the courtroom he replied:

'Madam, your hopes and wishes have misled you. Your husband was a guilty man; as guilty a man as any judge ever passed sentence upon.'

'Oh!' she wailed forth, reeling heavily back and almost succumbing to the shock, she had so thoroughly convinced herself that what she said was true. But hers was a courageous soul. She rallied instantly and approaching him again with face uncovered and her whole potent personality alive with magnetism, she retorted:

'You say that, eye to my eye, hand on my hand, heart beating with my heart above the grave of our children's mutual happiness?'

'I do.'

Convinced; for there was no wavering in his eye, no trembling in the hand she had clasped; convinced but ready notwithstanding to repudiate her own convictions, so much of the mother-passion, if not the wife's, tugged at her heart, she remained immovable for a moment, waiting for the impossible, hoping against hope for a withdrawal of his words and the re-illumination of hope. Then her hand fell away from his; she gave a great sob, and, lowering her head, muttered:

'John Scoville smote down Algernon Etheridge! O God! O God! what horror!'

A sigh from her one auditor welled up in the silence, holding a note which startled her erect and brought back a memory which drove her again into passionate speech:

'But he swore the day I last visited him in the prison, with his arms pressed tight about me and his eye looking straight into mine as you are looking now, that he never struck that blow.

I did not believe him then, there were too many dark spots in my memory of old lies premeditated and destructive of my happiness; but I believed him later, and I believe him now.'

'Madam, this is quite unprofitable. A jury of his peers condemned him as guilty and the law compelled me to pass sentence upon him. That his innocent child should be forced, by the inexorable decrees of fate, to suffer for a father's misdoing, I regret as much, perhaps more, than you do; for my son – beloved, though irreconcilably separated from me – suffers with her, you say. But I see no remedy; no remedy, I repeat. Were Oliver to forget himself so far as to ignore the past and marry Reuther Scoville, a stigma would fall upon them both for which no amount of domestic happiness could ever compensate. Indeed, there can be no domestic happiness for a man and woman so situated. The inevitable must be accepted. Madam, I have said my last word.'

'But not heard mine,' she panted. 'For me to acknowledge the inevitable where my daughter's life and happiness are concerned would make me seem a coward in my own eyes. Helped or unhelped, with the sympathy or without the sympathy of one who I hoped would show himself my friend, I shall proceed with the task to which I have dedicated myself. You will forgive me, judge. You see that John's last declaration of innocence goes further with me than your belief, backed as it is by the full weight of the law.'

Gazing at her as at one gone suddenly demented, he said:

'I fail to understand you, Mrs – I will call you Mrs Averill. You speak of a task. What task?'

'The only one I have heart for: the proving that Reuther is not the child of a wilful murderer; that another man did the deed for which he suffered. I can do it. I feel confident that I can do it; and if you will not help me –'

'Help you! After what I have said and reiterated that he is guilty, guilty, guilty?'

Advancing upon her with each repetition of the word, he towered before her, an imposing, almost formidable figure. Where was her courage now? In what pit of despair had it finally gone down? She eyed him fascinated, feeling her inconsequence and all the madness of her romantic, ill-digested effort, when from somewhere in the maze of confused memories there came to her a cry, not of the disappointed heart but of a daughter's shame, and she saw again the desperate, haunted look with which the stricken child had said in answer to some plea, 'A criminal's daughter has no place in this world but with the suffering and the lost'; and nerved anew, she faced again his anger which might well be righteous, and with almost preternatural insight, boldly declared:

'You are too vehement to quite convince me, Judge Ostrander. Acknowledge it or not, there is more doubt than certainty in your mind; a doubt which ultimately will lead you to help me. You are too honest not to. When you see that I have some reason for the hopes I express, your sense of justice will prevail and you will confide to me the point untouched or the fact unmet, which has left this rankling dissatisfaction to fester in your mind. That known, my way should broaden; a way, at the end of which I see a united couple – my daughter and your son. Oh, she is worthy of him –' the woman broke forth, as he made another repellent and imperative gesture. 'Ask anyone in the town where we have lived.'

Abruptly, and without apology for his rudeness, Judge Ostrander again turned his back and walked away from her to an old-fashioned bookcase which stood in one corner of the room. Halting mechanically before it, he let his eyes roam up and down over the shelves, seeing nothing, as she was well aware, but weighing, as she hoped, the merits of the problem she had propounded him. She was, therefore, unduly startled when with a quick whirl about which brought him face to face with her once more, he impetuously asked:

'Madam, you were in my house this morning. You came in through a gate which Bela had left unlocked. Will you explain how you came to do this? Did you know that he was going down street, leaving the way open behind him? Was there collusion between you?'

Her eyes looked up clearly into his. She felt that she had nothing to disguise or conceal.

'I had urged him to do this, Judge Ostrander. I had met him more than once in the street when he went out to do your errands, and I used all my persuasion to induce him to give me this one opportunity of pleading my cause with you. He was your devoted servant, he showed it in his death, but he never got over his affection for Oliver. He told me that he would wake oftentimes in the night feeling about for the boy he used to carry in his arms. When I told him –'

'Enough! He knew who you were then?'

'He remembered me when I lifted my veil. Oh, I know very well that I had not the right to influence your own man to disobey your orders. But my cause was so pressing and your seclusion seemingly so arbitrary. How could I dream that your nerves could not bear any sudden shock? or that Bela – that giant among negroes – would be so affected by his emotions that he would not see or hear an approaching automobile? You must not blame me for these tragedies; and you must not blame Bela. He was torn by conflicting duties, and only yielded because of his great love for the absent.'

'I do not blame Bela.'

Startled, she looked at him with wondering eyes. There was a brooding despair in his tone which caught at her heart, and for an instant made her feel the full extent of her temerity. In a vain endeavour to regain her confidence, she falteringly remarked.

'I had listened to what folks said. I had heard that you would receive nobody; talk to nobody. Bela was my only resource.'

'Madam, I do not blame you.'

He was scrutinising her keenly and for the first time understandingly. Whatever her station past or present, she was certainly no ordinary woman, nor was her face without beauty, lit as it was by passion and every ardour of which a loving woman is capable. No man would be likely to resist it unless his armour were thrice forged. Would he himself be able to? He began to experience a cold fear – a dread which drew a black veil over the future; a blacker veil than that which had hitherto rested upon it.

But his face showed nothing. He was master of that yet. Only his tone. That silenced her. She was therefore scarcely surprised when, with a slight change of attitude which brought their faces more closely together, he proceeded, with a piercing intensity not to be withstood:

'When you entered my house this morning, did you come directly to my room?'

'Yes. Bela told me just how to reach it.'

'And when you saw me indisposed – unable, in fact, to greet you – what did you do then?'

With the force and meaning of one who takes an oath, she brought her hand, palm downward on the table before her, as she steadily replied:

'I flew back into the room through which I had come, undecided whether to fly the house or wait for what might happen to you, I had never seen anyone in such an attack before, and almost expected to hear you fall forward to the floor. But when you did not and the silence, which seemed so awful, remained unbroken, I pulled the curtain aside and looked in again. There was no change in your posture; and, alarmed now for your sake rather than for my own, I did not dare to go till Bela came back. So I stayed watching.'

'Stayed where?'

'In a dark corner of that same room. I never left it till the crowd came in. Then I slid out behind them.'

'Was the child with you – at your side I mean, all this time?'

'I never let go her hand.'

'Woman, you are keeping nothing back?'

'Nothing but my terror at the sight of Bela running in all bloody to escape the people pressing after him. I thought then that I had been the death of servant as well as master. You can imagine my relief when I heard that yours was but a passing attack.'

Sincerity was in her manner and in her voice. The judge breathed more easily, and made the remark:

'No one with hearing unimpaired can realise the suspicion of the deaf, nor can anyone who is not subject to attacks like mine conceive the doubts with which a man so cursed views those who have been active about him while the world to him was blank.'

Thus he dismissed the present subject, to surprise her by a renewal of the old one.

'What are your reasons,' said he, 'for the hopes you have just expressed? I think it your duty to tell me before we go any further.'

It was an acknowledgment, uttered after his own fashion, of the truth of her plea and the correctness of her woman's insight. She contemplated his face anew, and wondered that the dart she had so inconsiderately launched should have found the one weak joint in this strong man's armour. But she made no immediate reply, rather stopped to ponder, finally saying, with drooped head and nervously working fingers:

'Excuse me for tonight. What I have to tell – or rather, what I have to show you, – requires daylight.' Then, as she became conscious of his astonishment, added falteringly:

'Have you any objection to meeting me tomorrow on the bluff overlooking Dark –'

The voice of the clock, and that only! Tick! Tick! Tick! Tick! That only! Why then had she felt it impossible to finish her sentence? The judge was looking at her; he had not moved; nor had an eyelash stirred, but the rest of that sentence had stuck in her throat, and she found herself standing as immovably quiet as he.

Then she remembered. He had loved Algernon Etheridge. Memory still lived. The spot she had mentioned was a horror to him. Weakly she strove to apologise.

'I am sorry,' she began, but he cut her short at once.

'Why there?' he asked.

'Because' – her words came slowly, haltingly, as she tremulously, almost fearfully, felt her way with him – 'because… there… is… no… other place… where… I can make… my point.'

He smiled. It was his first smile in years and naturally was a little constrained, – and to her eyes at least, almost more terrifying than his frown.

'You have a point, then, to make?'

'A good one.'

He started as if to approach her, and then stood stock-still.

'Why have you waited till now?' he called out, forgetful that they were not alone in the house, forgetful apparently of everything but his surprise and repulsion. 'Why not have made use of this point before it was too late? You were at your husband's trial; you were even on the witness stand?'

She nodded, thoroughly cowed at last both by his indignation and the revelation contained in this question of the judicial mind – 'Why now, when the time was then?'

Happily, she had an answer.

'Judge Ostrander, I had a reason for that too; and, like my point, it is a good one. But do not ask me for it tonight. Tomorrow I will tell you everything. But it will have to be in the place I have mentioned. Will you come to the bluff where the ruins are one half hour before sunset? Please, be exact as to the time. You will see why, if you come.'

He leaned across the table – they were on opposite sides of it – and plunging his eyes into hers stood so, while the clock ticked out one slow minute more, then he drew back, and remarking with an aspect of gloom but with much less appearance of distrust:

'A very odd request, madam. I hope you have good reason for it,' adding, 'I bury Bela tomorrow and the cemetery is in this direction. I will meet you where you say and at the hour you name.'

And, regarding him closely as he spoke, she saw that for all the correctness of his manner and the bow of respectful courtesy with which he instantly withdrew, that deep would be his anger and unquestionable the results to her if she failed to satisfy him at this meeting of the value of her point in reawakening justice and changing public opinion.

Excerpts

One of the lodgers at the Claymore Inn had great cause for complaint the next morning. A restless tramping over his head had kept him awake all night. That it was intermittent had made it all the more intolerable. Just when he thought it had stopped, it would start up again, to and fro, to and fro, as regular as clockwork and much more disturbing.

But the complaint never reached Mrs Averill. The landlady had been restless herself. Indeed, the night had been one of thought and feeling to more than one person in whom we are interested. The feeling we can understand; the thought – that is, Mrs Averill's thought – we should do well to follow.

The one great question which had agitated her was this: Should she trust the judge? Ever since the discovery which had changed Reuther's prospects, she had instinctively looked to this one source for aid and sympathy. Her reasons she has already given. His bearing during the trial, the compunction he showed in uttering her husband's sentence were sufficient proof to her that for all his natural revulsion against the crime which had robbed him of his dearest friend, he was the victim of an undercurrent of sympathy for the accused which could mean but one thing – a doubt of the prisoner's actual guilt.

But her faith had been sorely shaken in the interview just related. He was not the friend she had hoped to find. He had insisted upon her husband's guilt, when she had expected consideration and a thoughtful recapitulation of the evidence; and he had remained unmoved, or but very little moved, by the disappointment of his son – his only remaining link to life.

Why? Was the alienation between these two so complete as to block out natural sympathy? Had the separation of years rendered them callous to every mutual impression? She dwelt in tenderness upon the bond uniting herself and Reuther and could not believe in such unresponsiveness. No parent could carry resentment or even righteous anger so far as that. Judge Ostrander might seem cold – both manner and temper would naturally be much affected by his unique and solitary mode of life – but at heart he must love Oliver. It was not in nature for it to be otherwise. And yet –

It was at this point in her musing that there came one of the breaks in her restless pacing. She was always of an impulsive temperament, and always giving way to it. Sitting down before paper and ink she wrote the following lines:

My Darling if Unhappy Child:

I know that this sudden journey on my part must strike you as cruel, when, if ever, you need your mother's presence and care. But the love I feel for you, my Reuther, is deep enough to cause you momentary pain for the sake of the great good I hope to bring you out of this shadowy quest. I believe, what I said to you on leaving, that a great injustice was done your father. Feeling so, shall I remain quiescent and see youth and love slip from you, without any effort on my part to set this matter straight? I cannot. I have done you the wrong of silence when knowledge would have saved you shock and bitter disillusion, but I will not add to my fault the inertia of a cowardly soul. Have patience with me, then; and continue to cherish those treasures of truth and affection which you may one day feel free to bestow once more upon one who has a right to each and all of them.

This is your mother's prayer.

DEBORAH SCOVILLE.

It was not easy for her to sign herself thus. It was a name which she had tried her best to forget for twelve long, preoccupied years. But how could she use any other in addressing her daughter who had already declared her intention of resuming her father's name, despite the opprobrium it carried and the everlasting bar it must in itself raise between herself and Oliver Ostrander?

Deborah Scoville!

A groan broke from her lips as she rapidly folded that name in, and hid it out of sight in the envelope she as rapidly addressed.

But her purpose had been accomplished, or would be when once this letter reached Reuther. With these words in declaration against her she could not retreat from the stand she had therein taken. It was another instance of burning one's ships upon disembarking, and the effect made upon the writer showed itself at once in her altered manner. Henceforth, the question should be not what awaited her, but how she should show her strength in face of the opposition she now expected to meet from this clear-minded, amply equipped lawyer and judge she had called to her aid.

'A task for his equal, not for an ignorant, untried woman like myself,' she thought; and, following another of her impulses, she leaped from her seat at the table and rushed across to her dresser on which she placed two candles, one at her right and another at her left. Then she sat down between them and in the stillness of midnight surveyed herself in the glass, as she might survey the face of a stranger.

What did she see? A countenance no longer young, and yet with some of the charm of youth still lingering in the brooding eyes and in the dangerous curves of a mobile and expressive mouth. But it was not for charm she was looking, but for some signs of power quite apart from that of sex. Did her face express intellect, persistence and, above all, courage? The brow was good; she would so characterise it in another. Surely a woman with such a forehead might do something even against odds. Nor was her chin weak; sometimes she had thought it too pronounced for beauty; but what had she to do with beauty now? And the neck so proudly erect! the heaving breast! the heart all aflame! Defeat is not for such; or only such defeat as bears within it the germ of future victory.

Is her reading correct? Time will prove. Meanwhile she will have confidence in herself, and that this confidence might be well founded she decided to spend the rest of the night in formulating her plans and laying out her imaginary campaign.

Leaving the dresser she recommenced that rapid walking to and fro which was working such havoc in the nerves of the man in the room below her. When she paused, it was to ransack a trunk and bring out a flat wallet filled with newspaper clippings, many of them discoloured by time, and all of them showing marks of frequent handling.

A handling now to be repeated. For after a few moments spent in arranging them, she deliberately set about their complete reperusal, a task in which it has now become necessary for us to join her.

The first was black with old headlines:

CRIME IN DARK HOLLOW

Algernon Etheridge, One of Our Most Esteemed Citizens, Waylaid and Murdered at Long Bridge.

A DIRECT CLUE TO THE MURDERER

The Stick With Which the Crime was Committed Easily Traced to Its Owner. The Landlord of Claymore Tavern in the Toils. He Denies His Guilt But Submits Sullenly to Arrest.

Particulars followed.

Last evening Shelby's clean record was blackened by outrageous crime. Sometime after nightfall a carter was driving home by Factory Road, when just as he was nearing Long Bridge one of his horses shied so violently that he barely escaped being thrown from his seat. As he had never known the animal to shy like this before, he was curious enough to get down and look about him for the cause. Dark Hollow is never light, but it is impenetrable after dark, and not being able to see anything, he knelt down in the road and began to feel about with his hand. This brought results. In a few moments he came upon the body of a man lying without movement, and seemingly without life.

Long Bridge is not a favourite spot at night, and, knowing that in all probability an hour might elapse before assistance would arrive in the shape of another passer-by, he decided to carry his story straight to Claymore Tavern. Afterwards he was heard to declare that it was fortunate his horses were headed that way instead of the other, or he might have missed seeing the skulking figure which slipped down into the ravine as he made the turn at the far end of the bridge – a figure which had no other response to his loud 'Hola!' than a short cough, hurriedly choked back. He could not see the face or identify the figure, but he knew the cough. He had heard it a hundred times; and, saying to himself, 'I'll find fellers enough at the tavern, but there's one I won't find there and that's John Scoville,' he whipped his horse up the hill and took the road to Claymore.

And he was right. A dozen fellows started up at his call, but Scoville was not among them. He had been out for two hours; which the carter having heard, he looked down, but said nothing except 'Come along, boys! I'll drive you to the turn of the bridge.'

But just as they were starting Scoville appeared. He was hatless and dishevelled and reeled heavily with liquor. He also tried to smile, which made the carter lean quickly down and with very little ceremony drag him up into the cart. So with Scoville amongst them they rode quickly back to the bridge, the landlord coughing, the men all grimly silent.

In crossing the bridge he made more than one effort to escape, but the men were determined, and when they finally stooped over the man lying in Dark Hollow, he was in their midst and was forced to stoop also.

One flash of the lantern told the dismal tale. The man was not only dead, but murdered. His forehead had been battered in with a knotted stick; all his pockets hung out empty; and from the general disorder of his dress it was evident that his watch had been torn away by a ruthless hand. But the face they failed to recognise till some people, running down from the upper town where the alarm had by this time spread, sent up the shout of 'It's Mr Etheridge! Judge Ostrander's great friend. Let someone run and notify the judge.'

But the fact was settled long before the judge came upon the scene, and another fact too. In beating the bushes, they had lighted on a heavy stick. When it was brought forward and held under the strong light made by a circle of lanterns, a big movement took place in the crowd. The stick had been recognised. Indeed, it was well known to all the Claymore men. They had seen it in Scoville's hands a dozen times. Even he could not deny its ownership; explaining, or trying to, that he had been in the ravine looking for this stick only a little while before, and adding, as he met their eyes:

'I lost it in these woods this afternoon. I hadn't anything to do with this killing.'

He had not been accused; but he found it impossible to escape after this, and when at the instance of Coroner Haines he was carefully looked over and a small red ribbon found in one of his pockets, he was immediately put under arrest and taken to the city lock-up. For the ribbon had been identified as well as the stick. Oliver Ostrander, who had accompanied his father to the scene of crime, declared that he had observed it that very afternoon, dangling from one end of Mr Etheridge's watch chain where it had been used to fasten temporarily a broken link.

As we go to press we hear that Judge Ostrander has been prostrated by this blow. The deceased had been playing chess up at his house, and in taking the shortcut home had met with his death.

Long Bridge should be provided with lights. It is a dangerous place for foot passengers on a dark night.'

A later paragraph.

The detectives were busy this morning, going over the whole ground in the vicinity of the bridge.

They were rewarded by two important discoveries. The impression of a foot in a certain soft place halfway up the bluff; and a small heap of fresh earth nearby which, on being dug into, revealed the watch of the murdered man. The broken chain lay with it.

The footprint has been measured. It coincides exactly with the shoe worn that night by the suspect.

The case will be laid before the Grand Jury next week.

The prisoner continues to deny his guilt. The story he gives out is to the effect that he left the tavern some few minutes before seven o'clock, to look for his child who had wandered into the ravine. That he entered the woods from the road running by his house, and was searching the bushes skirting the stream when he heard little Reuther's shout from somewhere up on the bluff. He had his stick with him, for he never went out without it, but, finding it in his way, he leaned it against a tree and went plunging up the bluff without it. Why he didn't call out the child's name he doesn't know; he guessed he thought he would surprise her; and why, when he got to the top of the bluff and didn't find her, he should turn about for his stick instead of hunting for her on the road, he also fails to explain, saying again, he doesn't know. What circumstances force him to tell and what he declares to be true is this: that instead of going back diagonally through the woods to the lone chestnut where he had left his stick, he crossed the bridge and took the path running along the edge of the ravine; that in doing this he came upon the body of a man in the black recesses of the hollow, a man so evidently beyond all help that he would have hurried by without a second look if it had not been for the watch he saw lying on the ground close to the dead man's side. It was a very fine watch, and it seemed like tempting Providence to leave it lying there exposed to the view of any chance tramp who might come along. It seemed better for him to take it into his own charge till he found some responsible person willing to carry it to Police Headquarters. So, without stopping to consider what the consequences might be to himself, he tore it away by the chain from the hold it had on the dead man's coat and put it in his pocket. He also took some other little things; after which he fled away into town, where the sight of a saloon was too much for him and he went in to have a drink to take the horrors out of him. Since then, the detectives have followed all his movements and know just how much liquor he drank and to whom, in tipsy bravado, he showed the contents of his pockets. But he wasn't so far gone as not to have moments of apprehension when he thought of the dead man lying with his feet in Dark Hollow, and of the hue and cry which would soon be raised, and what folks might think if that accursed watch he had taken so innocently should be found in his pocket. Finally his fears overcame his scruples, and, starting for home, he stopped at the bluff, meaning to run down over the bridge and drop the watch as near as possible to the spot where he had found it. But as he turned to descend, he heard a team approaching from the other side and, terrified still more, he dashed into the woods, and, tearing up the ground with his hands, buried his booty in the loose soil, and made for home. Even then he had no intention of appropriating the watch, only of safeguarding himself, nor did he have any hand at all in the murder of Mr Etheridge. This he would swear to; also, to the leaving of the stick where he said.

It is understood that in case of his indictment, his lawyer will follow the line of defence thus indicated.

Today, John Scoville was taken to the tree where he insists he left his stick. It is a big chestnut some hundred and fifty feet beyond the point where the ravine turns west. It has a big enough trunk for a stick to stand upright against it, as was shown by Inspector Snow who had charge of this affair. But we are told that after demonstrating this fact with the same bludgeon which had done its bloody work in the hollow, the prisoner showed a sudden interest in this weapon and begged to see it closer. This being granted, he pointed out where a splinter or two had been freshly whittled from the handle, and declared that no knife had touched it while it remained in his hands. But, as he had no evidence to support this statement (a knife having been found amongst the other effects taken from his pocket at the time of his arrest), the impression made by this declaration is not likely to go far towards influencing public opinion in his favour.

A true bill was found today against John Scoville for the murder of Algernon Etheridge.

A third clipping:

We feel it our duty, as the one independent paper of this city, to insist upon the right of a man to the consideration of the public till a jury of his peers has pronounced upon his guilt and thus rendered him a criminal before the law. The way our hitherto sufficiently respected citizen, John Scoville, has been maligned and his every fault and failing magnified for the delectation of a greedy public is unworthy of a Christian community. No man saw him kill Algernon Etheridge, and he himself denies most strenuously that he did so, yet from the first moment of his arrest till now, not a voice has been raised in his favour, or the least account taken of his defence. Yet he is the husband of an estimable wife and the father of a child of such exceptional loveliness that she has been the petted darling of high and low ever since John Scoville became the proprietor of Claymore Tavern.

Give the man a chance. It is our wish to see justice vindicated and the guilty punished; but not before the jury has pronounced its verdict.

'*The Star* was his only friend,' sighed Deborah Scoville, as she laid this clipping aside and took up another headed by a picture of her husband. This picture she subjected to the same scrutiny she had just given to her own reflection in the glass: 'Seeing him anew,' as she said to herself, 'after all these years of determined forgetfulness.'

It was not an unhandsome face. Indeed, it was his good looks which had prevailed over her judgement in the early days of their courtship. Reuther had inherited her harmony of feature from him – the chiselled nose, the well-modelled chin, and all the other physical graces which had made him a fine figure behind his bar. But even with the softening of her feelings towards him since she had thus set herself up in his defence,

Deborah could not fail to perceive under all these surface attractions an expression of unreliability, or, as some would say, of actual cruelty. Ruddy-haired and fair of skin, he should have had an optimistic temperament; but, on the contrary, he was of a gloomy nature, and only infrequently social. No company was better for his being in it. Never had she seen any man sit out the evening with him without effort. Yet the house had prospered. How often had she said to herself, in noting these facts: 'Yet the house prospers!' There was always money in the till even when the patronage was small. Their difficulties were never financial ones. She was still living on the proceeds of what they had laid by in those old days.

Her mind continued to plunge back. He had had no business worries; yet his temper was always uncertain. She had not often suffered from it herself, for her ascendency over men extended even to him. But Reuther had shrunk before it more than once – the gentle Reuther, who was the refined, the etherealised picture of himself. And he had loved the child as well as he could love anybody. Great gusts of fondness would come over him at times, and then he would pet and cajole the child almost beyond a parent's prerogative. But he was capable of striking her too – had struck her frequently. And for nothing – an innocent look; a shrinking movement; a smile when he wasn't in the mood for smiles. It was for this Deborah had hated him; and it was for this the mother in her now held him responsible for the doubts which had shadowed their final parting. Was not the man, who could bring his hand down upon so frail and exquisite a creature as Reuther was in those days, capable of any act of violence? Yes; but in this case he had been guiltless. She could not but concede this even while yielding to extreme revulsion as she laid his picture aside.

The next slip she took up contained an eulogy of the victim.

The sudden death of Algernon Etheridge has been in more than one sense a great shock to the community. Though a man of passive rather than active qualities, his scholarly figure, long, lean and bowed, has been seen too often in our streets not to be missed, when thus suddenly withdrawn. His method of living; the rigid habits of an almost ascetic life; such an hour for this thing, such an hour for that – his smile, which made you soon forget his irascibility and pride of learning; made up a character unique in our town and one that we can ill afford to spare. The closed doors of the little cottage, so associated with his name that it will be hard to imagine it occupied by anyone else, possess a pathos of their own which is felt by young and old alike. The gate that never would latch, the garden, where at a stated hour in the morning his bowed figure would always be seen hoeing or weeding or raking, the windows without curtains showing the stacks of books within, are eloquent of a presence gone, which can never be duplicated. Alone on its desolate corner, it seems to mourn the child, the boy, the man who gave it life, and made it, in its simplicity, more noted and more frequently pointed at than any other house in town.

Why he should have become the target of Fate is one of the mysteries of life. His watch, which aside from his books was his most valuable possession, was the gift of Judge Ostrander. That it should be associated in any way with the tragic circumstances of his death is a source of the deepest regret to the unhappy donor.

This excerpt she hardly looked at; but the following she studied carefully:

Judge Ostrander has from the first expressed a strong desire that some associate judge should be called upon to preside over the trial of John Scoville for the murder of Algernon

Etheridge. But Judge Saunders' sudden illness and Judge Dole's departure for Europe have put an end to these hopes. Judge Ostrander will take his seat on the bench as usual next Monday. Fortunately for the accused, his well-known judicial mind will prevent any unfair treatment of the defence.

The prosecution, in the able hands of District Attorney Foss, made all its points this morning. Unless the defence has some very strong plea in the background, the verdict seems foredoomed. A dogged look has replaced the callous and indifferent sneer on the prisoner's face, and sympathy, if sympathy there is, is centred entirely upon the wife, the able, agreeable and bitterly humiliated landlady of Claymore Tavern. She it is who has attracted the most attention during this trial, little as she seems to court it.

Only one new detail of evidence was laid before the jury today. Scoville has been known for some time to have a great hankering after a repeating watch. He had once seen that of Algernon Etheridge, and was never tired of talking about it. Several witnesses testified to his various remarks on this subject. Thus the motive for his dastardly assault upon an unoffending citizen, which to many minds has seemed lacking, has been supplied.

The full particulars of this day's proceedings will be found below.

We omit these to save repetition; but they were very carefully conned by Deborah Scoville. Also the following:

The defence is in a line with the statement already given out. The prisoner acknowledges taking the watch but from motives quite opposed to those of thievery. Unfortunately he can produce no witnesses to substantiate his declaration that he had heard voices in the direction of the bridge while he was wandering the woods in search of his lost child. No evidence of any other presence there is promised or likely to be produced. It was thought that when his wife was called to the stand she might have something to say helpful to his case. She had been the one to ultimately find and lead home the child, and, silent as she had been up to this time, it has been thought possible that she might swear to having heard these voices also.

But her testimony was very disappointing. She had seen nobody, heard nobody but the child whom she had found playing with stones in the old ruin. Though by a close calculation of time she could not have been far from Dark Hollow at the instant of the crime, yet neither on direct or cross-examination could anything more be elicited from her than what has been mentioned above. Nevertheless, we feel obliged to state that, irreproachable as her conduct was on the stand, the impression she made was, on the whole, whether intentionally or unintentionally, unfavourable to her husband.

Some anxiety was felt during the morning session that an adjournment would have to be called, owing to some slight signs of indisposition on the part of the presiding judge. But he rallied very speedily, and the proceedings continued without interruption.

'Ah!'

The exclamation escaped the lips of Deborah Scoville as she laid this clipping aside. 'I remember his appearance well. He had the ghost of one of those attacks, the full force of which I was a witness to this morning. I am sure of this now, though nobody thought of it then. I happened to glance his way as I left the stand, and he was certainly for one minute without consciousness of himself or his surroundings. But it passed so quickly it drew little attention; not so, the attack of today. What a misfortune rests upon this man. Will they let him continue on the bench when his full condition is known?' These were her thoughts, as she recalled that day and compared it with the present.

There were other slips, which she read but which we may pass by. The fate of the prisoner was in the hands of a jury. The possibility suggested by the defence made no appeal to men who had the unfortunate prisoner under their eye at every stage of the proceedings. The shifty eye, the hang-dog look, outweighed the plea of his counsel and the call for strict impartiality from the bench. He was adjudged guilty of murder in the first degree, and sentence called for.

This was the end; and as she read these words, the horror which overwhelmed her was infinitely greater than when she heard them uttered in that fatal courtroom. For then she regarded him as guilty and deserving his fate and now she knew him to be innocent.

Well, well! too much dwelling on this point would only unfit her for what lay before her on the morrow. She would read no more. Sleep were a better preparation for her second interview with the judge than this reconsideration of facts already known to their last detail.

Alas, when her eyelids finally obeyed the dictates of her will, the first glimmering rays of dawn were beginning to scatter the gloom of her darkened chamber!

The Shadow

Bela was to be buried at four. As Judge Ostrander prepared to lock his gate behind the simple cortege which was destined to grow into a vast crowd before it reached the cemetery, he was stopped by the sergeant who whispered in his ear:

'I thought your honour might like to know that the woman – you know the one I mean without my naming her – has been amusing herself this morning in a very peculiar manner. She broke down some branches in the ravine – small ones, of course – and would give no account of herself when one of my men asked her what she was up to. It may mean nothing, but I thought you would like to know.'

'Have you found out who she is?'

'No, sir. The man couldn't very well ask her to lift her veil, and at the tavern they have nothing to say about her.'

'It's a small matter. I will see her myself today and find out what she wants of me. Meanwhile, remember that I leave this house and grounds absolutely to your protection for the next three hours. I shall be known to be absent, so that a more careful watch than ever is necessary. Not a man, boy or child is to climb the fence. I may rely on you?'

'You may, judge.'

'On my return you can all go. I will guard my own property after today. You understand me, sergeant?'

'Perfectly, your honour.'

This ended the colloquy.

Spencer's Folly, as the old ruin on the bluff was called in memory of the vanished magnificence which was once the talk of the county, presented a very different appearance to the eye in broad daylight from what it did at night with a low moon sending its mellow rays through the great gap made in its walls by that ancient stroke of lightning. Even the enkindling beams of the westering sun striking level through the forest failed to adorn its broken walls and battered foundations. To the judge, approaching it from the highway, it was as ugly a sight as the world contained. He hated its arid desolation and all the litter of blackened bricks blocking up the site of former feastings and reckless merriment, and, above all, the incongruous aspect of the one gable still standing undemolished, with the zigzag marks of vanished staircases outlined upon its mildewed walls. But, most of all, he shrank from a sight of the one corner still intact where the ghosts of dead memories lingered, making the whole place horrible to his eye and one to be shunned by all men. How long it had been shunned by him he realised when he noticed the increased decay of the walls and the growth of the verdure encompassing the abominable place!

The cemetery from which he had come looked less lonesome to his eyes and far less ominous; and, for a passing instant, as he contemplated the scene hideous with old memories and threatening new sorrows, he envied Bela his narrow bed and honourable rest.

A tall figure and an impressive presence are not without their disadvantages. This he felt as he left the highway and proceeded up the path which had once led through a double box hedge to the high, pillared entrance. He abhorred scandal and shrank with almost a woman's distaste from anything which savoured of the clandestine. Yet here he was about to meet on a spot open to the view of every passing vehicle, a woman who, if known to him, was a mystery to everyone else. His expression showed the scorn with which he regarded his own compliance, yet he knew that no instinct of threatened dignity, no generous thought for her or selfish one for himself would turn him back from this interview till he had learned what she had to tell him and why she had so carefully exacted that he should hear her story in a spot overlooking the hollow it would beseem them both to shun.

There had originally been in the days of Spencer's magnificence a lordly portico at the end of this approach, girt by pillars of extraordinary height. But no sign remained of pillar, or doorway – only a gap, as I have said. Towards this gap he stepped, feeling a strange reluctance in entering it. But he had no choice. He knew what he should see – no, he did not know what he should see, for when he finally stepped in, it was not an open view of the hollow which met his eyes, but the purple-clad figure of Mrs Averill with little Peggy at her side. He had not expected to see the child, and, standing as they were with their backs to him, they presented a picture which, for some reason to be found in the mysterious recesses of his disordered mind, was exceedingly repellent to him. Indeed, he was so stricken by it that he had actually made a move to withdraw, when the exigency of the occasion returned upon him in full force, and, with a smothered oath, he overcame his weakness and stepped firmly up into the ruins.

The noise he made should have caused Deborah's tall and graceful figure to turn. But the spell of her own thoughts was too great; and he would have found himself compelled to utter the first word, if the child, who had heard him plainly enough, had not dragged at the woman's hand and so woke her from her dream.

'Ah, Judge Ostrander,' she exclaimed in a hasty but not ungraceful greeting, 'you are very punctual. I was not looking for you yet.' Then, as she noted the gloom under which he was labouring, she continued with real feeling, 'Indeed, I appreciate this sacrifice you have made to my wishes. It was asking a great deal of you to come here; but I saw no other way of making my point clear. Come over here, Peggy, and build me a little house out of these stones. You don't mind the child, do you, judge? She may offer a diversion if our retreat is invaded.'

The gesture of disavowal which he made was courteous but insincere. He did mind the child, but he could not explain why; besides he must overcome such folly.

'Now,' she continued as she rejoined him on the place where he had taken his stand, 'I will ask you to go back with me to the hour when John Scoville left the tavern on that fatal day. I am not now on oath, but I might as well be for any slip I shall make in the exact truth. I was making pies in the kitchen, when someone came running in to say that Reuther had strayed away from the front yard. She was about the age of the little one over there, and we never allowed her out alone for fear of her tumbling off the bluff. So I set down the pie I was just putting in the oven, and was about to run out after her when my husband called to me from the front, and said he would go. I didn't like his tone – it was sullen and impatient, but I knew he loved the child too well to see her suffer any danger, and so I settled back to work and was satisfied enough till the pies were all in. Then I got uneasy, and, hearing nothing of either of them, I started in this direction because they told me John had taken the other. And here I found her, sir, right in the heart of these ruins. She was playing with stones just as Peggy dear is doing now. Greatly relieved, I was taking her away when I thought I heard John calling. Stepping up to the edge just behind where you are standing, sir – yes, there, where you get such a broad outlook up and down the ravine, I glanced in the direction from which I had heard his call – just wait a moment, sir; I want to know the exact time.'

Stopping, she pulled out her watch and looked at it, while he, faltering up to the verge which she had pointed out, followed her movements with strange intensity as she went on to say in explanation of her act:

'The time is important, on account of a certain demonstration I am anxious to make. You will remember that I was expecting to see John, having heard his voice in the ravine. Now if you will lean a little forward and look where I am pointing, you will notice at the turn of the stream, a spot of ground more open than the rest. Please keep your eyes on that spot, for it was there I saw at this very hour twelve years ago the shadow of an approaching figure; and it is there you will presently see one similar, if the boy I have tried to interest in this experiment does not fail me. Now, now, sir! We should see his shadow before we see him. Oh, I hope the underbrush and trees have not grown up too thick! I tried to thin them out today. Are you watching, sir?'

He seemed to be, but she dared not turn to look. Both figures leaned, intent, and in another moment she had gripped his arm and clung there.

'Did you see?' she whispered, 'Don't mind the boy; it's the shadow I wanted you to notice. Did you observe anything marked about it?'

She had drawn him back into the ruins. They were standing in that one secluded corner under the ruinous gable, and she was gazing up at him very earnestly. 'Tell me, judge,' she entreated as he made no effort to answer.

With a hurried moistening of his lips, he met her look and responded, with a slight emphasis:

'The boy held a stick. I should say that he was whittling it.'

'Ah!' Her tone was triumphant. 'That was what I told him to do. Did you see anything else?'

'No. I do not understand this experiment or what you hope from it.'

'I will tell you. The shadow which I saw at a moment very like this, twelve years ago, showed a man whittling a stick and wearing a cap with a decided peak in front. My husband wore such a cap – the only one I knew of in town. What more did I need as proof that it was his shadow I saw?'

'And wasn't it?'

'Judge Ostrander, I never thought differently till after the trial – till after the earth closed over my poor husband's remains. That was why I could say nothing in his defence – why I did not believe him when he declared that he had left his stick behind him when he ran up the bluff after Reuther. The tree he pointed out as the one against which he had stood it, was far behind the place where I saw this advancing shadow. Even the oath he made to me of his innocence at the last interview we held in prison did not impress me at the time as truthful. But later, when it was all over, when the disgrace of his death and the necessity of seeking a home elsewhere drove me into selling the tavern and all its effects, I found something which changed my mind in this regard, and made me confident that I had done my husband a great injustice.'

'You found? What do you mean by that? What could you have found?'

'His peaked cap lying in a corner of the garret. He had not worn it that day.'

The judge stared. She repeated her statement, and with more emphasis:

'He had not worn it that day; for when he came back to be hustled off again by the crowd, he was without hat of any kind, and he never returned again to his home – you know that, judge. I had seen the shadow of some other man approaching Dark Hollow. Whose, I am in this town now to find out.'

'I will think about it'

Judge Ostrander was a man of keen perception, quick to grasp an idea, quick to form an opinion. But his mind acted slowly tonight. Deborah Scoville wondered at the blankness of his gaze and the slow way in which he seemed to take in this astounding fact.

At last he found voice and with it gave some evidence of his usual acumen.

'Madam, a shadow is an uncertain foundation on which to build such an edifice as you plan. How do you know that the fact you mention was coincident with the crime? Mr Etheridge's body was not found till after dark. A dozen men might have come down that path with or without sticks before he reached the bridge and fell a victim to the assault which laid him low.'

'I thought the time was pretty clearly settled by the hour he left your house. The sun had not set when he turned your corner on his way home. So several people said who saw him. Besides –'

'Yes; there is a besides. I'm sure of it.'

'I saw the tall figure of a man, whom I afterwards made sure was Mr Etheridge, coming down Factory Road on his way to the bridge when I turned about to get Reuther.'

'All of which you suppressed at the trial.'

'I was not questioned on this point, sir.'

'Madam,' – he was standing very near to her now, hemming her as it were into that decaying corner – 'I should have a very much higher opinion of your candour if you told me the whole story.'

'I have, sir.'

His hands rose, one to the right hand wall, the other to the left, and remained there with their palms resting heavily against the rotting plaster. She was more than ever hemmed in; but, though she felt a trifle frightened at his aspect which certainly was not usual, she faced him without shrinking and in very evident surprise.

'You went immediately home with the child after that glimpse you got of Mr Etheridge?'

'Yes; I had no reason in the world to suppose that anything was going to happen in the ravine below us. Of course, I went straight on; there were things to be done at home, and – you don't believe me, sir.'

His hands fell; an indefinable change had come over his aspect; he bowed and seemed about to utter an ironic apology. She felt puzzled and unconsciously she began to think. What was lacking in her statement? Something. Could she remember what? Something which he had expected; something which as presiding judge over John's trial he had been made aware of and now recalled to render her story futile. It couldn't be that one little thing – but yes, it might be. Nothing is little where a great crime is concerned. She smiled a dubious smile, then she said:

'It seems too slight a fact to mention, and, indeed, I had forgotten it till you pressed me, but after we had passed the gates and were well out on the highway, I found that Reuther had left her little pail behind her here, and we came back and got it. Did you mean that, sir?'

'I meant nothing; but I felt sure you had not told all you could about that fatal ten minutes. You came back. It is quite a walk from the road. The man whose shadow you saw must have reached the bridge by this time. What did you see then or... hear?'

'Nothing. Absolutely nothing, judge. I was intent on finding the baby's pail, and having found it I hurried back home all the faster.'

'And tragedy was going on or was just completed, in plain sight from this gap!'

'I have no doubt, sir; and if I had looked, possibly John might have been saved.'

The silence following this was broken by a crash and a little cry. Peggy's house had tumbled down.

The small incident was a relief. Both assumed more natural postures.

'So the shadow is your great and only point,' remarked the judge.

'It is sufficient for me.'

'Ah, perhaps.'

'But not enough for the public?'

'Hardly.'

'Not enough for you, either?'

'Madam, I have already told you that, in my opinion, John Scoville was a guilty man.'

'And this fact, with which I have just acquainted you, has done nothing to alter this opinion?'

'I can only repeat what I have just said.'

'Oh, Reuther! Oh, Oliver!'

'Do not speak my son's name. I am in no mood for it. The boy and girl are two and can never become one. I have other views for her – she is an innocent victim and she has my sympathy. You, too, madam, though I consider you as following a will-o'-the-wisp which will only lead you hopelessly astray.'

'I shall not desist, Judge Ostrander.'

'You are going to pursue this Jack-o'-Lanthorn?'

'I am determined to. If you deny me aid and advice, I shall seek another counsellor. John's name must be vindicated.'

'Obstinacy, madam.'

'No; conscience.'

He gave her a look, turned and glanced down at the child piling stone on stone and whimpering just a little when they fell.

'Watch that baby for a while,' he remarked, 'and you will learn the lesson of most human endeavour. Madam, I have a proposition to make you. You cannot wish to remain at the inn, nor can you be long happy separated from your daughter. I have lost Bela. I do not know how, nor would I be willing, to replace him by another servant. I need a housekeeper; someone devoted to my interests and who will not ask me to change my habits too materially. Will you accept the position, if I add as an inducement my desire to have Reuther also as an inmate of my home? This does not mean that I countenance or in any way anticipate her union with my son. I do not; but any other advantages she may desire, she shall have. I will not be strict with her.'

'Judge Ostrander!'

Deborah Scoville was never more taken aback in her life. The recluse opening his doors to two women! The man of mystery flinging aside the reticences of years to harbour an innocence which he refused to let weigh against the claims of a son he has seen fit to banish from his heart and home!

'You may take time to think of it,' he continued, as he watched the confused emotions change from moment to moment the character of her mobile features. 'I shall not have my affairs adjusted for such a change before a week. If you accept, I shall be very grateful. If you decline, I shall close up my two rear gates, and go into solitary seclusion. I can cook a meal if I have to.'

And she saw that he would do it; saw and wondered still more.

'I shall have to write to Reuther,' she murmured. 'How soon do you want my decision?'

'In four days.'

'I am too disturbed to thank you, judge. Should – should we have to keep the gates locked?'

'No. But you would have to keep out unwelcome intruders. And the rights of my library will have to be respected. In all other regards I should wish, under these new circumstances, to live as other people live. I have been very lonely these past twelve years.'

'I will think about it.'

'And you may make note of these two conditions: Oliver's name is not to be mentioned in my hearing, and you and Reuther are to be known by your real names.'

'You would –'

'Yes, madam. No secrecy is to be maintained in future as to your identity or my reasons for desiring you in my house. I need a housekeeper and you please me. That you have a past to forget and Reuther a disappointment to overcome, gives additional point to the arrangement.'

Her answer was:

'I cannot take back what I have said about my determined purpose.' In repeating this, she looked up at him askance.

He smiled. She remembered that smile long after the interview was over and only its memory remained.

Sounds in the Night

Dearest Mother:

Where could we go that disgrace would not follow us? Let us then accept the judge's offer. I am the more inclined to do this because of the possible hope that some day he may come to care for me and allow me to make life a little brighter for him. The fact that for some mysterious reason he feels himself cut off from all intercourse with his son, may prove a bond of sympathy between us. I, too, am cut off from all companionship with Oliver. Between us also a wall is raised. Do not mind that teardrop, mamma. It is the last.

Kisses for my comforter. Come soon.

REUTHER.

Over this letter Deborah Scoville sat for two hours, then she rang for Mrs Yardley.

The maid who answered her summons surveyed her in amazement. It was the first time that she had seen her uncovered face.

Mrs Yardley was not long in coming up.

'Mrs Averill –' she began in a sort of fluster, as she met her strange guest's quiet eye.

But she got no further. That guest had a correction to make.

'My name is not Averill,' she protested. 'You must excuse the temporary deception. It is Scoville. I once occupied your present position in this house.'

Mrs Yardley had heard all about the Scovilles; and, while a flush rose to her cheeks, her eyes snapped with sudden interest.

'Ah!' came in quick exclamation, followed, however, by an apologetic cough and the somewhat forced and conventional remark: 'You find the place changed, no doubt?'

'Very much so, and for the better, Mrs Yardley.' Then, with a straightforward meeting of the other's eye calculated to disarm whatever criticism the situation might evoke, she quietly added, 'You need no longer trouble yourself with serving me my meals in my room. I will eat dinner in the public dining room today with the rest of the boarders. I have no further reason for concealing who I am or what my future intentions are. I am going to live with Judge Ostrander, Mrs Yardley; keep house for him, myself and daughter. His man is dead and he feels very helpless. I hope that I shall be able to make him comfortable.'

Mrs Yardley's face was a study. In all her life she had never heard news that surprised her more. In fact, she was mentally aghast. Judge Ostrander admitting anyone into his home, and this woman above all! Yet, why not? He, certainly, would have to have someone. And this woman had always been known as a notable housekeeper. In another moment, she had accepted the situation, like the very sensible woman she was, and Mrs Scoville had the satisfaction of seeing the promise of real friendly support in the smile with which Mrs Yardley remarked:

'It's a good thing for you and a very good thing for the judge. It may shake him out of his habit of seclusion. If it does, you will be the city's benefactor. Good luck to you, madam. And you have a daughter, you say?'

After Mrs Yardley's departure, Mrs Scoville, as she now expected herself to be called, sat for a long time brooding. Would her quest be facilitated or irretrievably hindered by her presence in the judge's house? She had that yet to learn. Meanwhile, there was one thing more to be accomplished. She set about it that evening.

Veiled, but in black now, she went into town. Getting down at the corner of Colburn Avenue and Perry Street, she walked a short distance on Perry, then rang the bell of an attractive-looking house of moderate dimensions. Being admitted, she asked to see Mr Black, and for an hour sat in close conversation with him. Then she took a trolley-car which carried her into the suburbs. When she alighted, it was unusually late for a woman to be out alone; but she had very little physical fear, and walked on steadily enough for a block or two till she came to a corner, where a high fence loomed forbiddingly between her and a house so dark that it was impossible to distinguish between its chimneys and the encompassing trees whose swaying tops could be heard swishing about uneasily in the keen night air. An eerie accompaniment, this latter, to the beating of Deborah's heart already throbbing with anticipation and keyed to an unusual pitch by her own daring.

Was she quite alone in the seemingly quiet street? She could hear no one, see no one. A lamp burned in front of Miss Weeks' small house, but the road it illumined (I speak of the one running down to the ravine) showed only darkened houses.

She had left the corner and was passing the gate of the Ostrander homestead, when she heard, coming from some distant point within, a low and peculiar sound which held her immovable for a moment, then sent her on shuddering.

It was the sound of hammering.

What is there in a rat-tat-tat in the dead of night which rouses the imagination and fills the mind with suggestions which we had rather not harbour when in the dark and alone? Deborah Scoville was not superstitious, but she had keen senses and mercurial spirits and was easily moved by suggestion.

Hearing this sound and locating it where she did, she remembered, with a quick inner disturbance, that the judge's house held a secret; a secret of such import to its owner that the dying Bela had sought to preserve it at the cost of his life.

Oh, she had heard all about that! The gossip at Claymore Inn had been great, and nothing had been spared her curiosity. There was something in this house which it behooved the judge to secrete from sight yet more completely before her own and Reuther's entrance, and he was at work upon it now, hammering with his own hand while other persons slept! No wonder she edged her way along the fence with a shrinking, yet persistent, step. She was circling her future home and that house held a mystery.

And yet, like any other imaginative person under a stress of aroused feeling, she might very easily be magnifying some commonplace act into one of terrifying possibilities. One can hammer very innocently in his own house, even at night, when making preparations to receive fresh inmates after many years of household neglect.

She recognised her folly before reaching the adjoining field. But she went on. Where the fence turned, she turned, there being no obstruction to her doing so. This brought her into a wilderness of tangled grasses where free stepping was difficult. As she groped her way along, she had ample opportunity to hear again the intermittent sounds of the hammer, and to note that they reached their maximum at a point where the ell of the judge's study approached the fences.

Rat-tat-tat; rat-tat-tat. She hated the sound even while she whispered to herself:

'It is just some household matter he is at work upon – rehanging pictures or putting up shelves. It can be nothing else.'

Yet on laying her ear to the fence, she felt her sinister fears return; and, with shrinking glances into a darkness which told her nothing, she added in fearful murmur to herself:

'What am I taking Reuther into? I wish I knew. I wish I knew.'

Book II

The House and the Room

A Bit of Steel

'When are you going to Judge Ostrander's?'

'Tomorrow. This is my last free day. So if there is anything for me to do, do tell me, Mr Black, and let me get to work at once.'

'There is nothing you can do. The matter is hopeless.'

'You think so?'

There was misery in the tone, but the seasoned old lawyer, who had conducted her husband's defence, did not allow his sympathies to run away with his judgement.

'I certainly do, madam. I told you so the other night, and now, after a couple of days of thought on the subject, I am obliged to repeat my assertion. Your own convictions in the matter, and your story of the shadow and the peaked cap may appeal to the public and assure you some sympathy, but for an entire reversal of its opinion you will need substantial and incontrovertible evidence. You must remember – you will pardon my frankness – that your husband's character failed to stand the test of inquiry. His principles were slack, his temper violent. You have suffered from both and must know. A poor foundation I found it for his defence; and a poor one you will find it for that reversal of public opinion upon which you count, without very strong proof that the crime for which he was punished was committed by another man. You think you have such proof, but it is meagre, very meagre. Find me something definite to go upon and we will talk.'

'Discouragement; discouragement everywhere,' she complained. 'Yet I know John to have been innocent of this crime.'

The lawyer raised his brows, and toyed impatiently with his watch chain. If her convictions found any echo in his own mind, he gave no evidence of it. Doubtfully she eyed him.

'What you want,' she observed at length, with a sigh, 'is the name of the man who sauntered down the ravine ahead of my husband. I cannot give it to you now, but I do not despair of learning it.'

'Twelve years ago, madam; twelve years ago.'

'I know; but I have too much confidence in my cause to be daunted even by so serious an obstacle as that. I shall yet put my finger on this man. But I do not say that it will be immediately. I have got to renew old acquaintances; revive old gossip; possibly, recall to life almost obliterated memories.'

Mr Black, dropping his hand from his vest, gave her his first look of unqualified admiration.

'You ring true,' said he. 'I have met men qualified to lead a Forlorn Hope; but never before a woman. Allow me to express my regret that it is such a forlorn one.' Then, with a twinkle in his eye which bespoke a lighter mood, he remarked in a curiously casual tone.

'Talking of gossip, there is but one person in town who is a complete repository of all that is said or known this side of Colchester.' (The next town.) 'I never knew her to forget anything; and I never knew her to be very far from the truth. She lives near Judge Ostrander – a quaint little body, not uninteresting to talk to; a regular character, in fact. Do you know what they say about her house? That everything on God's earth can be found in it. That you've but to name an object, and she will produce it. She's had strange opportunities for collecting odds and ends, and she's never neglected one of them. Yet her house is but a box. Miss Weeks is her name.'

'I will remember it.'

Mrs Scoville rose. Then she sat down again, with the remark:

'I have a strange notion. It's a hard thing to explain and you may not understand me, but I should like to see, if it still exists, the stick – my husband's stick – with which this crime was committed. Do the police retain such things? Is there any possibility of my finding it laid away in some drawer at headquarters or on some dusty shelf?'

Mr Black was again astonished. Was this callousness or a very deep and determined purpose?

'I don't know. I never go pottering about at headquarters. What do you want to see that for? What help can you get out of that?'

'None probably; but in the presence of defeat you grasp at every hope. I dreamt of that stick last night. I was in an awful wilderness, all rocks, terrific gorges and cloud-covered, unassailable peaks. A light – one ray and one only – shone on me through the darkness. Towards this ray I was driven through great gaps in the yawning rocks and along narrow galleries sloping above an unfathomable abyss. Hope lay beyond, rescue, light. But a wall reared its black length between. I came upon it suddenly; a barrier mighty and impenetrable with its ends lost in obscurity. And the ray! the one long beam! It was still there. It shone directly upon me from an opening in this wall. It marked a gate, a gate for which I only lacked the key. Where should I find one to fit a lock so gigantic! Nowhere! unless the something which I held – which had been in my hands from the first – would be found to move its stubborn wards. I tried it and it did! it did! I hear the squeak of those tremendous hinges now, and – Mr Black, you must have guessed what that something was. My husband's stick! the bludgeon with whose shape I was so familiar twelve years ago! It is that and that only which will lead us to the light. Of this I feel quite sure.'

A short and ironical grunt answered her. Mr Black was not always the pink of politeness even in the presence of ladies.

'Most interesting,' he commented sarcastically. 'The squeak you heard was probably the protest of the bed you were reclining on against such a misuse of the opportunities it offered you. A dream listened to as evidence in this office! You must have a woman's idea of the value of my time.'

Flushing with discomfiture, she attempted to apologise, when he cut her short. 'Nevertheless, you shall see the stick if it is still to be found. I will take you to Police Headquarters if you will go heavily veiled. We don't want any recognition of you there yet.'

'You will take me –'

'The fact that I never go there may make my visit not unwelcome. I'll do it; yes, I'll do it.'

'Mr Black, you are very good. How soon –'

'Now,' he announced, jumping up to get his hat. 'A woman who can take up a man's time, with poetry and dreams, might as well have the whole afternoon. Are you ready? Shall we go?'

All alacrity, in spite of the irony of his bow and smile, he stood at the door waiting for her to follow him. This she did slowly and with manifest hesitation. She did not understand the man. People often said of her that she did not understand her own charm.

There was one little fact of which Mr Black was ignorant – that the police had had their eye on the veiled lady at Claymore Inn for several days now and knew who his companion was the instant they stepped into headquarters. In vain his plausible excuses for showing his lady friend the curiosities of the place; her interest in the details of criminology was well understood by Sergeant Doolittle, though of course he had not sounded its full depths, and could not know from anyone but Judge Ostrander himself, her grave reasons for steeping her mind again in the horrors of her husband's long-since expiated crime. And Judge Ostrander was the last man who would be likely to give him this information.

Therefore, when he saw the small, mocking eye of the lawyer begin to roam over the shelves, and beheld his jaw drop as it sometimes did when he sought to veil his purpose in an air of mild preoccupation, he knew what the next request would be, as well as if the low sounds which left Mr Black's lips at intervals had been words instead of inarticulate grunts. He was, therefore, prepared when the question did come.

'Any memorial of the Etheridge case?'

'Nothing but a stick with blood-marks on it. That, I'm afraid, wouldn't be a very agreeable sight for a lady's eye.'

'She's proof,' the lawyer whispered in the officer's ear. 'Let's see the stick.'

The sergeant considered this a very interesting experience – quite a jolly break in the dull monotony of the day. Hunting up the stick, he laid it in the lawyer's hands, and then turned his eye upon the lady.

She had gone pale, but it took her but an instant to regain her equanimity and hold out her own hand for the weapon.

With what purpose? What did she expect to see in it which others had not seen many times? She did not know, herself. She was simply following an impulse, just as she had felt herself borne on by some irresistible force in her dream. And so, the three stood there, the men's faces ironic, inquisitive, wondering at the woman's phlegm if not at her motive; hers, hidden behind her veil, but bent forward over the weapon in an attitude of devouring interest. Thus for a long, slow minute; then she impulsively raised her head and, beckoning the two men nearer, she directed attention to a splintered portion of the handle and asked them what they saw there.

'Nothing; just stick,' declared the sergeant. 'The marks you are looking for are higher up.'

'And you, Mr Black?'

He saw nothing either but stick. But he was little less abrupt in his answer.

'Do you mean those roughnesses?' he asked. 'That's where the stick was whittled. You remember that he had been whittling at the stick –'

'Who?'

The word shot from her lips so violently that for a moment both men looked staggered by it. Then Mr Black, with unaccustomed forbearance, answered gently enough:

'Why, Scoville, madam; or so the prosecution congratulated itself upon having proved to the jury's satisfaction. It did not tally with Scoville's story or with common sense I know. You remember, pardon me, I mean that anyone who read a report of the case, will remember how I handled the matter in my speech. But the prejudice in favour of the prosecution – I will not say against the defence – was too much for me, and common sense, the defendant's declarations, and my eloquence all went for nothing.'

'Of course they produced the knife?'

'Yes, they produced the knife.'

'It was in his pocket?'

'Yes.'

'Have they that here?'

'No, we haven't that here.'

'But you remember it?'

'Remember it?'

'Was it a new knife, a whole one, I mean, with all its blades sharp and in good order?'

'Yes. I can say that. I handled it several times.'

'Then, whose blade left that?' And again she pointed to the same place on the stick where her finger had fallen before.

'I don't know what you mean.' The sergeant looked puzzled. Perhaps, his eyesight was not very keen.

'Have you a magnifying glass? There is something embedded in this wood. Try and find out what it is.'

The sergeant, with a queer look at Mr Black, who returned it with interest, went for a glass, and when he had used it, the stare he gave the heavily veiled woman drove Mr Black to reach out his own hand for the glass.

'Well,' he burst forth, after a prolonged scrutiny, 'there is something there.'

'The point of a knife blade. The extreme point,' she emphasised. 'It might easily escape the observation even of the most critical, without such aid as is given by this glass.'

'No one thought of using a magnifying glass on this,' blurted out the sergeant. 'The marks made by the knife were plain enough for all to see, and that was all which seemed important.'

Mr Black said nothing; he was feeling a trifle cheap – something which did not agree with his crusty nature. Not having seen Mrs Scoville for a half-hour without her veil, her influence over him was on the wane, and he began to regret that he had laid himself open to this humiliation.

She saw that it would be left for her to wind up the interview and get out of the place without arousing too much attention. With a self-possession which astonished both men, knowing her immense interest in this matter, she laid down the stick, and, with a gentle shrug of her shoulders, remarked in an easy tone:

'Well, it's curious! The ins and outs of a crime, I mean. Such a discovery ten years after the event (I think you said ten years) is very interesting.' Then she sighed: 'Alas! it's too late to benefit the one whose life it might have saved. Mr Black, shall we be going? I have spent a most entertaining quarter of an hour.'

Mr Black glanced from her to the sergeant before he joined her. Then, with one of his sour smiles directed towards the former, he said:

'I wouldn't be talking about this, sergeant. It will do no good, and may subject us to ridicule.'

The sergeant, none too well pleased, nodded slightly. Seeing which, she spoke up:

'I don't know about that, I should think it but proper reparation to the dead to let it be known that his own story of innocence has received this late confirmation.'

But the lawyer continued to shake his head, with a very sharp look at the sergeant. If he could have his way, he would have this matter stop just where it was.

Alas! he was not to have his way, as he saw, when at parting he essayed to make a final protest against a public as well as premature reopening of this old case. She did not see her position as he did, and wound up her plea by saying:

'The public must lend their aid, if we are to get the evidence we need to help us. Can we find the man who whittled that stick? Never. But someone else may. I am going to give the men and women of this town a chance. I'm too anxious to clear my husband's memory to shrink from any publicity. You see, I believe that the real culprit will yet be found.'

The lawyer dropped argument. When a woman speaks in that tone, persuasion is worse than useless. Besides, she had raised her veil. Strange, what a sensitive countenance will do!

All is Clear

'This is my daughter, Judge Ostrander, Reuther, this is the judge.'

The introduction took place at the outer gates whither the judge had gone to receive them.

Reuther threw aside her veil, and looked up into the face bent courteously towards her. It had no look of Oliver. Somehow she felt glad. She could hardly have restrained herself if he had met her gaze with Oliver's eyes. They were fine eyes notwithstanding, piercing by nature but just now misty with a feeling that took away all her fear. He was going to like her; she saw it in every trembling line of his countenance, and at the thought a smile rose to her lips which, if fleeting, lent such an ethereal aspect to her beauty that he forgave Oliver then and there for a love which never could be crowned, but which henceforth could no longer be regarded by him as despicable.

With a courteous gesture he invited them in, but stopping to lock one gate before leading them through the other, Mrs Scoville had time to observe that since her last visit with its accompanying inroad of the populace, the two openings which at this point gave access to the walk between the fences had been closed up with boards so rude and dingy that they must have come from some old lumber pile in attic or cellar.

The judge detected her looking at them.

'I have cut off my nightly promenade,' said he. 'With youth in the house, more cheerful habits must prevail. Tomorrow I shall have my lawn cut, and if I must walk after sundown I will walk there.'

The two women exchanged glances. Perhaps their gloomy anticipations were not going to be realised.

But once within the house, the judge showed embarrassment. He was conscious of its unfitness for their fastidious taste and yet he had not known how to improve matters. In his best days he had concerned himself very little with household affairs, and for the last few years he had not given a thought to anything outside his own rooms. Bela had done all – and Bela was pre-eminently a cook, not a general house-servant. How would these women regard the disorder and the dust?

'I have few comforts to offer,' said he, opening a door at his right and then hastily closing it again. 'This part of the house is, as you see, completely dismantled and not – very clean. But you shall have carte blanche to arrange to your liking one of these rooms for your sitting room and parlour. There is furniture in the attic and you may buy freely whatever else is necessary. I don't want to discourage little Reuther. As for your bedrooms –' He stopped, hemmed a little and flushed a vivid red as he pointed up the dingy flight of uncarpeted stairs towards which he had led them. 'They are above; but it is with shame I admit that I have not gone above this floor for many years. Consequently, I don't know how it looks up there or whether you can even find towels and things. Perhaps you will go up first, Mrs Scoville. I will stay here while you take a look. I really, couldn't have a strange cleaning-woman here, or anyone who would make remarks. Have I counted too much on your good nature?'

'No; not at all. In fact, you simply arouse all the housekeeping instincts within me. I will be down in a minute. Reuther, I leave you with the judge.'

She ran lightly up. The next instant they heard her sneeze, then they caught the sound of a window rattling up, followed by a streak of light falling slant-wise across the dismal stairs.

The judge drew a breath of relief and led Reuther towards a door at the end of the hall.

'This is the way to the dining room and kitchen,' he explained. 'I have been accustomed to having my meals served in my own room, but after this I shall join you at table. Here,' he continued, leading her up to the iron door, 'is the entrance to my den. You may knock here if you want me, but there is a curtain beyond, which no one lifts but myself. You understand, my dear, and will excuse an old man's eccentricities?'

She smiled, rejoicing only in the caressing voice, and in the yearning, almost fatherly, manner with which he surveyed her.

'I quite understand,' said she; 'and so will mother.'

'Reuther,' he now observed with a strange intermixture of gentleness and authority, 'there is one thing I wish to say to you at the very start. I may grow to love you – God knows that a little affection would be a welcome change in my life – but I want you to know and know now, that all the love in the world will not change my decision as to the impropriety of a match between you and my son Oliver. That settled, there is no reason why all should not be clear between us.'

'All is clear.'

Faint and far off the words sounded, though she was standing so near he could have laid his hand on her shoulder. Then she gave one sob as though in saying this she heard the last clod fall upon what would never see resurrection again in this life, and, lifting her head, looked him straight in the eye with a decision and a sweetness which bowed his spirit and caused his head in turn to fall upon his breast.

'What a father can do for a child, I will do for you,' he murmured, and led her back to her mother, who was now coming downstairs.

A week, and Deborah Scoville had evolved a home out of chaos. That is, within limits. There was one door on that upper story which she had simply opened and shut; nor had she entered the judge's rooms, or even offered to do so. The ban which had been laid upon her daughter she felt applied equally to herself; that is for the present. Later, there must be a change. So particular a man as the judge would soon find himself too uncomfortable to endure the lack of those attentions which he had been used to in Bela's day. He had not even asked for clean sheets, and sometimes she had found herself wondering, with a strange shrinking of her heart, if his bed was ever made, or whether he had not been driven at times to lie down in his clothes.

She had some reason for these doubtful conclusions. In her ramblings through the house she had come upon Bela's room. It was in a loft over the kitchen and she had been much amazed at its condition. In some respects it looked as decent as she could expect, but in the matter of bed and bedclothes it presented an aspect somewhat startling. The clothes were there, tossed in a heap on the floor, but there was no bed in sight nor anything which could have served as such.

It had been dragged out. Evidences of this were everywhere; dragged out, and down the narrow, twisted staircase which was the only medium of communication between the lower floor and this loft. As she noted the marks made by its passage down the steps, the unhappy vision rose before her of the judge, immaculate in attire and unaccustomed of hand, tugging at this bed and alternately pushing and pulling it by main strength down this contracted, many-cornered staircase. A smile, half pitiful, half self-scornful curved her lips as she remembered the rat-tat-tat she had heard on that dismal night when she clung listening to the fence, and wondered now if it had not been the bumping of this cot sliding from step to step.

But no! the repeated stroke of a hammer is unmistakable. He had played the carpenter that night as well as the mover, and with no visible results. Mystery still reigned in the house for all the charm and order she had brought into it; a mystery which deeply interested her, and which she yet hoped to solve, notwithstanding its remoteness from the real problem of her existence.

The Picture

Night! and Deborah Scoville waiting anxiously for Reuther to sleep, that she might brood undisturbed over a new and disturbing event which for the whole day had shaken her out of her wonted poise, and given, as it were, a new phase to her life in this house.

Already had she stepped several times to her daughter's room and looked in, only to meet Reuther's unquiet eye turned towards hers in silent inquiry. Was her own uneasiness infectious? Was the child determined to share her vigil? She would wait a little longer this time and see.

Their rooms were over the parlour and thus as far removed as possible from the judge's den. In her own, which was front, she felt at perfect ease, and it was without any fear of disturbing either him or Reuther that she finally raised her window and allowed the cool wind to soothe her heated cheeks.

How calm the aspect of the lawn and its clustering shrubs. Dimly seen though they were through the leaves of the vines she had but partially clipped, she felt the element of peace which comes with perfect quiet, and was fain to forget for a while the terrors it so frequently conceals. The moon, which had been invisible up to this moment, emerged from scurrying clouds as she quietly watched the scene; and in an instant her peace was gone and all the thronging difficulties of her position came rushing back upon her in full force, as all the details of the scene, so mercifully hidden just now, flashed again upon her vision.

Perched, as she was, in a window overlooking the lane, she had but to lift her eyes from the double fence (that symbol of sad seclusion) to light on the trees rising above that unspeakable ravine, black with memories she felt strangely like forgetting tonight. Beyond... how it stood out on the bluff! it had never seemed to stand out more threateningly!... the bifurcated mass of dismal ruin from which men had turned their eyes these many years now! But the moon loved it; caressed it; dallied with it, lighting up its toppling chimney and empty, staring gable. There, where the black streak could be seen, she had stood with the judge in that struggle of wills which had left its scars upon them both to this very day. There, hidden but always seen by those who remembered the traditions of the place, mouldered away the walls of that old closet where the timorous, God-stricken suicide had breathed out his soul. She had stood in it only the other day, penned from outsiders' view by the judge's outstretched arms. Then, she had no mind for bygone horrors, her own tragedy weighed too heavily upon her; but tonight, as she gazed, fascinated, anxious to forget herself, anxious to indulge in any thought which would relieve her from dwelling on the question she must settle before she slept, she allowed her wonder and her revulsion to have free course. Instead of ignoring, she would recall the story of the place as it had been told her when she first came to settle in its neighbourhood.

Spencer's Folly! Well, it had been that, and Spencer's den of dissipation too! There were great tales – but it was not of these she was thinking, but of the night of storm – (of the greatest storm of which any record remained in Shelby) when the wind tore down branches and toppled down chimneys; when cattle were smitten in the field and men on the highway; when the old bridge, since replaced, buckled up and sank in the roaring flood it could no longer span, and the bluff towering overhead, flared into flame, and the house which was its glory, was smitten apart by the descending bolt as by a Titan sword, and blazed like a beacon to the sky.

This was long before she herself had come to Shelby; but she had been told the story so often that it was quite as vivid to her as if she had been one of the innumerable men and women who had crowded the glistening, swimming streets to view this spectacle of destruction. The family had been gone for months, and so no pity mingled with the excitement. Not till the following day did the awful nature of the event break in its full horror upon the town. Among the ruins, in a closet which the flames had spared, they found hunched up in one corner, the body of a man, in whose seared throat a wound appeared which had not been made by lightning or fire. Spencer! Spencer himself, returned they knew not how, to die of this self-inflicted wound, in the dark corner of his grand but neglected dwelling.

And this was what made the horror of the place till the tragedy of the opposite hollow added crime to crime, and the spot became outlawed to all sensitive citizens. Folly and madness and the vengeance of high heaven upon unhallowed walls, spoke to her from that towering mass, bathed though it was just now in liquid light under the impartial moon.

But as she continued to survey it, the clouds came trooping up once more, and the vision was wiped out and with it all memories save those of a nearer trouble – a more pressing necessity.

Withdrawing from the window, she crept again to Reuther's room and peered carefully in. Innocence was asleep at last. Not a movement disturbed the closed lids on the wax-like cheek. Even the breath came so softly that it hardly lifted the youthful breast. Repose the most perfect and in the form of all others the sweetest to a tender mother, lay before her and touched her already yearning heart to tears. Lighting a candle and shielding it with her hand, she gazed long and earnestly at Reuther's sweet face. Yes, she was right. Sorrow was slowly sapping the fountain of her darling's youth. If Reuther was to be saved, hope must come soon. With a sob and a prayer, the mother left the room, and locking herself into her own, sat down at last to face the new perplexity, the monstrous enigma which had come into her life.

It had followed in natural sequence from a proposal made by the judge that some attention should be given his long-neglected rooms. He had said on rising from the breakfast table (the words are more or less important):

'I am really sorry to trouble you, Mrs Scoville; but if you have time this morning, will you clean up my study before I leave? The carriage is ordered for half-past nine.'

The task was one she had long desired to perform, and would have urged upon him daily had she dared, but the limitations he set for its accomplishment struck her aghast.

'Do you mean that you wish to remain there while I work? You will be choked, Judge.'

'No more than I have been for the last two days. You may enter any time.' And going in, he left the door open behind him.

'He will lock it when he goes out,' she commented to herself. 'I had better hasten.'

Giving Reuther the rest of the work to do, she presently appeared before him with pail and broom and a pile of fresh linen. Nothing more commonplace could be imagined, but to her, if not to him, there underlay this especial act of ordinary housewifery a possible enlightenment on a subject which had held the whole community in a state of curiosity for years. She was going to enter the room which had been barred from public sight by poor Bela's dying body. She was going to see – or had he only meant that she was to have her way with the library – the room where she had already been and much of which she remembered. The doubt gave a tremulous eagerness to her step and caused her eye to wander immediately to that forbidden corner soon as she had stepped over the threshold.

The bedroom door was open – proof that she was expected to enter there. Meanwhile, she felt the eye of the judge upon her and endeavoured to preserve a perfect composure and to sink the curious and inquiring woman in the diligent housekeeper.

But she could not, quite. Two facts of which she immediately became cognisant, prevented this. First, the great room before her presented a bare floor, whereas on her first visit it had been very decently, if not cheerfully, covered by a huge carpet rug. Secondly, the judge's chair, which had once looked immovable, had been dragged forward into such a position that he could keep his own eye on the bedroom door. Manifestly she was not to be allowed to pursue her duties unwatched. Certainly she had to take more than one look at the everyday implements she carried to retain that balance of judgement which should prevent her from becoming the dupe of her own expectations.

'I do not expect you to clean up here as thoroughly as you have your own rooms upstairs,' he remarked, as she passed him. 'You haven't the time, or I the patience for too many strokes of the broom. And Mrs Scoville,' he called out as she slipped through the doorway, 'leave the door open and keep away as much as possible from the side of the room where I have nailed up the curtain. I had rather not have that touched.'

She turned with a smile and nodded. She felt that she had been set to work with a string tied round her feet. Not touch the curtain! Why, that was the one thing in the room she wanted to touch; for in it she not only saw the carpet which had been taken up from the floor of the study, but a possible screen behind which anything might lurk – even his redoubtable secret.

Or had it another and much simpler explanation? Might it not have been hung there merely as a shield to the window. The room must have a window and there was none to be seen elsewhere. It would be like him to shut out light and air. She would ask.

'There is no window,' she observed, looking back at the judge.

'No,' was his short reply.

Slowly she set down her pail. One thing was settled. It was Bela's cot she saw before her – a cot without any sheets. These had been left behind in the dead negro's room, and the judge had been sleeping just as she had feared, wrapped in a rug and with uncovered pillow. This pillow was his own; it had not been brought down with the bed. She hastily slipped a cover on it, and without calling any further attention to her act, began to make up the bed.

Conscious that the papers he made a feint of reading were but a cover for his watchfulness, she moved about in a matter-of-fact way and did not spare him the clouds of dust which presently rose before her broom. She could have managed it more deftly, would have done so at another time, but it was her express intention just now to make him move back out of her way, if only to give her an opportunity to disturb by a backward stroke of her broom the folds of the carpet-rug and learn if she could what lay hidden behind it.

But the judge was impervious to discomfort. He coughed and shook his head, but did not budge an inch. Before she had begun to put things in order, the clock struck the half-hour.

'Oh!' she protested, with a pleading glance his way, 'I'm not half done.'

'There's another day to follow,' he dryly remarked, rising and taking a key from his pocket.

The act expressed his wishes; and she was proceeding to carry out her things when a quick sliding noise from the wall she was passing, drew her attention and caused her to spring forward in an involuntary effort to catch a picture which had slipped its cord and was falling to the floor.

A shout from the judge of 'Stand aside, let me come!' reached her too late. She had grasped and lifted the picture and seen –

But first, let me explain. This picture was not like the others hanging about. It was a veiled one. From some motive of precaution or characteristic desire for concealment on the part of the judge, it had been closely wrapped about in heavy brown paper before being hung, and in the encounter which ensued between the falling picture and the spear of an image standing on a table underneath, this paper had received a slit through which Deborah had been given a glimpse of the canvas beneath.

The shock of what she saw would have unnerved a less courageous woman.

It was a highly finished portrait of Oliver in his youth, with a broad band of black painted directly across the eyes.

'Don't! Don't!'

In recalling this startling moment, Deborah wondered as much at her own aplomb as at that of Judge Ostrander. Not only had she succeeded in suppressing all recognition of what had thus been discovered to her, but had carried her powers of self-repression so far as to offer, and with good grace too, to assist him in rehanging the picture. This perfection of acting had its full reward. With equal composure he excused her from the task, and, adding some expression of regret at his well-known carelessness in not looking better after his effects, bowed her from the room with only a slight increase of his usual courteous reserve.

But later, when thought came and with it certain recollections, what significance the incident acquired in her mind, and what a long line of terrors it brought in its train!

It was no casual act, this defacing of a son's well-loved features. It had a meaning – a dark and desperate meaning. Nor was the study-wall the natural home of this picture. An unfaded square which she had noted on the wallpaper of the inner room showed where its original place had been. There in full view of the broken-hearted father when he woke and in darksome watchfulness while he slept, it had played its heavy part in his long torment – a galling reminder of – what?

It was to answer this question – to face this new view of Oliver and the bearing it had on the relations she had hoped to establish between him and Reuther, that she had waited for the house to be silent and her child asleep. If the defacing marks she had seen meant that the cause of separation between father and son lay in some past fault of Oliver himself, serious enough for such a symbol to be necessary to reconcile the judge to their divided lives, she should know it and know it soon. The night should not pass without that review of the past by which alone she could now judge Oliver Ostrander.

She had spoken of him as noble; she had forced herself to believe him so, and in profession and in many of his actions he had been so, but had she ever been wholly pleased with him? To go back to their first meeting, what impression had he made upon her then? Had it been altogether favourable and such as would be natural in one of his repute? Hardly; but then the shock of her presentation to one who had possibly seen her under other and shameful conditions had been great, and her judgement could scarcely have full play while her whole attention was absorbed in watching for some hint of recognition on his part.

But when this apprehension had vanished; when quite assured that he had failed to see in the widowed Mrs Averill the wife of the man who had died a felon's death in Shelby, had her spirits risen and her eyes cleared to his great merits as she had heard them extolled by people of worth and intellectual standing? Alas, no. There had been something in his look – a lack of spontaneity which had not fitted in with her expectations.

And in the months which followed, when as Reuther's suitor she saw him often and intimately – how had she regarded him then? More leniently of course. In her gratification at prospects so far beyond any she had a right to expect for her child, she had taken less note of this successful man's defects. Peculiarities of conversation and manner which had seemed to bespeak a soul far from confident in its hopes, resolved themselves into the uneasy moods of a man who had a home he never visited, a father he never saw.

But had she been really justified in this easy view of things? If the break between his father and himself was the result of nothing deeper than a difference of temperament, tastes or even opinions, why should he have shrunk with such morbid distaste from all allusions to that father? Was it natural? She may have looked upon it as being so in the heyday of her hopes and when she had a secret herself to hide, but could she so degrade her judgement now?

And what of his conduct towards Reuther? Had that been all her mother heart could ask of a man of his seemingly high instincts? She had assured his father in her first memorable interview with him that it had been perfectly honourable and above all reproach. And so it had been as far as mere words went. But words are not all; it is the tender look, the manly bearing, the tone which springs from the heart which tells in great crises; and these had all been lacking. Generous as he attempted to show himself, there was nothing in his bearing to match that of Reuther as she took her quiet leave of him and entered upon a fate so much bitterer for her than for him.

This lack of grace in him had not passed unnoted by her even at the time, but being herself so greatly in fault she had ascribed it to the recoil of a proud man from the dread of social humiliation. But it took another aspect under the strong light just thrown upon his early life by her discovery in the room below. Nothing but some act, unforgivable and unforgettable would account for that black mark drawn between a father's eyes and his son's face. No bar sinister could tell a stronger tale. But this was no bar sinister; rather the deliberate stigmatising of one yet loved, but banned for a reason which was little short of – here her conclusions stopped; she would not allow her imagination to carry her any further.

Unhappy mother, just as she saw something like a prospect of releasing her long-dead husband from the odium of an unjust sentence, to be shaken by this new doubt as to the story and character of the man for whose union with her beloved child she was so anxiously struggling! Should it not make her pause? Should she not show wisdom in giving a different meaning from any she had hitherto done, to that stern and inexorable dictum of the father, that no marriage between the two could or should ever be considered?

It was a question for which no ready answer seemed possible in her present mood. Better to await the time when some move had to be made or some definite decision reached. Now she must rest – rest and not think.

Have any of us ever made the like acknowledgment and then tried to sleep? In half an hour Mrs Scoville was again upon her feet, this time with a determination which ignored the hour and welcomed night as though it were broad noon day.

There was a room on this upper floor into which neither she nor Reuther had ever stepped. She had once looked in but that was all. Tonight – because she could not sleep; because she must not think – she was resolved to enter it. Oliver's room! left as he had left it years before! What might it not tell of a past concerning which she longed to be reassured?

The father had laid no restrictions upon her, in giving her this floor for her use. Rights which he ignored she could afford to appropriate. Dressing sufficiently for warmth, she lit a candle, put out the light in her own room and started down the hall.

If she paused on reaching the threshold of this long-closed room, it was but natural. The clock on Reuther's mantel had sent its three clear strokes through the house as her hand fell on the knob, and to her fearing heart and now well-awakened imagination these strokes had sounded in her ear like a 'don't! don't!' The silence, so gruesome, now that this shrill echo had ceased, was poor preparation for her task. Yet would she have welcomed any sound – the least which could have been heard? No, that were a worse alternative than silence; and, relieved of that momentary obsession consequent upon an undertaking of doubtful outcome, she pushed the door fully open and entered.

A smother of dust – an odour of decay – a lack of all order in the room's arrangements and furnishings – even a general disarray, hallowed, if not affected, by time – for all this she was prepared. But not for the wild confusion – the inconceivable litter and all the other signs she saw about her of a boy's mad packing and reckless departure. Here her imagination, so lively at times, had failed her; and, as her eye became accustomed to the semi-obscurity, and she noted the heaps of mouldering clothing lying amid overturned chairs and trampled draperies, she felt her heart grow cold with a nameless dread she could only hope to counteract by quick and impulsive action.

But what action? Was it for her to touch, to rearrange, to render clean and orderly this place of unknown memories? She shrank with inconceivable distaste from the very idea of such meddling; and, though she saw and noted all, she did not put out so much as a finger towards any object there till – there was an inner door, and this some impulse drove her to open. A small closet stood revealed, empty but for one article. When she saw this article she gave a great gasp; then she uttered a low pshaw! and with a shrug of the shoulders drew back and flung to the door. But she opened it again. She had to. One cannot live in hideous doubt, without an effort to allay it. She must look at that small, black article again; look at it with candle in hand; see for herself that her fears were without foundation; that a shadow had made the outline on the wall which –

She found herself laughing. There was nothing else to do. She with thoughts like these; she, Reuther's mother! Verily, the early hours of morning were unsuited for any such work as this. She would go back to her own room and bed – But she only went as far as the bureau where she had left the candlestick, which having seized, she returned to the closet and slowly, reluctantly reopened the door. Before her on the wall hung a cap, and it was no shadow which gave it that look like her husband's; the broad peak was there. She had not been mistaken; it was the duplicate of the one she had picked up in the attic of the Claymore Inn when that inn was simply a tavern.

Well, and what if it was! – such was her thought a moment later. She would take down the cap, set it before her and look at it till her brain grew clear of its follies.

But after she had it in her hand she found herself looking anywhere but at the cap. She stared at the floor, the walls about, the desk she had mechanically approached. She even noticed the books lying about on the shelves before her and took down one or two, to glance at their title-pages in a blind curiosity she could not account for the next minute. Then she found herself looking into a drawer half drawn out and filled with all sorts of heterogeneous articles: sealing-wax, a roll of pins, a pen-holder, a knife – a knife! Why should she recoil again at that? Nothing could be more ordinary than to find a knife in the desk-drawer of a young man! The fact was not worth a thought; yet before she knew it, her fingers were creeping towards this knife, had picked it up from among the other scattered articles, had closed upon it, let it drop again, only to seize hold of it yet more determinedly and carry it straight to the light.

Who spoke? Had anyone spoken? Was there any sound in the air at all? She heard none, yet the sense of sound was in her ear, as though it had been and passed. When the glance she threw about her came back to her outstretched hand, she knew that the cry, if cry it were, had been within, and that the echoes of the room had remained undisturbed. The knife was lying open on her palm, and from one of the blades the end had been nipped, just enough of it to match –

Was she mad! She thought so for a moment; then she laid down the knife close against the cap and contemplated them both for more minutes than she ever reckoned.

And the stillness, which had been profound, became deeper yet. Not even Reuther's clock sounded its small note.

The candle fluttering low in its socket roused her at last from her abstraction. Catching up the two articles which had so enthralled her, she restored the one to the closet, the other to the drawer, and, with swift but silent step, regained her own room where she buried her head in her pillow, weeping and praying until the morning light, breaking in upon her grief, awoke her to the obligations of her position and the necessity of silence concerning all the experiences of this night.

Unwelcome Truths

Silence. Yes, silence was the one and only refuge remaining to her. Yet, after a few days, the constant self-restraint which it entailed, ate like a canker into her peace, and undermined a strength which she had always considered inexhaustible. Reuther began to notice her pallor, and the judge to look grave. She was forced to complain of a cold (and in this she was truthful enough) to account for her alternations of feverish impulse and deadly lassitude.

The trouble she had suppressed was having its quiet revenge. Should she continue to lie inert and breathless under the threatening hand of Fate, or risk precipitating the doom she sought to evade, by proceeding with inquiries upon the result of which she could no longer calculate?

She recalled the many mistakes made by those who had based their conclusions upon circumstantial evidence (her husband's conviction in fact) and made up her mind to brave everything by having this matter out with Mr Black. Then the pendulum swung back, and she found that she could not do this because, deep down in her heart, there burrowed a monstrous doubt (how born or how cherished she would not question), which Mr Black, with an avidity she could not combat, would at once detect and pounce upon. Better silence and a slow death than that.

But was there no medium course? Could she not learn from some other source where Oliver had been on the night of that old-time murder? Miss Weeks was a near neighbour and saw everything. Miss Weeks never forgot; to Miss Weeks she would go.

With instructions to Reuther calculated to keep that diligent child absorbed and busy in her absence, she started out upon her quest. She had reached the first gate, passed it and was on the point of opening the second one, when she saw on the walk before her a small slip of brown paper. Lifting it, she perceived upon it an almost illegible scrawl which she made out to read thus:

For Mrs Scoville:
Do not go wandering all over the town for clues. Look closer home.

And below:

You remember the old saying about jumping from the frying pan into the fire. Let your daughter be warned. It is better to be singed than consumed.

Warned! Reuther? Better be singed than consumed? What madness was this? How singed and how consumed? Then because Deborah's mind was quick, it all flashed upon her, bowing her in spirit to the ground. Reuther had been singed by the knowledge of her father's ignominy, she would be consumed if inquiry were carried further and this ignominy transferred to the proper culprit. Consumed! There was but one person whose disgrace could consume Reuther. Oliver alone could be meant. The doubts she had tried to suppress from her own mind were shared by others, others!

The discovery overpowered her and she caught herself crying aloud in utter self-abandonment:

'I will not go to Miss Weeks. I will take Reuther and fly to some wilderness so remote and obscure that we can never be found.'

Yet in five minutes she was crossing the road, her face composed, her manner genial, her tongue ready for any encounter. The truth must be hers at all hazards. If it could be found here, then here would she seek it. Her long struggle with fate had brought to the fore every latent power she possessed.

One stroke on the tiny brass knocker, old-fashioned and quaint like everything else in this doll-house, brought Miss Weeks' small and animated figure to the door. She had seen Mrs Scoville coming, and was ready with her greeting. A dog from the big house across the way would have been welcomed there. The eager little seamstress had never forgotten her hour in the library with the half-unconscious judge.

'Mrs Scoville!' she exclaimed, fluttering and leading the way into the best room; 'how very kind you are to give me this chance for making my apologies. You know we have met before.'

'Have we?' Mrs Scoville did not remember, but she smiled her best smile and was gratified to note the look of admiration with which Miss Weeks surveyed her more than tasty dress before she raised her eyes to meet the smile to whose indefinable charm so many had succumbed. 'It is a long time since I lived here,' Deborah proceeded as soon as she saw that she had this woman, too, in her net. 'The friends I had then, I scarcely hope to have now; my trouble was of the kind which isolates one completely. I am glad to have you acknowledge an old acquaintance. It makes me feel less lonely in my new life.'

'Mrs Scoville, I am only too happy.' It was bravely said, for the little woman was in a state of marked embarrassment. Could it be that her visitor had not recognised her as the person who had accosted her on that memorable morning she first entered Judge Ostrander's forbidden gates?

'I have been told –' thus Deborah easily proceeded, 'that for a small house yours contains the most wonderful assortment of interesting objects. Where did you ever get them?'

'My father was a collector, on a very small scale of course, and my mother had a passion for hoarding which prevented anything from going out of this house after it had once come into it, and a great many strange things have come into it. There have even been bets made as to the finding or not finding of a given object under this roof. Pardon me, perhaps I bore you.'

'Not at all. It's very interesting. But what about the bets?'

'Oh, just this. One day two men were chaffing each other in one of the hotel lobbies, and the conversation turning upon what this house held, one of them wagered that he knew of something I could not fish out of my attic, and when the other asked what, he said an aeroplane – why he didn't say a locomotive, I don't know; but he said an aeroplane, and the other, taking him up, they came here together and put me the question straight. Mrs Scoville, you may not believe it, but my good friend won that bet. Years ago when people were just beginning to talk about air-sailing machines, my brother who was visiting me, amused his leisure hours in putting together something he called a 'flyer'. And what is more, he went up in it, too, but he came down so rapidly that he kept quite still about it, and it fell to me to lug the broken thing in. So when these gentlemen asked to see an aeroplane, I took them into a lean-to where I store my least desirable things, and there pointed out a mass of wings and bits of tangled wire, saying as dramatically as I could: "There she is!" And they first stared, then laughed; and when one complained: "That's a ruin, not an aeroplane," I answered with all the demureness possible; "and what is any aeroplane but a ruin in prospect? This has reached the ruin stage; that's all." So the bet was paid and my reputation sustained. Don't you find it a little amusing?'

'I do, indeed,' smiled Deborah. 'Now, if I wanted to make the test, I should take another course from these men. I should not pick out something strange, or big, or unlikely. I should choose some everyday object, some little matter –' She paused as if to think.

'What little matter?' asked the other complacently.

'My husband once had a cap,' mused Mrs Scoville thoughtfully. 'It had an astonishingly broad peak in front. Have you a cap like that?'

Miss Weeks' eyes opened. She stared in some consternation at Mrs Scoville, who hastened to say:

'You wonder that I can mention my husband. Perhaps you will not be so surprised when I tell you that in my eyes he is a martyr, and quite guiltless of the crime for which he was punished.'

'You think that?' There was real surprise in the manner of the questioner. Mrs Scoville's brow cleared. She was pleased at this proof that her affairs had not yet reached the point of general gossip.

'Miss Weeks, I am a mother. I have a young and lovely daughter. Can I look in her innocent eyes and believe her father to have so forgotten his responsibilities as to overshadow her life with crime? No, I will not believe it. Circumstances were in favour of his conviction, but he never lifted the stick which struck down Algernon Etheridge.'

Miss Weeks, who had sat quite still during the utterance of these remarks, fidgeted about at their close, with what appeared to the speaker, a sudden and quite welcome relief.

'Oh!' she murmured; and said no more. It was not a topic she found easy of discussion.

'Let us go back to the cap,' suggested Deborah, with another of her fascinating smiles. 'Are you going to show me one such as I have described?'

'Let me see. A man's cap with an extra broad peak! Mrs Scoville, I fear that you have caught me. There are caps hanging up in various closets, but I don't remember any with a peak beyond the ordinary.'

'Yet they are worn? You have seen such?'

A red spot sprang out on the faded cheek of the woman as she answered impulsively:

'Oh, yes. Young Mr Oliver Ostrander used to wear one. I wish I had asked him for it,' she pursued, naively. 'I should not have had to acknowledge defeat at your very first inquiry.'

'Oh! you needn't care about that,' laughed Deborah, in rather a hard tone for her. She had made her point, but was rather more frightened than pleased at her success. 'There must be a thousand articles you naturally would lack. I could name –'

'Don't, don't!' the little woman put in breathlessly. 'I have many odd things but of course not everything. For instance –' But here she caught sight of the other's abstracted eye, and dropped the subject. The sadness which now spread over the very interesting countenance of her visitor, offered her an excuse for the introduction of a far more momentous topic; one she had burned to introduce but had not known how.

'Mrs Scoville, I hear that Judge Ostrander has got your daughter a piano. That is really a wonderful thing for him to do. Not that he is so close with his money, but that he has always been so set against all gaiety and companionship. I suppose you did not know the shock it would be to him when you asked Bela to let you into the gates.'

'No! I didn't know. But it is all right now. The judge seems to welcome the change. Miss Weeks, did you know Algernon Etheridge well enough to tell me if he was as good and irreproachable a man as they all say?'

'He was a good man, but he had a dreadfully obstinate streak in his disposition and very set ideas. I have heard that he and the judge used to argue over a point for hours. And he was most always wrong. For instance, he was wrong about Oliver.'

'Oliver?'

'Judge Ostrander's son, you know. Mr Etheridge wanted him to study for a professorship; but the boy was determined to go into journalism, and you see what a success he has made of it. As a professor he would probably have been a failure.'

'Was this difference of opinion on the calling he should pursue, the cause of Oliver's leaving home in the way he did?' continued Deborah, conscious of walking on very thin ice.

But Miss Weeks rather welcomed than resented this curiosity. Indeed she was never tired of enlarging upon the Ostranders. It was, therefore, with a very encouraging alacrity she responded:

'I have never thought so. The judge would not quarrel with Oliver on so small a point as that. My idea is, though I never talk of it much, that they had a great quarrel over Mr Etheridge. Oliver never liked the old student; I've watched them and I've seen. He hated his coming to the house so much; he hated the way his father singled him out and deferred to him and made him the confidant of all his troubles. When they went on their walks, Oliver always hung back, and more than once I have seen him make a grimace of distaste when his father urged him forward. He was only a boy, I know, but his dislikes meant something, and if it ever happened that he spoke out his whole mind, you may be sure that some very bitter words passed.'

Was this meant as an innuendo? Could it be that she shared the very serious doubts of Deborah's anonymous correspondent?

Impossible to tell. Such nervous, fussy little bodies often possess minds of unexpected subtlety. Deborah gave up all hope of understanding her, and, accepting her statements at their face value, effusively remarked:

'You must have a very superior mind to draw such conclusions from the little you have seen. I have heard many explanations given for the breach you name, but never any so reasonable.'

A flash from the spinster's wary eye, then a burst of courage and the quick retort:

'And what explanation does Oliver himself give? You ought to know, Mrs Scoville.'

The attack was as sudden as it was unexpected. Deborah flushed and trimmed her sails for this new tack, and insinuating gently, 'Then you have heard –' waited for the enlightenment these words were likely to evoke.

It came quickly enough.

'That he expected to marry your daughter? Oh, yes, Mrs Scoville; it's the common talk here now. I hope you don't mind my mentioning it.'

Deborah's head went up. She faced the other fairly, with the look born of mother passion, and mother passion only.

'Reuther is blameless in this matter,' she protested. 'She was brought up in ignorance of what I felt sure would prove a handicap and misery to her. She loves Oliver as she will never love any other man, but when she was told her real name and understood fully what that name carries with it, she declined to saddle him with her shame. That's her story, Miss Weeks; one that hardly fits her appearance which is very delicate. And, let me add, having once accepted her father's name, she refuses to be known by any other. I have brought her to Shelby where to our own surprise and Reuther's great happiness, we have been taken in by Judge Ostrander, an act of kindness for which we are very grateful.' Miss Weeks got up, took down one of her rarest treasures from an old etagere standing in one corner and laid it in Mrs Scoville's hand.

'For your daughter,' she declared. 'Noble girl! I hope she will be happy.'

The mother was touched. But not quite satisfied yet of the giver's real feelings towards Oliver, she was not willing to conclude the interview until she understood her small hostess better. She, therefore, looked admiringly at the vase (it was really choice); and, after thanking its donor warmly, proceeded to remark:

'There is but one thing that will ever make Reuther happy, and that she cannot have unless a miracle occurs.'

'Oliver?' suggested the other, with a curious, wan little smile.

Deborah nodded.

'And what miracle –'

'Oh, I do not wonder you pause. This is not the day of miracles. But if my belief in my husband could be shared; if by some fortuitous chance I should be enabled to clear his name, might not love and loyalty be left to do the rest? Wouldn't the judge's objections, in that case, be removed? What do you think, Miss Weeks?'

The warmth, the abandon, the confidence she expressed in this final question were indescribable. Miss Weeks' conventional mannerisms melted before it. She could no more withstand the witchery of this woman's tone and manner than if she had been a man subdued by the charm of sex. But nothing, not even her newly awakened sympathy for this agreeable woman, could make her untruthful. She might believe in the miracle of a reversal of judgment in the case of a falsely condemned criminal, but not of an Ostrander accepting humiliation, even at the hands of Love. She felt that in justice to this new friendship she should say so.

'Do you ask me?' she began. 'Then I feel that I must admit to you that the Ostrander pride is proverbial. Oliver may think he would be happy if he married your daughter under these changed conditions; but I should be fearful of the reaction which would certainly follow when he found that old shames are not so easily outlived. There is temper in the family, though you would never think it to hear the judge speak; and if your daughter is delicate –'

'Is it of her you are thinking?' interrupted Deborah, with a new tone in her voice.

'Not altogether; you see I knew Oliver first.'

'And are fond of him?'

'Fond is a big word. But I cannot help having some feeling for the boy I have seen grow up from a babe in arms to a healthy, brilliant manhood.'

'And having this feeling – there! we will say no more about it.' The little woman's attitude and voice were almost prayerful.

'You have judgement enough for two. Besides the miracle has not happened,' she interjected, with a smile which seemed to say it never would be.

Deborah sighed. Whether or not it was quite an honest expression of her feeling we will not inquire. She was there for a definite purpose and her way to it was, as yet, far from plain. All that she had really learned was this: that it was she, and not Miss Weeks who was playing a part, and that whatever her inquiries, she need have no fear of rousing suspicion against Oliver in a mind already dominated by a belief in John Scoville's guilt. The negative with which she followed up this sigh was consequently one of sorrowful acceptance. She made haste, however, to qualify it with the remark:

'But I have not given up all hope. My cause is too promising. True, I may not succeed in marrying Reuther into the Ostrander family, even if it should be my good lot to clear her father's name; but my efforts would have one good result, as precious – perhaps more precious than the one I name. She would no longer have to regard that father as guilty of a criminal act. If such relief can be hers she should have it. But how am I to proceed? I know as well as anyone how impossible the task must prove, unless I can light upon fresh evidence. And where am I to get that? Only from some new witness.'

Miss Weeks' polite smile took on an expression of indulgence. This roused Deborah's pride, and, hesitating no longer, she anxiously remarked:

'I have sometimes thought that Oliver Ostrander might be that witness. He certainly was in the ravine the night Algernon Etheridge was struck down.'

Had she been an experienced actress of years she could not have thrown into this question a greater lack of all innuendo. Miss Weeks, already under her fascination, heard the tone but never thought to notice the quick rise and fall of her visitor's uneasy bosom, and so unwarned, responded with all due frankness:

'I know he was. But how will that help you? He had no testimony to give in relation to this crime, or he would have given it.'

'That is true.' The admission fell mechanically from Deborah's lips; she was not conscious, even, of making it. She was struggling with the shock of the simple statement, confirming her own fears that Oliver had actually been in the ravine at the hour of Etheridge's murder. 'Not even a boy would hide knowledge of that kind,' she stumblingly continued. Then, as her emotion choked her into silence, she sat with piteous eyes searching Miss Weeks' face, till she had recovered her voice, when she added this vital question:

'How did you know that Oliver was in the ravine that night? I only guessed it.'

'Well, it was in this way. I do not often keep my eye on my neighbours (oh, no, Miss Weeks!), but that night I chanced to be looking over the way just at the minute Mr Etheridge came out, and something I saw in his manner and in that of the judge who had followed him to the door, and in that of Oliver who, cap on head, was leaning towards them from a window over the porch, made me think that a controversy was going on between the two old people of which Oliver was the subject. This naturally interested me, and I watched them long enough to see Oliver suddenly raise his fist and shake it at old Etheridge; then, in great rage, slam down the window and disappear inside. The next minute, and before the two below had done talking; I caught another glimpse of him as he dashed around the corner of the house on his way to the ravine.'

'And Mr Etheridge?'

'Oh, he left soon after. I watched him as he went by, his long cloak flapping in the wind. Little did I think he would never pass my window again.'

So interested were they both, the one in telling to new and sympathetic ears the small experiences of her life, the other in listening for the chance phrase or the unconscious admission which would fix the suspicion already struggling into strong life within her breast, that neither for the moment realised the strangeness of the situation or that it was in connection with a crime for which the husband of one of them had suffered, they were raking up this past, and gossiping over its petty details. Possibly recollection returned to them both, when Mrs Scoville sighed and said:

'It couldn't have been very long after you saw him that Mr Etheridge was struck?'

'Only some twenty minutes. It takes just that long for a man to walk from this corner to the bridge.'

'And you never heard where Oliver went?'

'It was never talked about at the time. Later, when some hint got about of his having been in the ravine that night, he said he had gone up the ravine not down it. And we all believed him, madam.'

'Of course, of course. What a discriminating mind you have, Miss Weeks, and what a wonderful memory! To think that after all these years you can recall that Oliver had a cap on his head when he looked out of the window at his father and Mr Etheridge. If you were asked, I have no doubt you could tell its very colour. Was it the peaked one? – the like of which you haven't in your marvellous collection?'

'Yes, I could swear to it.' And Miss Weeks gave a little laugh, which sounded incongruous enough to Deborah in whose heart at that moment, a leaf was turned upon the past, which left the future hopelessly blank.

'Must you go?' Deborah had risen mechanically. 'Don't, I beg, till you have relieved my mind about Judge Ostrander. I don't suppose that there is really anything behind that door of his which it would alarm anyone to see?'

Then, Deborah understood Miss Weeks.

But she was ready for her.

'I've never seen anything of the sort,' said she, 'and I make up his bed in that very room every morning.'

'Oh!' And Miss Weeks drew a deep breath. 'No article of immense value such as that rare old bit of real Satsuma in the cabinet over there?'

'No,' answered Deborah, with all the patience she could muster. 'Judge Ostrander seems very simple in his tastes. I doubt if he would know Satsuma if he saw it.'

Miss Weeks sighed. 'Yes, he has never expressed the least wish to look over my shelves. So the double fence means nothing?'

'A whim,' ejaculated Deborah, making quietly for the door. 'The judge likes to walk at night when quite through with his work; and he doesn't like his ways to be noted. But he prefers the lawn now. I hear his step out there every night.'

'Well, it's something to know that he leads a more normal life than formerly!' sighed the little lady as she prepared to usher her guest out. 'Come again, Mrs Scoville; and, if I may, I will drop in and see you some day.'

Deborah accorded her permission and made her final adieux. She felt as if a hand which had been stealing up her chest had suddenly gripped her throat, choking her. She had found the man who had cast that fatal shadow down the ravine, twelve years before.

Reflections

Deborah re-entered the judge's house a stricken woman. Evading Reuther, she ran upstairs, taking off her things mechanically on the way. She must have an hour alone. She must learn her first lesson in self-control and justifiable duplicity before she came under her daughter's eyes. She must –

Here she reached her room door and was about to enter, when at a sudden thought she paused and let her eyes wander down the hall, till they settled on another door, the one she had closed behind her the night before, with the deep resolve never to open it again except under compulsion.

Had the compulsion arisen? Evidently, for a few minutes later she was standing in one of the dim corners of Oliver's musty room, reopening a book which she had taken down from the shelves on her former visit. She remembered it from its torn back and the fact that it was an Algebra. Turning to the fly leaf, she looked again at the names and schoolboy phrases she had seen scribbled all over its surface, for the one which she remembered as, I hate algebra.

It had not been a very clearly written algebra, and she would never have given this interpretation to the scrawl, had she been in a better mood. Now another thought had come to her, and she wanted to see the word again. Was she glad or sorry to have yielded to this impulse, when by a closer inspection she perceived that the word was not algebra at all, but Algernon, I hate A Etheridge. – I hate A. E. – I hate Algernon E. all over the page, and here and there on other pages, sometimes in characters so rubbed and faint as to be almost unreadable and again so pressed into the paper by a vicious pencil-point as to have broken their way through to the leaf underneath.

The work of an ill-conditioned schoolboy! but – this hate dated back many years. Paler than ever, and with hands trembling almost to the point of incapacity, she put the book back, and flew to her own room, the prey of thoughts bitter almost to madness.

It was the second time in her life that she had been called upon to go through this precise torture. She remembered the hour only too well, when first it was made known to her that one in closest relation to herself was suspected of a hideous crime. And now, with her mind cleared towards him and readjusted to new developments, this crushing experience of seeing equal indications of guilt in another almost as dear and almost as closely knit into her thoughts and future expectations as John had ever been. Can one endure a repetition of such horror? She had never gauged her strength, but it did not seem possible. Besides of the two blows, this seemed the heaviest and the most revolting. Then, only her own happiness and honour were involved; now it was Reuther's; and the fortitude which sustained her through the ignominy of her own trouble, failed her at the prospect of Reuther's. And again, the two cases were not equal. Her husband had had traits which, in a manner, had prepared her for the ready suspicion of people. But Oliver was a man of reputation and kindly heart; and yet, in the course of time this had come, and the question once agitating her as to whether Reuther was a fit mate for him had now evolved itself into this: was he a fit mate for her?

She had rather have died, nay, have had Reuther die than to find herself forced to weigh and decide so momentous a question.

For, however she might feel about it, not a single illusion remained as to whose hand had made use of John Scoville's stick to strike down Algernon Etheridge. How could she have when she came to piece the whole story together, and weigh the facts she had accumulated against Oliver with those which had proved so fatal to her husband.

First: the uncontrolled temper of the lad, hints of which she was daily receiving.

Secondly: his absolute, if unreasonable, hatred of the man thus brutally assailed. She knew what such hatred was and how it eats into an undeveloped mind. She had gone through its agonies herself when she was a young girl, and knew its every stage. With jealousy and personal distaste for a start, it was easy to trace the revolt of this boyish heart from the intrusive, ever present mentor who not only shared his father's affections but made use of them to influence that father against the career he had chosen, in favour of one he not only disliked but for which he lacked all aptitude.

She saw it all from the moment his pencil dug into the paper these tell-tale words: I hate old E to that awful and final one when the detested student fell in the woods and his reign over the judgement, as well as over the heart, of Judge Ostrander was at an end.

In hate, bitter, boiling, long-repressed hate, was found the motive for an act so out of harmony with the condition and upbringing of a lad like Oliver. She need look for no other.

But motive goes for little if not supported by evidence. Was it possible, with this new theory for a basis, to reconstruct the story of this crime without encountering the contradiction of some well-known fact?

She would see.

First, this matter of the bludgeon left, as her husband declared, leaning against the old oak in the bottom of the ravine. All knew the tree and just where it stood. If Oliver, in his eagerness to head off Etheridge at the bridge, had rushed straight down into the gully from Ostrander Lane, he would almost strike this tree in his descent. The diagram sketched on page 143 will make this plain. What more natural, then, than for him to catch up the stick he saw there, even if his mind had not been deliberately set on violence. A weapon is a weapon; and an angry man feels easier with something of the kind in hand.

Armed, then, in this unexpected way, but evidently not yet decided upon crime (or why his nervous whittling of the stick) he turned towards the bridge, following the meandering of the stream which in time led him across the bare spot where she had seen the shadow. That it was his shadow no one could doubt who knew all the circumstances, and that she should have leant just long enough from the ruins to mark this shadow and take it for her husband's – and not long enough to see the man himself and so detect her error, was one of those anomalies of crime which make for judicial errors. John scurrying away through the thicket towards Claymore, Oliver threading his way down the ravine, and she hurrying away from the ruin above with her lost Reuther in hand! Such was the situation at this critical moment. Afterwards when she came back for the child's bucket, some power had withheld her from looking again into the ravine or she might have been witness to the meeting at the bridge, and so been saved the misery and shame of believing as long as she did that the man who intercepted Algernon Etheridge at that place was her unhappy husband.

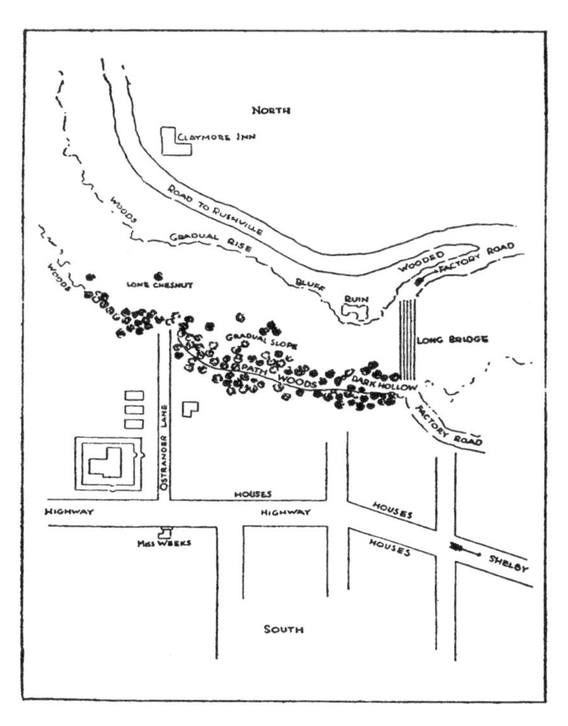

The knife with the broken point, which she had come upon in her search among the lad's discarded effects, proved only too conclusively that it was his hand which had whittled the end of the bludgeon; for the bit of steel left in the wood and the bit lost from the knife were to her exact eye of the same size and an undoubted fit.

Oliver's remorse, the judge's discovery of his guilt (a discovery which may have been soon but probably was late – so late that the penalty of the doing had already been paid by the innocent), can only be guessed from the terrible sequel: a son dismissed, a desolated home in which the father lived as a recluse.

How the mystery cleared, as she looked at it! The house barred from guests – the double fence where, hidden from all eyes, the wretched father might walk his dreary round when night forbade him rest or memory became a whip of scorpions to lash him into fury or revolt – the stairs never passed – (how could he look upon rooms where his wife had dreamed the golden dreams of motherhood and the boy passed his days of innocent youth) – aye, and his own closed-up room guarded by Bela from intrusion as long as breath remained to animate his sinking body! What was its secret? Why, Oliver's portrait! Had this been seen, marked as it was for all men's reprobation, nothing could have stemmed inquiry; and inquiry was to be dreaded as Judge Ostrander's own act had shown. Not till he had made his clumsy attempt to cover this memorial of love and guilt and rehanging it, thus hidden, where it would attract less attention, had she been admitted to his room. Alas! alas! that he had not destroyed it then and there. That, clinging to habits old as his grief and the remorse which had undoubtedly devoured him for the part he had played in this case of perverted justice, he had trusted to a sheet of paper to cover what nothing on earth could cover, once Justice were aroused or the wrath of God awakened.

Deborah shuddered. Aye, the mystery had cleared, but only to enshroud her spirits anew and make her long with all her bursting heart and shuddering soul that death had been her portion before ever she had essayed to lift the veil held down so tightly by these two remorseful men.

But was her fault irremediable? The only unanswerable connection between this old crime and Oliver lay in the evidence she had herself collected. As she had every intention of suppressing this evidence, and as she had small dread of anyone else digging out the facts to which she only possessed a clue, might she not hope that any suspicions raised by her inquiries would fall like a house of cards when she withdrew her hand from the toppling structure?

She would make her first effort and see. Mr Black had heard her complaint; he should be the first to learn that the encouragement she had received was so small that she had decided to accept her present good luck without further query, and not hark back to a past which most people had buried.

Alanson Black

'You began it, as women begin most things, without thought and a due weighing of consequences. And now you propose to drop it in the same freakish manner. Isn't that it?'

Deborah Scoville lifted her eyes in manifest distress and fixed them deprecatingly upon her interrogator. She did not like his tone which was dry and suspiciously sarcastic, and she did not like his attitude which was formal and totally devoid of all sympathy. Instinctively she pushed her veil still further from her features as she deprecatingly replied:

'You are but echoing your sex in criticising mine as impulsive. And you are quite within your rights in doing this. Women are impulsive; they are even freakish. But it is given to one now and then to recognise this fact and acknowledge it. I hope I am of this number; I hope that I have the judgement to see when I have committed a mistake and to stop short before I make myself ridiculous.'

The lawyer smiled, a tight-lipped, acrid sort of smile which nevertheless expressed as much admiration as he ever allowed himself to show.

'Judgement, eh?' he echoed. 'You stop because your judgement tells you that you were on the point of making a fool of yourself? No other reason, eh?'

'Is not that the best which can be given a hard-headed, clear-eyed lawyer like yourself? Would you have me go on, with no real evidence to back my claims; rouse up this town to reconsider his case when I have nothing to talk about but my husband's oath and a shadow I cannot verify?'

'Then Miss Weeks' neighbourliness failed in point? She was not as interesting as you had a right to expect from my recommendation?'

'Miss Weeks is a very chatty and agreeable woman, but she cannot tell what she does not know.'

Mr Black smiled. The woman delighted him. The admiration which he had hitherto felt for her person and for the character which could so develop through misery and reproach as to make her in twelve short years, the exponent of all that was most attractive and bewitching in woman, seemed likely to extend to her mind. Sagacious, eh? and cautious, eh? He was hardly prepared for such perfection, and let the transient lighting up of his features speak for him till he was ready to say:

'You find the judge very agreeable, now that you know him better?'

'Yes, Mr Black. But what has that got to do with the point at issue?'

And she smiled, but not just in his manner nor with quite as little effect.

'Much,' he growled. 'It might make it easier for you to reconcile yourself to the existing order of things.'

'I am reconciled to them simply from necessity,' was her gentle response. 'Nothing is more precious to me than Reuther's happiness. I should but endanger it further by raising false hopes. That is why I have come to cry halt.'

'Madam, I commend your decision. It is that of a wise and considerate woman. Your child's happiness is, of course, of paramount importance to you. But why should you characterise your hopes as false, just when there seems to be some justification for them.'

Her eyes widened, and she regarded him with a simulation of surprise which interested without imposing upon him.

'I do not understand you,' said she. 'Have you come upon some clue? Have you heard something which I have not?'

The smile with which he seasoned his reply was of a very different nature from that which he had previously bestowed upon her. It prepared her, possibly, for the shock of his words:

'I hardly think so,' said he. 'If I do not mistake, we have been the recipients of the same communications.'

She started to her feet, but sat again instantly. 'Pray explain yourself,' she urged. 'Who has been writing to you? And what have they written?' she added, presuming a little upon her fascinations as a woman to win an honest response.

'Must I speak first?'

If it was a tilt, it was between even forces.

'It would be gentlemanly in you to do so.'

'But I am not of a gentlemanly temper.'

'I deal with no other,' said she; but with what a glance and in what a tone!

A man may hold out long – and if a lawyer and a bachelor more than long, but there is a point at which he succumbs. Mr Black had reached that point. Smoothing his brow and allowing a more kindly expression to creep into his regard, he took two or three crushed and folded papers from a drawer beside him and, holding them, none too plainly in sight, remarked very quietly, but with legal firmness:

'Do not let us play about the bush any longer. You have announced your intention of making no further attempt to discover the man who in your eyes merited the doom accorded to John Scoville. Your only reason for this – if you are the woman I think you – lies in your fear of giving further opportunity to the misguided rancour of an irresponsible writer of anonymous epistles. Am I not right, madam?'

Beaten, beaten by a direct assault, because she possessed the weaknesses, as well as the pluck, of a woman. She could control the language of her lips, but not their quivering; she could meet his eye with steady assurance but she could not keep the pallor from her cheeks or subdue the evidences of her heart's turmoil. Her pitiful glance acknowledged her defeat, which she already saw mirrored in his eyes.

Taking it for an answer, he said gently enough:

'That we may understand each other at once, I will mention the person who has been made the subject of these attacks. He –'

'Don't speak the name,' she prayed, leaning forward and laying her gloved hand upon his sleeve. 'It is not necessary. The whole thing is an outrage.'

'Of course,' he echoed, with some of his natural brusqueness, 'and the rankest folly. But to some follies we have to pay attention, and I fear that we shall have to pay attention to this one if only for your daughter Reuther's sake. You cannot wish her to become the butt of these scandalous attempts?'

'No, no.' The words escaped her before she realised that in their utterance she had given up irretrievably her secret.

'You consider them scandalous?'

'Most scandalous,' she emphatically returned, with a vivacity and seeming candour such as he had seldom seen equalled even on the witness stand.

His admiration was quite evident. It did not prevent him, however, from asking quite abruptly:

'In what shape and by what means did this communication reach you?'

'I found it lying on the walk between the gates.'

'The same by which Judge Ostrander leaves the house?'

'Yes,' came in faint reply.

'I see that you share my fears. If one such scrap can be thrown over the fence, why shouldn't another be? Men who indulge themselves in writing anonymous accusations seldom limit themselves to one effusion. I will stake my word that the judge has found more than one on his lawn.'

She could not have responded if she would; her mouth was dry, her tongue half paralysed. What was coming? The glint in the lawyer's eye forewarned her that something scarcely in consonance with her hopes and wishes might be expected.

'The judge has seen and read these barefaced insinuations against his son and has not turned this whole town topsy-turvy! What are we to think of that? A lion does not stop to meditate; he springs. And Archibald Ostrander has the nature of a lion.

There is nothing of the fox or even of the tiger in him. Mrs Scoville, this is a very serious matter. I do not wonder that you are a trifle overwhelmed by the results of your ill-considered investigations.'

'Does the town know? Has the thing become a scandal – a byword? Miss Weeks gave no proof of ever having heard one word of this dreadful not-to-be-foreseen business.'

'That is good news. You relieve me. Perhaps it is not a general topic as yet.' Then shortly and with lawyer-like directness, 'Show me the letter which has disturbed all your plans.'

'I haven't it here.'

'You didn't bring it?'

'No, Mr Black. Why should I? I had no premonition that I should ever be induced to show it to anyone, least of all to you.'

'Look over these. Do they look at all familiar?'

She glanced down at the crumpled sheets and half-sheets he had spread out before her. They were similar in appearance to the one she had picked up on the judge's grounds but the language was more forcible, as witness these:

When a man is trusted to defend another on trial for his life, he's supposed to know his business. How came John Scoville to hang, without a thought being given to the man who hated A. Etheridge like poison? I could name a certain chap who more than once in the old days boasted that he'd like to kill the fellow. And it wasn't Scoville or anyone of his low-down stamp either.

A high and mighty name shouldn't shield a man who sent a poor, unfriended wretch to his death in order to save his own bacon.

'Horrible!' murmured Deborah, drawing back in terror of her own emotion. 'It's the work of some implacable enemy taking advantage of the situation I have created. Mr Black, this man must be found and made to see that no one will believe, not even Scoville's widow –'

'There! you needn't go any further with that,' admonished the lawyer. 'I will manage him. But first we must make sure to rightly locate this enemy of the Ostranders. You do detect some resemblance between this writing and the specimen you have at home?'

'They are very much alike.'

'You believe one person wrote them?'

'I do.'

'Have you any idea who this person is?'

'No; why should I?'

'No suspicion?'

'Not the least in the world.'

'I ask because of this,' he explained, picking out another letter and smilingly holding it out towards her.

She read it with flushed cheeks.

Listen to the lady. You can't listen to anyone nicer. What she wants she can get. There's a witness you never saw or heard of.

A witness they had never heard of! What witness? Scarcely could she lift her eyes from the paper. Yet there was a possibility, of course, that this statement was a lie.

'Stuff, isn't it?' muttered the lawyer. 'Never mind, we'll soon have hold of the writer.' His face had taken on a much more serious aspect, and she could no longer complain of his indifference or even of his sarcasm.

'You will give me another opportunity of talking with you on this matter,' pursued he. 'If you do not come here, you may expect to see me at Judge Ostrander's. I do not quite like the position into which you have been thrown by these absurd insinuations from some unknown person who may be thinking to do you a service, but who you must feel is very far from being your friend. It may even lead to your losing the home which has been so fortunately opened for you. If this occurs, you may count on my friendship, Mrs Scoville. I may have failed you once, but I will not fail you twice.'

Surprised, almost touched, she held out her hand, with a cordial thank you, in which emotion struggled with her desire to preserve an appearance of complete confidence in Judge Ostrander, and incidentally in his son. Then, being on her feet by this time, she turned to go, anxious to escape further embarrassment from a perspicacity she no longer possessed the courage to meet.

The lawyer appeared to acquiesce in the movement of departure. But when he saw her about to vanish through the door, some impulse of compunction, as real as it was surprising, led him to call her back and seat her once more in the chair she had so lately left.

'I cannot let you go,' said he, 'until you understand that these insinuations from a self-called witness would not be worth our attention if there were not a few facts to give colour to his wild claims. Oliver Ostrander was in that ravine connecting with Dark Hollow, very near the time of the onslaught on Mr Etheridge; and he certainly hated the man and wanted him out of the way. The whole town knows that, with one exception. You know that exception?'

'I think so,' she acceded, taking a fresh grip upon her emotions.

'That this was anything more than a coincidence has never been questioned. He was not even summoned as a witness. With the judge's high reputation in mind I do not think a single person could have been found in those days to suggest any possible connection between this boy and a crime so obviously premeditated. But people's minds change with time and events, and Oliver Ostrander's name uttered in this connection today would not occasion the same shock to the community as it would have done then. You understand me, Mrs Scoville?'

'You allude to the unexplained separation between himself and father, and not to any failure on his part to sustain the reputation of his family?'

'Oh, he has made a good position for himself, and earned universal consideration. But that doesn't weigh against the prejudices of people, roused by such eccentricities as have distinguished the conduct of these two men.'

'Alas!' she murmured, frightened to the soul for the first time, both by his manner and his words.

'You know and I know,' he went on with a grimness possibly suggested by his subject, 'that no mere whim lies back of such a preposterous seclusion as that of Judge Ostrander behind his double fence. Sons do not cut loose from fathers or fathers from sons without good cause. You can see, then, that the peculiarities of their mutual history form but a poor foundation for any light refutation of this scandal, should it reach the public mind. Judge Ostrander knows this, and you know that he knows this; hence your distress. Have I not read your mind, madam?'

'No one can read my mind any more than they can read Judge Ostrander's,' she avowed in a last desperate attempt to preserve her secret. 'You may think you have done so, but what assurance can you have of the fact?'

'You are strong in their defence,' said he, 'and you will need to be if the matter ever comes up. The shadows from Dark Hollow reach far, and engulf all they fall upon.'

'Mr Black' – she had re-risen the better to face him – 'you want something from me – a promise, or a condition.'

'No,' said he, 'this is my affair only as it affects you. I simply wished to warn you of what you might have to face; and what Judge Ostrander will have to face (here I drop the lawyer and speak only as a man) if he is not ready to give a more consistent explanation of the curious facts I have mentioned.'

‘I cannot warn him, Mr Black.’

‘You? Of course not. Nobody can warn him; possibly no one should warn him. But I have warned you; and now, as a last word, let us hope that no warning is necessary and that we shall soon see the last of these calumniating letters and everything readjusted once more on a firm and natural basis. Judge Ostrander’s action in reopening his house in the manner and for the purpose he has, has predisposed many in his favour. It may, before we know it, make the past almost forgotten.’

‘Meanwhile you will make an attempt to discover the author of these anonymous attacks?’

‘To save you from annoyance.’

Obliged to make acknowledgment of the courtesy if not kindness prompting these words, Mrs Scoville expressed her gratitude and took farewell in a way which did not seem to be at all displeasing to the crusty lawyer; but when she found herself once more in the streets, her anxiety and suspense took on a new phase. What was at the bottom of Mr Black’s contradictory assertions? Sympathy with her, as he would have her believe, or a secret feeling of animosity towards the man he openly professed to admire?

What Had Made the Change?

'Reuther, sit up here close by mother and let me talk to you for a little while.'

'Yes, mother; oh, yes, mother.' Deborah felt the beloved head pressed close to her shoulder and two soft arms fall about her neck.

'Are you very unhappy? Is my little one pining too much for the old days?'

A closer pressure of the head, a more vehement clasp of the encircling arms, but no words.

'You have seemed brighter lately. I have heard you sing now and then as if the joy of youth was not quite absent from your heart. Is that true, or were you merely trying to cheer your mother?'

'I am afraid I was trying to cheer the judge,' came in low whisper to her ear. 'When I hear his step in the study – that monotonous tramp, tramp, which we both dread, I feel such an ache here, such a desire to comfort him, that I try the one little means I have to divert him from his thoughts. He must be so lonely without –'

'Reuther, you forget how many years have passed since he had a companion. A man becomes used to loneliness. A judge with heavy cases on his mind must think and think very closely, you know.'

'Oh, mamma, it's not of his cases our judge is thinking when he walks like that. I know him too well, love him too well, not to feel the trouble in his step. I may be wrong, but all the sympathy and understanding I may not give to Oliver I devote to his father, and when he walks like that he seems to drag my heart after him. Mamma, mamma, do not blame me. I have just as much affection for you, and I suffer just as keenly when I see you unhappy. And, mamma, are you sure that you are quite happy today? You look as if something had happened to trouble you – something more than usual, I mean.'

They were sitting in the dark, with just the light of the stars shining through the upper panes of the one unshaded window. Deborah, therefore, had little to fear from her daughter's eye, only from the sensitiveness of her touch and the quickness of her ear. Alas, in this delicately organised girl these were both attuned to the nicest discrimination, and before the mother could speak, Reuther had started up, crying:

'Oh, how your heart beats! Something has happened, darling mother; something which –'

'Hush, Reuther; it is only this: When I came to Shelby it was with a hope that I might some day smooth the way to your happiness. But it was only a wild dream, Reuther; and the hour has come for me to tell you so. What joys are left us must come in other ways; love unblessed must be put aside resolutely and forever.'

She felt the shudder pass through the slender form which had thrown itself again at her side; but when the young girl spoke it was with unexpected bravery and calm.

'I have long ago done that, mamma. I've had no hopes from the first. The look with which Oliver accepted my refusal to go on with the ceremony was one of gratitude, mother. I can never forget that. Relief struggled with grief. Would you have me cherish any further illusions after that?'

Mrs Scoville was silent. So, after all, Reuther had not been so blind on that day as she had always feared.

'Oliver has faults – Oh, let me talk about him just for once, darling mother,' the poor, stricken child babbled on. 'His temper is violent, or so he has often told me, coming and going like a gust of – no, mamma, don't make me stop. If he has faults he has good traits too. He was always gentle with me and if that far away look you did not like would come at times and take him, as it were, out of our world, such a sweet awakening would follow when he realised that I was waiting for his spirit to come back, that I never minded the mystery, in my joy at the comfort which my love gave him.'

'My child, my child!'

'Mother, I can soothe the father, but I can no longer soothe Oliver. That is my saddest thought. It makes me wish, sometimes, that he would find another loving heart on which he could lean without any self-reproach. I should soon learn to bear it. It would so assure his future and rid me of the fear that he may fail to hold the place he has won by such hard work and persistence.'

A moment's silence, then a last appeal on the part of the mother.

'Reuther, have I ever been harsh to you?'

'No, no.'

'Then you will not think me unkind or even untender if I say that every loving thought you give now to Oliver is hurtful both to yourself and to me. Don't indulge in them, my darling. Put your heart into work or into music, and your mother will bless you. Won't it help you to know this, Reuther? Your mother, who has had her griefs, will bless you.'

'Mother, mother!'

That night, at a later hour, Deborah struggled with a great temptation.

The cap which hung in Oliver's closet – the knife which lay in the drawer of Oliver's desk – were to her mind positive proofs of his actual connection with the crime she now wished to see buried for all time in her husband's grave. The threat of that unknown indicter of mysterious letters, I know a witness, had sunk deep into her mind. A witness of what? Of anything which the discovery of these articles might substantiate? If so, what peril remained in their continued preservation when an effort on her part might so easily destroy them.

Sleep, long a stranger to her pillow, forsook her entirely as she faced this question and realised the gain in peace which might be hers if cap and knife were gone. Why then did she allow them to remain, the one in the closet, the other in the drawer? Because she could not help herself. Instinct was against her meddling with these possible proofs of crime.

But this triumph of conscience cost her dear. The next morning found her pale – almost as pale as Reuther. Was that why the judge surveyed her so intently as she poured out the coffee, and seemed more than once on the point of addressing her particularly, as she went through the usual routine of tidying up his room?

She asked herself this question more than once, and found it answered every time she hurried by the mirror. Certainly she showed a remarkable pallor.

Knowing its cause herself, she did not invite his inquiries; and another day passed. With the following morning she felt strong enough to open the conversation which had now become necessary for her peace of mind.

She waited till the moment when, her work all done, she was about to leave his presence. Pausing till she caught his eye, which seemed a little loth, she thought, to look her way, she observed, with perhaps unnecessary distinctness:

'I hope that everything is to your mind, Judge Ostrander. I should be sorry not to make you as comfortable as is possible under the circumstances.'

Roused a little suddenly, perhaps, from thoughts quite disconnected with those of material comfort, he nodded with the abstraction of one who recognises that some sort of acknowledgment is expected from him; then, seeing her still waiting, added politely:

'I am very well looked after, if that is what you mean, Mrs Scoville. Bela could not do any better – if he ever did as well.'

'I am glad,' she replied, thinking with what humour this would have struck her once. 'I – I ask because, having nothing on my mind but housekeeping, I desire to remedy anything which is not in accordance with your exact wishes.'

His attention was caught and by the very phrase she desired.

'Nothing on your mind but housekeeping?' he repeated. 'I thought you had something else of a very particular nature with which to occupy yourself.'

'I had; but I have been advised against pursuing it. The folly was too great.'

'Who advised you?'

The words came short and sharp just as they must have come in those old days when he confronted his antagonists at the bar.

'Mr Black. He was my husband's counsel, you remember. He says that I should only have my trouble for my pains, and I have come to agree with him. Reuther must content herself with the happiness of living under this roof; and I, with the hope of contributing to your comfort.'

Had she impressed him? Had she played her part with success? Dare she lift her eye and meet the gaze she felt concentrated upon her? No. He must speak first. She must have some clue to the effect she had produced before she risked his penetration by a direct look.

She had to wait longer than her beating heart desired. He had his own agitation to master, and possibly his own doubts. This was not the fiery, determined woman he had encountered amid the ruins of Spencer's Folly. What had made the change? Black's discouraging advice? Hardly. Why should she take from that hard-faced lawyer what she had not been willing to take from himself? There must have been some other influencing cause.

His look, his attitude, his voice, betrayed his hesitations, as he finally remarked:

'Black is a man of excellent counsel, but he is hard as a stone and not of the sort whose monitions I should expect to have weight with one like you. What did he put in the balance, or what have others put in the balance, to send your passionate intentions flying up to the beam? I should be glad to hear.'

Should she tell him? She had a momentary impulse that way. Then the irrevocableness of such a move frightened her; and, pale with dismay at what she felt to be a narrow escape from a grave error of judgement, she answered with just enough truth, for her to hope that the modicum of falsehood accompanying it would escape his attention:

'What has changed my intentions? My experience here, Judge Ostrander. With every day I pass under this roof, I realise more and more the mistake I made in supposing that any change in circumstances would make a union between our two children proper or feasible. Headstrong as I am by nature, I have still some sense of the fitness of things, and it is that sense awakened by a better knowledge of what the Ostrander name stands for, which has outweighed my hopes and mad intentions. I am sorry that I ever troubled you with them.'

The words were ambiguous; startlingly so, she felt; but, in hope that they would strike him otherwise, she found courage at last to raise her eyes in search of what lay in his. Nothing, or so she thought at first, beyond the glint of a natural interest; then her mind changed, and she felt that it would take one much better acquainted with his moods than herself to read to its depths a gaze so sombre and inscrutable.

His answer, coming after a moment of decided suspense, only deepened this impression. It was to this effect:

'Madam, we have said our say on this subject. If you have come to see the matter as I see it, I can but congratulate you upon your good sense, and express the hope that it will continue to prevail. Reuther is worthy of the best –' he stopped abruptly. 'Reuther is a girl after my own heart,' he gently supplemented, with a glance towards his papers lying in a bundle at his elbow, 'and she shall not suffer because of this disappointment to her girlish hopes. Tell her so with my love.'

It was a plain dismissal. Mrs Scoville took it as such, and quietly left the room. As she did so she was approached by Reuther who handed her a letter which had just been delivered. It was from Mr Black and read thus:

We have found the rogue and have succeeded in inducing him to leave town. He's a man in the bill-sticking business and he owns to a grievance against the person we know.

Deborah's sleep that night was without dreams.

In the Courtroom

About this time, the restless pacing of the judge in his study at nights became more frequent and lasted longer. In vain Reuther played her most cheerful airs and sang her sweetest songs, the monotonous tramp kept up with a regularity nothing could break.

'He's worried by the big case now being tried before him,' Deborah would say, when Reuther's eyes grew wide and misty in her sympathetic trouble. And there was no improbability in the plea, for it was a case of much moment, and of great local interest. A man was on trial for his life and the circumstances of the case were such that the feeling called forth was unusually bitter; so much so, indeed, that every word uttered by the counsel and every decision made by the judge were discussed from one end of the county to the other, and in Shelby, if nowhere else, took precedence of all other topics, though it was a Presidential year and party sympathies ran high.

The more thoughtful spirits were inclined to believe in the innocence of the prisoner; but the lower elements of the town, moved by class prejudice, were bitterly antagonistic to his cause and loud for his conviction.

Did the judge realise his position and the effect made upon the populace by his very evident leaning towards this dissipated but well-connected young man accused of a crime so brutal, that he must either have been the sport of most malicious circumstances, or a degenerate of the worst type? The time of Judge Ostrander's office was nearly up, and his future continuance on the bench might very easily depend upon his attitude at the present hearing. Yet *he*, without apparent recognition of this fact, showed without any hesitancy or possibly without self-consciousness, the sympathy he felt for the man at the bar, and ruled accordingly almost without variation.

No wonder he paced the floor as the proceedings drew towards its close and the inevitable hour approached when a verdict must be rendered. Mrs Scoville, reading his heart by the light of her recent discoveries, understood as nobody else, the workings of his conscience and the passion of sympathy which this unhappy father must have for misguided youth. She began to fear for his health and count the days till this ordeal was over.

In other regards, quiet had come to them all and less tempestuous fears. Could the judge but weather the possible conviction of this man and restrain himself from a disclosure of his own suffering, more cheerful days might be in store for them, for no further missives were to be seen on the lawn, nor had anything occurred for days to recall to Deborah's mind the move she had made towards re-establishing her husband's innocence.

A week passed, and the community was all agog, in anticipation of the judge's charge in the case just mentioned. It was to be given at noon, and Mrs Scoville, conscious that he had not slept an hour the night before (having crept down more than once to listen if his step had ceased), approached him as he prepared to leave the house for the courtroom, and anxiously asked if he were quite well.

'Oh, yes, I'm well,' he responded sharply, looking about for Reuther.

The young girl was standing a little behind him, with his gloves in her hand – a custom she had fallen into in her desire to have his last look and fond good morning.

'Come here, child,' said he, in a way to make her heart beat; and, as he took the gloves from her hand, he stooped and kissed her on the forehead – something he had never done before. 'Let me see you smile,' said he. 'It's a memory I like to take with me into the courtroom.'

But when in her pure delight at his caress and the fatherly feeling which gave a tremor to his simple request, she lifted her face with that angelic look of hers which was far sweeter and far more moving than any smile, he turned away abruptly as though he had been more hurt than comforted, and strode out of the house without another word.

Deborah's hand went to her heart, in the dark corner whither she had withdrawn herself, and when she turned again towards the spot where Reuther had stood, it was in some fear lest she had betrayed her understanding of this deeply tried father's passionate pain. But Reuther was no longer there. She had fled quickly away with the memory of what was to make this day a less dreary one for her.

Morning passed and the noon came, bringing Deborah an increased uneasiness. When lunch was over and Reuther sat down to her piano, the feeling had grown into an obsession, which soon resolved itself into a definite fear.

'What if an attack, such as I once saw, should come upon him while he sits upon the bench! Why have I not thought of this before? O God! these evil days! When will they be over!'

She found herself so restless that she decided upon going out. Donning her quietest gown and veil, she looked in on Reuther and expressed her intention; then slipped out of the front door, hardly knowing whither her feet would carry her.

They did not carry her far, not at this moment at least. On the walk outside she met Miss Weeks hurrying towards her from the corner, stumbling in her excitement and so weakened in body or spirit that she caught at the unresponsive fence for the support which its smooth surface refused to give her.

At sight of Deborah's figure, she paused and threw up her hands.

'Oh, Mrs Scoville, such a dreadful thing!' she cried. 'Look here!' And, opening one of her hands, she showed a few torn scraps of paper whose familiarity made Deborah's blood run cold.

'On the bridge,' gasped the little lady, leaning against the fence for support. 'Pasted on the railing of the bridge. I should never have seen it, nor looked at it, if it hadn't been that I –'

'Don't tell me here,' urged Deborah. 'Let's go over to your house. See, there are people coming.'

The little lady yielded to the other's constraining hand and together they crossed the street. Once in the house, Deborah allowed her full apprehension to show itself.

'What were the words? What was on the paper? Anything about –'

The little woman's look of horror stopped her.

'It's a lie, an awful, abominable lie. But think of such a lie being pasted up on that dreadful bridge for anyone to see. After twelve years, Mrs Scoville! After –' But here indignation changed suddenly into suspicion, and eyeing her visitor with sudden disfavour she cried: 'This is your work, madam. Your inquiries and your talk of John Scoville's innocence has set wagging all the villainous tongues in town. And I remember something else. How you came smirking into this very room one day, with your talk about caps and Oliver Ostrander's doings on the day when Algernon Etheridge was murdered. You were in search of information, I see; information against the best, the brightest – well, why don't you speak? I'll give you the chance if you want it. Don't stand looking at me like that. I'm not used to it, Mrs Scoville. I'm a peaceable woman and I'm not used to it.'

'Miss Weeks –' Ah, the oil of that golden speech on troubled waters! What was its charm? What message did it carry from Deborah's warm, true heart that its influence should be so miraculous? 'Miss Weeks, you have forgotten my interest in Oliver Ostrander. He was my daughter's lover. He was my own ideal of a gifted, kind-hearted, if somewhat mysterious, young man. No calumny uttered against him can awaken in you half the sorrow and indignation it does in me. Let me see those lines or what there is left of them so that I may share your feelings. They must be dreadful –'

'They are more than dreadful. I don't know how I had strength to pull these pieces off. I couldn't have done it if they had been quite dry. But what do you want to see them for? I'd have left them there if I had been willing to have them seen. They are for the kitchen fire. Wait a moment and then we will talk.'

But Deborah had no mind to let these pieces escape her eye. Sick as she felt at heart, she exerted herself to win the little woman's confidence; and when Deborah exerted herself, even under such adverse conditions as these, she seldom failed to succeed.

Nor did she fail now. At the end of fifteen minutes she had the torn bits of paper arranged in their proper position and was reading these words:

The scene of Oliv der's crime.

Nothing could be more explicit, nothing more damaging. As the glances of the two women met, it would be difficult to tell on which face Distress hung out the whiter flag.

'The beginning of the end!' was Deborah's thought. 'If after Mr Black's efforts, a charge like this is found posted up in the public ways, the ruin of the Ostranders is determined upon, and nothing we can do can stop it.'

In five minutes more she had said goodbye to Miss Weeks and was on her way to the courthouse.

This building occupied one end of a large paved square in the busiest part of the town. As Deborah approached it, she was still further alarmed by finding this square full of people, standing in groups or walking impatiently up and down with their eyes fixed on the courthouse doors. The case which had agitated the whole country for days was now in the hands of the jury and a verdict was momentarily expected.

So much for appearances outside. Within, there was the uneasy hum, the anxious look, the subdued movement which marks an universal suspense. Announcement had been made that the jury had reached their verdict, and counsel were resuming their places and the judge his seat.

Those who had eyes only for the latter – and these were many – noticed a change in him. He looked older by years than when he delivered his charge. Not the prisoner himself gave greater evidence of the effect which this hour of waiting had had upon a heart whose covered griefs were, consciously or unconsciously, revealing themselves to the public eye. He did not wish this man sentenced. This was shown by his charge – the most one-sided one he had given in all his career. Yet the man awaiting verdict had small claim to his consideration – none, in fact, save that he was young and well connected; facts in his favour with which the people who packed the courthouse that day had little sympathy, as their cold looks proved.

To Deborah, who had succeeded in getting a seat in a remote and inconspicuous corner, these looks conveyed a spirit of so much threat that she gazed about her in wonder that so few saw where the real tragedy in this room lay.

But the jury is now seated, and the clatter of moving feet which but a moment before filled the great room, sinks as if under a charm, and silence, that awesome precursor of doom, lay in all its weight upon every ear and heart, as the clerk advancing with the cry, 'Order in the court,' put his momentous question:

'Gentlemen of the jury, are you ready with your verdict?'

A hush! – then, the clear voice of the foreman:

'We are.'

'How do you find? Guilty or not guilty?'

Another hesitation. Did the foreman feel the threat lurking in the air about him? If so, he failed to show it in his tones as he uttered the words which released the prisoner:

'Not guilty.'

A growl from the crowd, almost like that of a beast stirring its lair, then a quick cessation of all hubbub as everyone turned to the judge to whose one-sided charge they attributed this release.

Again he was a changed man. With the delivery of this verdict he had regained his natural poise, and never had he looked more authoritative or more pre-eminently the dominating spirit of the court than in the few following moments in which he expressed the thanks of the court to the jury and dismissed the prisoner. And yet, though each person there, from the disappointed prosecutor to the least aggressive spectator, appeared to feel the influence of a presence and voice difficult to duplicate on the bench of this country, Deborah experienced in her quiet corner no alleviation of the fear which had brought her into this forbidding spot and held her breathless through all these formalities.

For the end was not yet. Through all the turmoil of noisy departure and the drifting out into the square of a vast, dissatisfied throng, she had caught the flash of a bit of paper (how introduced into this moving mass of people no one ever knew) passing from hand to hand, towards the solitary figure of the judge who had not as yet left his seat.

She knew – no one better – what this meant, and instinct bade her cry out and bid those thoughtless hands to cease their work and let this letter drop. But her discretion still held, and, subduing the mad impulse, she watched with dilating eyes and heaving breast the slow passage of this fatal note through the now rapidly thinning crowd, its delay as it reached the open space between the last row of seats and the judge's bench and its final delivery by some officious hand, who thrust it upon his notice just as he was rising to leave.

The picture he made in that instant of hesitation never left her mind. To the end of her days she will carry a vision of his tall form, imposing in his judicial robes and with the majesty of his office still upon him, fingering this envelope in sight of such persons as still lingered in his part of the room. Nemesis was lowering its black wings over his devoted head, and, with feelings which left her dazed and transfixed in silent terror,

Deborah saw his finger tear its way through the envelope and his eyes fall frowningly on the paper he drew out.

Then the People's counsel and the counsel for the Defence and such clerks and hangers-on as still lingered in the upper end of the room experienced a decided sensation.

The judge, who a moment before had towered above them all in melancholy but impressive dignity, shrunk with one gasp into feebleness and sank back stricken, if not unconscious, into his chair.

Was it a stroke, or just one of his attacks of which all had heard? Was he aware of his own condition and the disturbance it caused or was he, on the contrary, dead to his own misery and oblivious of the rush which was made from all sides to his assistance? Even Deborah could not tell, and was forced to sit quiet in her corner, waiting for the parting of the group which hid the judge from her sight.

It happened suddenly and showed her the same figure she had seen once before – a man with faculties suspended, but not impaired, facing them all with open gaze but absolutely dead for the moment to his own condition and to the world about.

But, horrible as this was, what she saw going on behind him was infinitely worse. A man had caught up the bit of paper Judge Ostrander had let fall from his hand and was opening his lips to read it to the curious people surrounding him.

She tried to stop him. She forced a cry to her lips which should have rung through the room, but which died away on the air unheard. The terror which had paralysed her limbs had choked her voice.

But her ears remained true. Low as he spoke, no trumpet-call could have made its meaning clearer to Deborah Scoville than did these words:

'We know why you favour criminals. Twelve years is a long time, but not long enough to make wise men forget.'

Had she not caught the words themselves she would have recognised their import from the blighting effect they produced upon the persons grouped within hearing.

Schooled as most of them were to face with minds secure and tempers quite unruffled the countless surprises of a court-room, they paled at the insinuation conveyed in these two sentences, and with scarcely the interchange of glance or word, drew aside in a silence which no man seemed inclined to break.

As for the people still huddled in the doorway, they rushed away helter-skelter into the street, there to proclaim the judge's condition and its probable cause – an event which to many quite eclipsed in interest the more ordinary one which had just released to freedom a man seemingly doomed.

Few persons were now left in the great room, and Deborah, embarrassed to find that she was the only woman present, was on the point of escaping from her corner when she perceived a movement take place in the rigid form from which she had not yet withdrawn her eyes, and, regarding Judge Ostrander more attentively, she caught the gleam of his suspicious eye as it glanced this way and that to see if his lapse of consciousness had been noticed by those about him.

Would the man still in possession of the paper whose contents had brought about this attack understand these evidences of apprehension? Yes; and what is more, he seems to take such means as offers to hide from the judge all knowledge of the fact that any other eyes than his own have read these invidious words. With unexpected address, he waits for the judge to turn his head aside when with a quick and dextrous movement he so launches the paper from his hand that it falls softly and without flurry within an inch of the judicial seat. Then he goes back to his papers.

This suggestion, at once so marked and so delicate, did not fail of its effect upon those about. Wherever the judge looked he saw abstracted faces and busy hands, and, taking heart at not finding himself watched, he started to rise. Then memory came, blasting, overwhelming memory of the letter he had been reading; and, rousing with a start, he looked down at his hand, then at the floor before him, and, seeing the letter lying there, picked it up with a secret, side-long glance to right and left, which sank deep into the heart of the still watchful Deborah.

If those about him saw, they made no motion. Not an eye looked round and not a head turned as he straightened himself and proceeded to leave the room. Only Deborah noted how his steps faltered and how little he was to be trusted to find his way unguided to the door. It lay to the right and he was going left. Now he stumbles – isn't there anyone to – yes, she is not the sole one on watch. The same man who had read aloud the note and then dropped it within his reach, had stepped after him, and kindly, if artfully, turned him towards the proper place of exit. As the two disappear, Deborah wakes from her trance, and, finding herself alone among the seats, hurries to quit her corner and leave the building.

The glare – the noise of the square, as she dashes down into it seems for the moment unendurable. The pushing, panting mass of men and women of which she has now become a part, closes about her, and for the moment she can see nothing but faces, faces with working mouths and blazing eyes, a medley of antagonistic expression, all directed against herself; or so she felt in the heat of her self-consciousness. But after the first recoil she knew that no such universal recognition could be hers; that she was merely a new and inconsiderable atom caught in a wave of feeling which engulfed all it met; that this mob was not raised from the stones to overwhelm her but *him*, and that if she flew, it should be to his aid, and not to save herself. But how was she to reach him? He would not come out by the main entrance;

that she knew. Where look for him, then? Suddenly she remembered; and using some of her strength of which she had good measure, and more of that address to which I have already alluded, she began to worm herself along through this astounding collection of people much too large already for the ordinary force of police to handle, to that corner of the building where a small door opened upon a rear street. She remembered it from those old days when she had once entered this courthouse as a witness.

But alas, others knew it also, and thick as the crowd was in front, it was even thicker here, and far more tumultuous. Word had gone about that the father of Oliver Ostrander had been given his lesson at last, and the curiosity of the populace had risen to fever-heat in their anxiety to see how the proud Ostrander would bear himself in his precipitate downfall. They had crowded there to see and they would see. Were he to shirk the ordeal! Were he to wait for the square to be cleared – but they knew him too well to fear this. He will come – nay, he is coming now – and coming alone! No other figure looms so grandly in a doorway, nor is there any other face in Shelby whose pallor could strike so coldly to the heart, or rouse such conflicting emotions.

He was evidently not prepared to see his path quite so heavily marked out for him by the gaping throng; but after one look, he assumed some show of his old commanding presence and advanced bravely down the steps, awing some and silencing all, until he had reached his carriage step and the protection of the officers on guard.

Then a hoot rose from some far-off quarter of the square, and he turned short about and the people saw his face. Despair had seized it, and if anyone there desired vengeance, he had it. The knell of active life had been rung for this man. He would never remount the courthouse steps, or face again a respectful jury.

As for Deborah, she had shrunk out of sight at his approach, but as soon as he had ridden off, she looked eagerly for a taxicab to carry her in his wake. She could not let him ride that mile alone. She was still fearful for him, though the mass of people about her was rapidly dissolving away, and the streets growing clear.

But an apprehension still greater, because more personal, seized her when she found herself behind him on the long road. Several minutes had been lost in obtaining a taxicab and she feared that she would be unable to overtake him before he reached his own gates. This would be to subject Reuther to a shock which the poor child had little strength to meet. She could not escape the truth long. Soon, very soon she would have to be told that the man who stood so high in her esteem was now regarded as a common criminal. But she must be prepared for the awful news. She must be within reach of her mother's arms when the blow fell destroying her past as well as her future.

Were minutes really so long – the house really so far away? Deborah gazes eagerly forward. There is very little traffic in the streets today and the road ahead looks clear – too clear, she cannot even see the dust raised by the judge's rapidly disappearing carriage. Can he have arrived home already? No, or the carriage would be coming back, and not a vehicle is in view.

Her anxiety increases. She has reached the road debouching towards the bridge – has crossed it – is drawing near – nearer – when, what is this? Men – women – coming from the right, coming from the left, running out of houses, flocking from every side street, filling up the road! A lesser mob than that from which she had just escaped, but still, a mob, and all making for one point – the judge's house! And he? She can see his carriage now. Held up for a moment by the crowd, it has broken through, and is rolling quickly towards Ostrander Lane. But the mob is following, and she is yet far behind.

Shouting to the chauffeur to hasten, the insistent honk! honk! of the cab adds its raucous note to the turmoil. They have dashed through one group; they are dashing through another; naught can withstand an on-rushing automobile. She catches glimpses of raised arms threatening retaliation; of eager, stolid, uncertain and furious faces – and her breath held back during that one instant of wild passage rushes pantingly forth again. Ostrander Lane is within sight. If only they can reach it! – if only they can cross it! But they cannot without sowing death in their track. No scattered groups here, the mob fills the corner. It is packed close as a wall. Brought up against it, the motor necessarily comes to a standstill.

Balked? No, not yet. Opening the door, Deborah leaps to the ground and in one instant finds herself but a mote in this seethe of humanity. In vain her efforts, she cannot move arm or limb. The gate is but a few paces off, but all hope of reaching it is futile. She can only hold herself still and listen as all around are listening. But to what? To nothing. It is expectation which holds them all silent. She will have to wait until the crowd sways apart, allowing her to – Ah, there, some heads are moving now! She catches one glimpse ahead of her, and sees – What does she see? The noble but shrunk figure of the judge drawn up before his gate. His lips are moving, but no sound issues from them; and while those about are waiting for his words, they peer, with an insolence barely dashed by awe, at his white head and his high fence and now at the gate swerving gently inward under the hand of someone whose figure is invisible.

But no words coming, a change passes like a stroke of lightning over the surging mass. Someone shouts out *coward*! another, *traitor*! and the lifted head falls, the moving lips cease from their efforts and in place of the great personality which filled their eyes a moment before, they see a man entrapped, waking to the horror of a sudden death in life for which no visions of the day, no dreams of the night, had been able to prepare him.

It was a sight to waken pity not derision. But these people had gathered here in a bitter mood and their rancour had but scented the prey. Calls of 'Oliver!' and such threats as 'You saved him at a poor man's expense, but we'll have him yet, we'll have him yet!' began to rise about him; followed by endless repetitions of the name from near and far: 'Oliver! Oliver!'

Oliver! His own lips seemed to re-echo the word. Then like a lion baited beyond his patience the judge lifted his head and faced them all with a fiery intensity which for the moment made him a terrible figure to contemplate.

'Let no one utter that name to me here!' shot from his lips in tones of unspeakable menace and power. 'Spare me that name, or the curse of my ruined life be upon you. I can bear no more today.'

Thrilled by his aspect, cowering under his denunciation, emphasised as it was by a terrifying gesture, the people, pressing closest about him, drew back and left the passage open to the gate. He took it with a bound, and would have entered but that from the outskirts of the crowd where his voice had not reached, the cry arose again of 'Oliver! Oliver! The sons of the rich go free, but ours have to hang!'

At which he turned his head about, gave them one stare and fell back against the door. It yielded and a woman's arms received him. The gentle Reuther in that hour of dire extremity, showed herself stronger than her mother who had fallen in a faint amid the crowd.

The Misfortunes of my House

To one who swoons but seldom, the moment of returning consciousness is often fraught with great pain and sometimes with unimaginable horror. It was such to Deborah; the pain and horror holding her till her eyes, accustomed to realities again, saw in the angel face which floated before her vision amid a swarm of demon masks, the sweet and solicitous countenance of Reuther.

As she took this in, she took in other facts also: that there were no demons, no strangers even about her: That she and her child were comparatively alone in their own little parlour, and that Reuther's sweet face wore a look of lofty courage which reminded her of something she could not at the moment grasp, but which was so beautiful. At that instant her full memory came, and, uttering a low cry, she started up, and struggling to her feet, confronted her child, this time with a look full of agonised inquiry.

Reuther seemed to understand her; for, taking her mother's hand in hers, she softly said:

'I knew you were not seriously ill, only frightened by the crowd and their senseless shoutings. Don't think of it any more, dear mother. The people are dispersing now, and you will soon be quite restored and ready to smile with us at an attack so groundless it is little short of absurd.'

Astounded at such tranquillity where she had expected anguish if not stark unreason, doubting her eyes, her ears – for this was no longer her delicate, suffering Reuther to be shielded from all unhappy knowledge, but a woman as strong if not as wise to the situation as herself – she scrutinised the child closely, then turned her gaze slowly about the room, and started in painful surprise, as she perceived standing in the space behind her the tall figure of Judge Ostrander.

He! and she must face him! the man whom she by her blind and untimely efforts to regain happiness for Reuther, had brought to this woeful pass! The ordeal was too bitter for her broken spirit and, shrinking aside, she covered her face with her hands like one who stands detected in a guilty act.

'Pardon,' she entreated, forgetting Reuther's presence in her consciousness of the misery she had brought upon her benefactor. 'I never meant – I never dreamed –'

'Oh, no apologies!' Was this the judge speaking? The tone was an admonitory, not a suffering one. It was not even that of a man humiliated or distressed. 'You have had an unfortunate experience, but that is over now and so must your distress be.' Then, as in her astonishment she dropped her hands and looked up, he added very quietly, 'Your daughter has been much disturbed about you, but not at all about Oliver or his good name. She knows my son too well, and so do you and I, to be long affected by the virulent outcries of a mob seeking for an object upon which to expend their spleen.'

Swaying yet in body and mind, quite unable in the turmoil of her spirits to reconcile this strong and steady man with the crushed and despairing figure she had so lately beheld shrinking under the insults of the crowd, Deborah was glad to sit silent under this open rebuke and listen to Reuther's ingenuous declarations, though she knew that they brought no conviction and distilled no real comfort either to his mind or hers.

'Yes, mother darling,' the young girl was saying. 'These people have not seen Oliver in years, but we have, and nothing they can say, nothing that anyone can say but himself could ever shake my belief in him as a man incapable of a really wicked act. He might be capable of striking a sudden blow – most men are under great provocation – but to conceal such a fact – to live for years enjoying the respect of all who knew him, with the knowledge festering in his heart of another having suffered for his crime – that, *that* would be impossible to Oliver Ostrander.'

Some words ring in the heart long after their echo has left the ear. *Impossible*! Deborah stole a look at the judge. But he was gazing at Reuther, where he well might gaze, if his sinking heart craved support or his abashed mind sought to lose itself in the enthusiasm of this pure soul, with its loving, uncalculating instincts.

'Am I not right, mother?'

Ah! must she answer that?

'Tell the judge who is as confident of Oliver as I am myself that you are confident, too. That you could no more believe him capable of this abominable act than you could believe it of my father.'

'I will – tell – the judge,' stammered the unhappy mother. 'Judge,' she briefly declared, as she rose with the help of her daughter's arm, 'my mind agrees with yours in this matter. What you think, I think.' And that was all she could say.

As she fell again into her seat, the judge turned to Reuther:

'Leave your mother for a little while,' he urged with that rare gentleness he always showed her. 'Let her rest here a few minutes longer, alone with me.'

'Yes, Reuther,' murmured Deborah, seeing no way of avoiding this inevitable interview. 'I am feeling better every minute. I will come soon.'

The young girl's eye faltered from one to the other, then settled, with a strange and imploring look upon her mother. Had her clear intelligence pierced at last to the core of that mother's misery? Had she seen what Deborah would have spared her at the cost of her own life? It would seem so, for when the mother, with great effort, began some conciliatory speech, the young girl smiled with a certain sad patience, and, turning towards Judge Ostrander, said as she softly withdrew:

'You have been very kind to allow me to mention a name and discuss a subject you have expressly forbidden. I want to show my gratitude, Judge Ostrander, by never referring to it again without your permission. That you know my mind,' – here her head rose with a sort of lofty pride which lent a dazzling quality to her usually quiet beauty, 'and that I know yours, is quite enough for me.'

'A noble girl! a mate for the best!' fell from the judge's lips after a silence disturbed only by the faint, far-off murmur of a slowly dispersing throng.

Deborah made no answer. She could not yet trust her courage or her voice.

The judge, who was standing near, concentrated his look upon her features. Still she made no effort to meet his eye. He did not speak, and the silence grew appalling. To break it, he stepped away and took a glance out of the window. There was nothing to be seen there; the fence hid all, but he continued to look, the shadows from his soul settling deeper and deeper upon his countenance as each heavy moment dragged by. When he finally turned, it was with a powerful effort which communicated itself to her and forced her long-bowed head to rise and her troubled mind to disclose itself.

'You wish to express your displeasure, and hesitate on account of Reuther,' she faltered. 'You need not. We are quite prepared to leave your house if our presence reminds you too much of the calamity I have brought upon you by my inconsiderate revival of a past you had every reason to believe buried.'

His reply was uttered with great courtesy.

'Madam,' said he, 'I have never had a thought from the first moment of your coming, of any change in the arrangements we then entered into; nor is the demonstration we have just witnessed a calamity of sufficient importance to again divide this household. To connect my high-minded son with a crime for which he had no motive and from which he could reap no benefit is, if you will pardon my plain speaking at a moment so critical, even greater folly than to exculpate, after all these years, the man whom a conscientious jury found guilty. Only a mob could so indulge itself; individuals will not dare.'

She thought of the letter which had been passed up to him in court, and surveyed him with an astonishment she made no effort to conceal. Never had she felt at a greater disadvantage with him. Never had she understood him less. Was this attempt at unconcern, so pitiably transparent to her, made in an endeavour to probe her mind or to deceive his own? In her anxiety to determine, she hesitatingly remarked:

'Not the man who writes those anonymous letters?'

'Letters?' Involuntarily his hand flew to one of his inner pockets.

'Yes, you have found them, have you not, lying about the grounds?'

'No.' He looked startled. 'Explain yourself,' said he. 'What letters? Not such as –' Again his hand went to his pocket, but shrunk hastily back as she pulled out a crumpled bit of paper and began to smooth it out for his perusal.

'What have you there?' he cried.

'Such a letter as I speak of, Judge Ostrander. I picked it up from the walk a day or so ago. Perhaps you have come upon the like?'

'No; why should I?'

He had started back, but his eye falling involuntarily upon the words she had spread out before him, he rapidly read them, and aghast at their import, glanced from the paper to her face and back again, crying:

'He means Oliver! We have an enemy, Mrs Scoville, an enemy! Do you know' – here he leaned forward, and plunged his eye, now burning with many passions, into hers – 'who this enemy is?'

'Yes.' Softly as the word came, it seemed to infuriate him. Seizing her by the arm, he was about to launch against her the whole weight of his aroused nature, when she said simply: 'He is a common bill-poster. I took pains to find this out. I was as interested as you could be to discover the author of such an outrage.'

'A bill-poster?'

'Yes, Judge Ostrander.'

'What is his name?'

'I do not know. I only know that he is resolved upon making you trouble. It was he who incited this riot. He did it by circulating anonymous missives and by – forgive me for telling you this – affixing scrawls of the same ambiguous character on fences and on walls, and even on – on –' (Here terror tied her tongue, for his hand had closed about her arm in a forceful grip, and the fire in the eye holding hers was a consuming one) 'the rails – of – of *bridges*.'

'Ah!'

The cry was involuntary, but not so the steady settling of the lips which followed it and the determined poise of his body as he waited for her next word.

'Miss Weeks, the little lady opposite, saw the latter and tore it off. But the mischief had already spread. Oh, strike me! Send me from your house!'

He gave no token of hearing her.

'Why is this man my enemy?' he asked. 'I do not know any such person as you describe.'

'Nor I,' she answered more quietly.

'A bill-poster! Well, he has done his worst. I shall think no more about him.' And the burning eye grew mild and the working lip calm again, with a determination too devoid of sarcasm to be false.

It was a change for which Deborah was in no wise prepared. She showed her amazement as ingenuously as a child, and he, observing it, remarked in a different tone from any he had used yet:

'You do not look well. You are still suffering from the distress and confusion into which this wretched swoon has thrown you. Or can it be that you are not yet convinced of our wisdom in ignoring this diabolic attack upon one whose reputation is as dear to us as our own? If that is so, and I see that it is, let me remind you of a fact which cannot be new to you if it is to others of happier memories, that no accusation of this kind, however plausible – and this is not plausible – can hold its own for a day without evidence to back it. And there is no evidence against my son in this ancient matter of my friend Etheridge's violent death, save the one coincidence known to many, that he chanced to be somewhere in the ravine at that accursed hour. A petty point upon which to hang this late and elaborate insult of suspicion!' And his voice rang out in a laugh, but not as it would have rung, or as Deborah thought it would have rung, had his mind been as free as his words.

When it had quite ceased, Deborah threw off the last remnant of physical as well as moral weakness, and deliberately rose to her feet. She believed she understood him now; and she respected the effort he was making, and would have seconded it gladly had she dared.

But she did not dare. If he were really as ignorant as he appeared of the extent of the peril threatening Oliver's good name; if he had cheated himself during these long years into supposing that the secret which had undermined his own happiness was an unshared one, and that his own conduct since that hour he had characterised as accursed, had given no point to the charges they had just heard hurled against his son, then he ought to be undeceived and that right speedily. Evidence did exist connecting Oliver with this crime; evidence as sure, nay, yet surer, than that raised against her husband; and no man's laughter, no, not even his father's – least of all his father's –

could cover up the fact or avail against the revelations which must follow, now that the scent was on. Honouring as she did the man before her, understanding both his misery and the courage he displayed in this superhuman effort to hide his own convictions, she gathered up all her resources, and with a resolution no less brave than his, said firmly:

'You are too much respected in this town, Judge Ostrander, for any collection of people, however thoughtless or vile, to so follow the lead of a low-down miscreant as to greet you to your face with these damaging assertions, unless they *thought* they had evidence, and good evidence, too, with which to back these assertions.'

It was the hurling of an arrow poisoned at the point; the launching of a bomb into the very citadel of his security. Had he burst into outbreak – gripped her again or fiercely shown her the door, she would not have been astonished. Indeed, she was prepared for some such result, but it did not come. On the contrary, his answer was almost mild, though tinged for the first time with a touch of that biting sarcasm for which he had once been famous.

'If they had not *thought*!' he repeated. 'If you had said if they had not *known*, then I might indeed have smelt danger. People *think* strange things. Perhaps *you* think them, too.'

'I?' The moment was critical. She saw now that he was sounding her, had been sounding her from the first. Should she let everything go and let him know her mind, or should she continue to conceal it? In either course lay danger, if not to herself and Reuther, then to himself and Oliver. She decided for the truth. Subterfuge had had its day. The menace of the future called for the strongest weapons which lie at the hand of man. She, therefore, answered:

'Yes; I have been thinking, and this is the result: you must either explain publicly and quite satisfactorily to the people of this town, the mystery of your long separation from Oliver and the life you have since led in this trebly barred house, or accept the opprobrium of such accusations as we have listened to today. There is no middle course, Judge Ostrander. I who have loved Oliver almost like a son; who have a daughter who not only loves him but regards him as a perfect model of noble manhood, tell you so, though it breaks my heart to do it. I cannot see you both fall headlong to destruction for lack of understanding the nearness or the depth of the precipice you are approaching.'

'So!'

The ejaculation came after a moment of intense silence – a silence during which she seemed to discern the sturdiness of years drop slowly away from him.

'So that is the explanation which people give to my desire for retirement and a life of contemplation. Well,' he slowly added, with the halting utterance of one to whom each word is an effort, 'I can see some justification for their conclusions now. I have been too self-centred, and too short-sighted to recognise my own folly. I might have known that anything out of the common course rouses a curiosity which supplies its own explanation at any cost to propriety or respect. I have courted my own doom. I am the victim of my own mistake. But,' he continued, with a flash of his old fire which made him a dignified figure again, 'I'm not going to cringe because I have lost ground in the first skirmish. I come of fighting blood. Oliver's reputation shall not suffer long, whatever I may have done in my parental confidence to endanger it. I have not spent ten years at the bar, and fifteen on the bench for nothing. Let the people look to it! I will stand by my own.'

He had as completely forgotten her as if she had never existed. John Scoville, his widow, even the child bowed under troubles not unlike his own, had faded alike from his consciousness. But the generous Deborah felt no resentment at the determination which would only press her and hers deeper into contumely.

She had seen the father in the man for the first time, and her whole heart went out in passionate sympathy which blinded her to everything but her present duty. Alas, that it should be so hard a one! Alas, that instead of encouraging him, she must point out the one weakness of his cause which he did not or would not see, that is, his own conviction of his absent son's guilt as typified by the line he had deliberately smeared across Oliver's pictured countenance. The task seemed so difficult, the first steps so blind, that she did not know how to begin and stood staring at him with interest and dread struggling for mastery in her heavily labouring breast.

Did he perceive this or was it the silence which drew his attention to her condition and the evils still threatening him? Whichever it was, the light vanished from his face as he surveyed her and it was with a return of his old manner, that he finally observed:

'You are keeping something from me – some fancied discovery – some clue, as they call it, to what you may consider my dear boy's guilt.'

With a deep breath she woke from her trance of indecision and letting forth the full passion of her nature, she cried out in her anguish:

'I have but one answer for that, Judge Ostrander. Look into your own heart! Question your own conscience. I have seen what reveals it. I –'

She stopped appalled. Rage, such as she had never even divined spoke from every feature. He was no longer the wretched but calmly reasoning man, but a creature hardly human, and when he spoke, it was in a frenzy which swept everything before it.

'You have *seen*!' he shouted. 'You have broken your promise! You have touched what you were forbidden to touch! You have –'

'Not so,' she broke in softly but very firmly. 'I have touched nothing that I was told not to, nor have I broken any promise.

I simply saw more than I was expected to, I suppose, of the picture which fell the day you first allowed me to enter your study.'

'Is that true?'

'It is true.'

They were whispering now.

Drawing a deep breath, he gathered up his faculties. 'Upon such accidents,' he muttered, 'hang the fate and honour of men. And you have gossiped about this picture,' he again vociferated with sudden and unrestrained violence, 'told Reuther – told others –'

'No.' The denial was peremptory, not to be disbelieved. 'What I have learned, I have kept religiously to myself. Alas!' she half moaned, half cried, 'that I should feel the necessity!'

'Madam!' – he was searching her eyes, searching her very soul, as men seldom search the mind of another. 'You believe in the truth of these calumnies that have just been shouted in our ears. You believe what they say of Oliver. You with every prejudice in his favour; with every desire to recognise his worth! You, who have shown yourself ready to drop your husband's cause though you consider it an honest one, when you saw what havoc it would entail to my boy's repute. *You* believe – and on what evidence?' he broke in. 'Because of the picture?'

'Yes.'

'And the coincidence of his presence in the ravine?'

'Yes.'

'But these are puerile reasons.' He was speaking peremptorily now and with all the weight of a master mind. 'And you are not the woman to be satisfied with anything puerile. There is something back of all this; something you have not imparted. What is that something? Tell – tell –'

'Oliver was a mere boy in those days and a very passionate one. He hated Etheridge – the obtrusive mentor who came between him and yourself.'

'Hated?'

'Yes.'

'*Hated?*'

'Yes, there is proof.'

'Of his hate?'

'Yes, judge.'

He did not ask where. Possibly he knew. And because he did not ask, she did not tell him, holding on to her secret in a vague hope that so much at least might never see light.

'I knew the boy shrank sometimes from Algernon's company,' the judge admitted, after another glance at her face; 'but that means nothing in a boy full of his own affairs. What else have you against him? Speak up! I can bear it all.'

'He handled the stick that – that –'

'Oliver?'

'Yes.'

'Never! Now you have gone mad, madam.'

'I would be willing to end my days in an asylum if that would disprove this fact.'

'But, madam, what proof – what reason can you have for an assertion so monstrous?'

'You remember the shadow I saw which was not that of John Scoville? The person who made that shadow was whittling a stick; that was a trick of Oliver's. I have heard that he even whittled furniture.'

'Good God!' The judge's panoply was pierced at last.

'They tried to prove, as you will remember, that it was John who thus disfigured the bludgeon he always carried with pride. But the argument was a sorry one and in itself would have broken down the prosecution had he been a man of better repute. Now, those few chips taken from the handle of this weapon will carry a different significance. For in my folly I asked to see this stick which still exists at Police Headquarters, and there in the wood I detected and pointed out a trifle of steel which never came from the unbroken blades of the knife taken from John's pocket.'

Fallen was the proud head now and fallen the great man's aspect. If he spoke it was to utter a low 'Oliver! Oliver!'

The pathos of it – the heart-rending wonder in the tone brought the tears to Deborah's eyes and made her last words very difficult.

'But the one great thing which gives to these facts their really dangerous point is the mystery you have made of your life and of this so-called hermitage. If you can clear up that, you can afford to ignore the rest.'

'The misfortunes of my house!' was his sole response. 'The misfortunes of my house!'

Suddenly he faced Deborah again. The crisis of feeling had passed, and he looked almost cold.

'You have had advisers,' said he. 'Who are they?'

'I have talked with Mr Black.'

The judge's brows met.

'Well, you were wise,' said he. Then shortly, 'What is his attitude?'

Feeling that her position was fast becoming intolerable she falteringly replied, 'Friendly to you and Oliver but, even without all the reasons which move me, sharing my convictions.'

'He has told you so?'

'Not directly; but there was no misjudging his opinion of the necessity you were under to explain, the mysteries of your life. *And it was yesterday we talked*; *not* Today.'

Like words thrown into a void, these slow, lingering, half-uttered phrases seemed to awaken an echo which rung not only in his inmost being, but in hers. Not till in both natures silence had settled again (the silence of despair, not peace), did he speak. When he did, it was simply to breathe her name.

'Deborah?'

Startled, for it had always before been Madam, she looked up to find him standing very near her and with his hand held out.

'I am going through deep waters,' said he. 'Am I to have your support?'

'O, Judge Ostrander, how can you doubt it?' she cried, dropping her hand into his, and her eyes swimming with tears. 'But what can I do? If I remain here I will be questioned. If I fly – but, possibly, that is what you want; for me to go – to disappear – to take Reuther and sink out of all men's sight forever. If this is your wish, I am ready to do it. Gladly will we be gone – now – at once – this very night if you say so.'

His disclaimer was peremptory.

'No; not that. I ask no such sacrifice. Neither would it avail. There is but one thing which can reinstate Oliver and myself in the confidence and regard of these people. Cannot you guess it, madam? I mean your own restored conviction that the sentence passed upon John Scoville was a just one. Once satisfied of this, your temperament is such that you would be our advocate whether you wished it or no. Your very silence would be eloquent.'

'Convince me; I am willing to have you, Judge Ostrander. But how can you do so? A shadow stands between my wishes and the belief you mention. The shadow cast by Oliver as he made his way towards the bridge, with my husband's bludgeon in his hand.'

'Did you see him strike the blow? Were there any opportune shadows to betray what happened between the instant of – let us say Oliver's approach and the fall of my friend? Much can happen in a minute, and this matter is one of minutes. Granted that the shadow you saw was that of Oliver, and the stick he carried was the one under which Algernon succumbed, what is to hinder the following from, having occurred. The stick which Oliver may have caught up in an absent frame of mind becomes burdensome; he has broken his knife against a knot in the handle and he is provoked. Flinging the bludgeon down, he hurries up the embankment and so on into town. John Scoville, lurking in the bushes, sees his stick fall and regains it at or near the time Algernon Etheridge steps into sight at the end of the bridge beyond Dark Hollow. Etheridge carries a watch greatly desired by the man who finds himself thus armed. The place is quiet; the impulse to possess himself of this watch is sudden and irresistible, and the stick falls on Etheridge's head. Is there anything impossible or even improbable about all this? Scoville had a heart open to crime, Oliver not. This I knew when I sat upon the bench at his trial; and now you shall know it too. Come! I have something to show you.'

He turned towards the door and mechanically she followed. Her thoughts were all in a whirl. She did not know what to make of him or of herself. The rooted dread of weeks was stirring in its soil. This suggestion of the transference of the stick from hand to hand was not impossible. Only Scoville had sworn to her, and that, too, upon their child's head, that he had not struck this blow. And she had believed him after finding the cap; *And she believed him now.* Yes, against her will, she believed him now. Why? and again, why?

They had crossed the hall and he was taking the turn to his room.

'Enter,' said he, lifting the curtain.

Involuntarily she recoiled. Not from him, but from the revelation she felt to be awaiting her in this place of unguessed mystery. Looking back into the space behind her, she caught a fleeting glimpse of Reuther hovering on a distant threshold. Leaving the judge, without even a murmured word of apology, she ran to the child, embraced her, and promised to join her soon; and then, satisfied with the comfort thus gained, she returned quickly to where the judge still awaited her, with his hand on the curtain.

'Forgive me,' said she; and meeting with no reply, stood trembling while he unlocked the door and ushered her in.

A new leaf in the history of this old crime was about to be turned.

Once within the room, he became his courteous self once more. 'Be seated,' he begged, indicating a chair in the half gloom. As she took it, the room sprang into sudden light. He had pulled the string which regulated the curtains over the glazed panes in the ceiling. Then as quickly all was gloom again; he had let the string escape from his hand.

'Half-light is better,' he muttered in vague apology.

It was a weird beginning to an interview whose object was as yet incomprehensible to her. One minute a blinding glimpse of the room whose details were so varied that many of them still remained unknown to her – the next, everything swept again into shadow through which the tall form of the genius of the place loomed with melancholy suggestion!

She was relieved when he spoke.

'Mrs Scoville (not Deborah now) have you any confidence in Oliver's word?'

She did not reply at once. Too much depended upon a simple yes or no. Her first instinctive cry would have been *yes*, but if Oliver had been guilty and yet held back his dreadful secret all these years, how could she believe his word, when his whole life had been a lie?

'Has there ever been anything in his conversation as you knew it in Detroit to make you hesitate to reply?' the judge persisted, as she continued speechless.

'No; nothing. I had every confidence in his assertions. I should have yet, if it were not for this horror.'

'Forget it for a moment. Recall his effect upon you as a man, a prospective son-in-law, for you meant him to marry Reuther.'

'I trusted him. I would trust him in many ways yet.'

'Would you trust him enough to believe that he would tell you the truth if you asked him point-blank whether his hands were clean of crime?'

'Yes.' The word came in a whisper; but there was no wavering in it. She had felt the conviction dart like an arrow through her mind that Oliver might slay a man in his hate – might even conceal his guilt for years – but that he could not lie about it when brought face to face with an accuser like herself.

'Then I will let you read something he wrote at my request these many years ago: an experience – the tale of one awful night, the horrors of which, locked within his mind and mine, have never been revealed to a third person. That you should share our secret now, is not only necessary but fitting. It becomes the widow of John Scoville to know what sort of a man she persists in regarding innocent. Wait here for me.'

With a quick step he wound his way among the various encumbering pieces of furniture, to the door opening into his bedroom. A breathless moment ensued, during which she heard his key turn in the lock, followed by the repeating sound of his footsteps, as he wended his way inside to a point she could only guess at from her knowledge of the room, to be a dresser in one of the corners. Here he lingered so long that, without any conscious volition of her own, almost in spite of her volition which would have kept her where she was, she found herself on her feet, then moving step by step, more cautiously than he, in and out of huddling chairs and cluttering tables till she came to a standstill before the reflection (in some mirror, no doubt) of the judge's tall form, bending not over the dresser, as she had supposed, but before a cupboard in the wall – a cupboard she had never seen, in a wall she had never seen, but now recognised for the one hitherto concealed by the great carpet rug. He had a roll of paper in his hand, which he bundled together as he dropped the curtain back into place and then stopped to smooth it out over the floor with the precision of long habit. All this she saw in the mirror as though she had been at his back in the other room; but when she beheld him turn, then panic seized her and she started breathlessly for the spot where he had left her, glad that there was so little light, and praying that he might be deaf to her steps, which, gently as they fell, sounded portentously loud in her own ears.

She had reached her chair, but she had not had time to re-seat herself when she beheld him approaching with the bundle of loose sheets clutched in his hand.

'I want you to sit here and read,' said he, laying the manuscript down on a small table near the wall under a gas-jet which he immediately lighted. 'I am going back to my own desk. If you want to speak, you may; I shall not be working.' And she heard his footsteps retreating again in and out among the furniture till he reached his own chair and sat before his own table.

This ended all sound in the room excepting the beating of her own heart, which had become tumultuous.

How could she sit there and read words, with the blood pounding in her veins and her eyes half blind with terror and excitement? It was only the necessity of the case which made it possible. She knew that she would never be released from that spot until she had read what had been placed before her. Thank God! the manuscript was legible. Oliver's handwriting possessed the clearness of print. She had begun to read before she knew it, and having begun, she never paused till she reached the end.

I was fifteen. It was my birthday and I had my own ideas of how I wanted to spend it. My hobby was modelling. My father had no sympathy with this hobby. To him it was a waste of time better spent in study or such sports as would fit me for study. But he had never absolutely forbidden me to exercise my talent this way, and when on the day I mention I had a few hours of freedom, I decided to begin a piece of work of which I had long dreamed. This was the remodelling in clay of an exquisite statue which had greatly aroused my admiration.

This statue stood in a forbidden place. It was one of the art treasures of the great house on the bluff commonly called Spencer's Folly. I had seen this marble once, when dining there with father, and was so impressed by its beauty, that it haunted me night and day, standing out white and wonderful in my imagination, against backgrounds of endless variation. To copy its lovely lines, to caress with a creative hand those curves of beauty instinct, as I then felt, with soul, became my one overmastering desire – a desire which soon deepened into purpose. The boy of fifteen would attempt the impossible. I procured my clay and then awaited my opportunity. It came, as I have said, on my birthday.

There was no one living in the house at this time. Mr Spencer had gone West for the winter. The servants had been dismissed, and the place closed. Only that morning I had heard one of his boon companions say, 'Oh, Jack's done for. He's found a pretty widow in the Sierras, and there's no knowing now when we'll drink his health again in Spencer's Folly,' a statement which wakened but one picture in my mind and that was a long stretch of empty rooms teeming with art treasures amid which one gem rose supreme – the gem which through his reckless carelessness, I now proposed to make my own, if loving fingers and the responsive clay would allow it.

What to every other person in town would have seemed an insuperable obstacle to this undertaking, was no obstacle to me. I knew how to get in. *One day in my restless wanderings about a place which had something of the nature of a shrine to me, I had noticed that one of the windows (a swinging one) overlooking the ravine, moved as the wind took it. Either the lock had given way or it had not been properly fastened. If I could only bring myself to disregard the narrowness of the ledge separating the house from the precipice beneath, I felt that I could reach this window and sever the vines sufficiently for my body to press in; and this I did that night, finding, just as I had expected, that once a little force was brought to bear upon the sash, it yielded easily, offering a free passage to the delights within.*

In all this I experienced little fear, but once inside, I began to realise the hazard of my adventure, as hanging at full length from the casement, I meditated on the drop I must take into what to my dazed eyes looked like an absolute void. This taxed my courage; but after a moment of sheer fright, I let myself go – I had to – and immediately found myself standing upright in a space so narrow I could touch the walls on either side. It was a closet I had entered, opening, as I soon discovered, into the huge dining-hall where I had once sat beside my father at the one formal meal of my life.

I remembered that room; it had made a great impression upon me, and some light finding its way through the panes of uncurtained glass which topped each of the three windows overlooking the ravine, I soon was able to find the door leading into the drawing room.

I had brought a small lantern in the bag slung to my shoulders, but I had not hitherto dared to use it on account of the transparency of the panes I have mentioned; but once in the perfectly dark recesses of the room beyond, I drew it out, and without the least fear of detection boldly turned it upon the small alcove where stood the object of my adoration.

It was another instance of the reckless confidence of youth. I was on the verge of one of the most appalling adventures which could befall a man, and yet no premonition disturbed the ecstasy with which I knelt before the glimmering marble and unrolled my bundle of wet clay.

I was not a complete fool. I only meant to attempt a miniature copy, but my presumption led me to expect it to be like – yes, like – oh, I never doubted it!

But when, after a few minutes of rapturous contemplation of the proportions which have been the despair of all lesser adepts than the great sculptor who conceived them, I began my work, oh, then I began to realise a little the nature of the task I had undertaken and to ask myself whether if I stayed all night I could finish it to my mind. It was during one of these moments of hesitation that I heard the first growl of distant thunder. But it made little impression upon me, and I returned to my work with renewed glow, renewed hope. I felt so secure in my shell of darkness, with only the one small beam lighting up my model and my own fingers busy with the yielding clay.

But the thunder growled again and my head rose, this time in real alarm. Not because of that far-off struggle of the elements with which I had nothing to do and hardly sensed, but because of a nearer sound, an indistinguishable yet strangely perturbing sound, suggesting a step – no, it was a voice, or if not a voice, some equally sure token of an approaching presence on the porch in front. Someone going by on the road two hundred feet away must have caught the gleam of my lantern through some unperceived crack in the parlour shutters. In another minute I should hear a shout at the window, or, perhaps, the pounding of a heavy hand on the front door. I hated the interruption, but otherwise I was but little disturbed. Whoever it was, he could not by any chance find his way in. Nevertheless, I discreetly closed the shutter of my lantern and began groping my way back to my own place of exit. I had reached the dining room door, when the blood suddenly stopped in my veins. Another sound had reached my ear; an unmistakable one this time – the rattling of a key in its lock. A man – two men were entering by the great front door. They came in on a swoop of wind which seemed to carry everything before it. I heard a loud laugh, coarsened by drink, and the tipsy exclamation of a voice I knew:

'There! shut the door, can't you, before it's blown from its hinges? You'll find everything jolly here. Wine, lights, solitude in which to finish our game and a roaring good opportunity to sleep afterwards. No servants, no porters, not a soul to disturb us. This is my house and it's a corker. I might be away for a year and' – here there was the crackling of a match – 'I've only to use my night-key to find everything a man wants right to my hand.'

The answer I failed to catch. I was simply paralysed by terror. Should their way lie through the drawing room! My clay, my tools were all lying there, and my unfinished model. Mr Spencer was not an unkind man, but he was very drunk, and I had heard that whisky makes a brute of the most good-natured. He would trample on my work; perhaps he would destroy my tools and then hunt the house till he found me. I did not know what to expect; meantime, lights began to flame up; the room where I stood was no longer a safe refuge, and creeping like a cat, I began to move towards the closet door. Suddenly I made a dart for it; the two men, trampling heavily on the marble floor of the hall were coming my way. I could hear their rude talk – rude to me, though one of them called himself a gentleman. As the door of the room opened to admit them, I succeeded in shutting that of the closet into which I had flung myself – or almost so. I did not dare to latch it, for they were already in the room and might hear me.

'This is the spot for us,' came in Spencer's most jovial tones. 'Big table, whisky handy, cards right here in my pocket. Wait, till I strike a light!'

But the lightning anticipated him. As he spoke, the walls which surrounded me, the walls which surrounded them, leapt into glaring view and I heard the second voice cry out:

'I don't like that! Let's wait till the storm is over. I can't play with such candles as those flaring about us.'

'Damn it! you won't know what candles you are playing by when once you see the pile I've got ready for you. I'm in for a big bout. You have ten dollars and I have a thousand. I'll play you for that ten. If, in the meantime, you get my thousand, why, it'll be because you're the better man.'

'I don't like it, I say. There, see!*'*

A flood of white light had engulfed the house. My closet, with its whitewashed walls flared about me like the mouth of a furnace.

'See, yourself!' came the careless retort, and with the words a gas-jet shot up, then two, then all that the room contained. 'How's that? What's a flash more or less now!'

I heard no answer, only the slap of the cards as they were flung onto the table; then the clatter of a key as it was turned in some distant lock and the quick question:

'Rum, or whisky. Irish or Scotch?'

'Whisky and Irish.'

'Good! but you'll drink it alone.'

The bottles were brought forward and they sat down one on each side of the dusty mahogany table. The man facing me was Spencer, the other sat with his back my way, but I could now and then catch a glimpse of his profile as he started at some flash or lifted his head in terror of the thunder-claps.

'We'll play till the hands point to three,' announced Spencer, taking out his watch and laying it down where both could see it. 'Do you agree to that? Unless I win and your funds go a-begging before the hour.'

'I agree.' The tone was harsh; it was almost smothered. The man was staring at the watch; there was a strange set look to his figure; a pausing as of thought – of sinister thought, I should now say; then I never stopped to characterise it; it was followed too quickly by a loud laugh and a sudden grab at the cards.

'You'll win! I feel it in my bones,' came in encouraging tones from the rich man. 'If you do' – here the storm lulled and his voice sank to an encouraging whisper – 'you can buy the old tavern up the road. It's going for a song; and then we'll be neighbours and can play – play –'

Thunder! – a terrific peal. It shook the house; it shook my boyish heart, but it no longer had power to move the two gamesters. The fever of play had reached its height, and I heard nothing more from their lips, but such phrases as belong to the game. Why didn't I take advantage of their absorption to fly? The sill above my head was within easy reach, the sash was open and no sound that I could make would reach them in this hurly-burly of storm. Why then, with all this invitation to escape, did I remain crouched in my dark retreat with eyes fixed on the narrow crack before me which, under some impulse of movement in the walls about, had widened sufficiently for me to see all that I have related? I do not know, unless I was hypnotised by the glare of expression on those men's faces.

I remember that it was my first glimpse of the human countenance under the sway of wicked and absorbing passions. Hitherto my dreams had all been of beauty – of lovely shapes or noble figures cast in heroic mould. Henceforth, these ideal groups must visit my imagination mixed with the bulging eyes of greed and the contortions of hate masking their hideousness under false smiles or hiding them behind the motions of riotous jollity. I was horrified, I was sickened, and I was frightened to the very soul, but the fascination of the spectacle held me; I watched the men and I watched the play and soon I forgot the tempest also, or remembered it only when my small retreat flared into sudden whiteness, or some gust, heavier than the rest, toppled the bricks from the chimneys above us and sent them crashing down upon the rain-soaked roof.

The stranger was winning. I saw the heap of bills beside him grow and grow while that of his opponent dwindled. I saw the latter smile – smile softly at each toss of his losings across the board; but there was no mirth in his smile, nor was there any common satisfaction in the way the other's hand closed over his gains.

'He will have it all,' I thought. 'The Claymore Tavern will soon change owners'; and I was holding my breath over the final stake when suddenly the house gave a lurch, resettled, then lurched again. The tempest had become a hurricane, and with its first swoop a change took place in the stranger's luck.

The bills which had all gone one way began slowly to recross the board, first singly, then in handfuls. They fell within Spencer's grasp, and the smile with which he hailed their return was not the smile with which he had seen them go, but a steady grin such as I had beheld on the faces of sculptured demons. It frightened me, this smile. I could see nothing else; but, when at another crashing peal I ducked my head, I found on lifting it that my eyes sought instinctively the rigid back of the stranger instead of the open face of Spencer. The passion of the winner was nothing to that of the loser; and from this moment on, I saw but the one figure, and thrilled to the one hope – that an opportunity would soon come for me to see the face of the man whose back told such a tale of fury and suspense.

But it remained fixed on Spencer, and the cards. The roof might fall – he was past heeding. A bill or two only lay now at his elbow, and I could perceive the further stiffening of his already rigid muscles as he dealt out the cards. Suddenly hard upon a rattling peal which seemed to unite heaven and earth, I heard shouted out:

'Half-past two! The game stops at three.'

'Damn your greedy eyes!' came back in a growl. Then all was still, fearfully still, both in the atmosphere outside and in that within, during which I caught sight of the stranger's hand moving slowly around to his back and returning as

slowly forward, all under cover of the table-top and a stack of half-empty bottles.

I was inexperienced. I knew nothing of the habits or the ways of such men as these, but the alarm of innocence in the face of untold, unsuspected but intuitively felt evil, seized me at this stealthy movement, and I tried to rise, tried to shriek, but could not; for events rushed upon us quicker than I could speak or move.

'I can buy the Claymore Tavern, can I? Well, I'm going to,' rang out into the air as the speaker leaped to his feet. 'Take that, you cheat! And that! And that!' And the shots rang out – one, two, three!

Spencer was dead in his Folly. I had seen him rise, throw up his hands and then fall in a heap among the cards and glasses.

Silence! Not even Heaven spoke.

Then the man who stood there alone turned slightly and I saw his face. I have seen it many times since; I have seen it at Claymore Tavern. Distorted up to this moment by a thousand emotions – all evil ones – it was calm now with the realisation of his act, and I could make no mistake as to his identity. Later I will mention his name.

Glancing first at his victim, then at the pistol still smoking in his hand, he put the weapon back in his pocket, and began gathering up the money for which he had just damned his soul. To get it all, he had to move an arm of the body sprawling along the board. But he did not appear to mind. When every bill was in his pockets, he reached out his hand for the watch. Then I saw him smile. He smiled as he shut the case, he smiled as he plunged it in after the bills. There was gloating in this smile. He seemed to have got what he wanted more than when he fingered the bills. I was stiff with horror. I was not conscious of noting these details, but I saw them every one. Small things make an impression when the mind is numb under the effect of a great blow.

Next moment I woke to a realisation of myself and all the danger of my own position. He was scanning very carefully the room about him. His eyes were travelling slowly – very slowly but certainly, in my direction. I saw them pause – concentrate their glances and fix them straight and full upon mine. Not that he saw me. The crack through which we were peering each in our several ways was too narrow for that. But the crack itself – that was what he saw and the promise it gave of some room beyond. I was a creature frozen. But when he suddenly turned away instead of plunging towards me with his still smoking pistol, I had the instinct to make a leap for the window over my head and clutch madly at its narrow sill in a wild attempt at escape.

But the effort ended precipitately. Terror had got me by the hair, and terror made me look back. The crack had widened still further, and what I now saw through it glued me to the wall and held me there transfixed, with dangling feet and starting eyeballs.

He was coming towards me – a straining, panting figure – half carrying, half dragging, the dead man who flopped aside from his arms.

God! what was I to do now! How meet those cold, indifferent eyes filled only with thoughts of his own safety and see them flare again with murderous impulse and that impulse directed towards myself! I couldn't meet them; I couldn't stay; but how fly when not a muscle responded. I had to stay – hanging from the sill and praying – praying – till my senses blurred and I knew nothing till on a sudden they cleared again, and I woke to the blessed realisation that the door had been pushed against my slender figure, hiding it completely from his sight, and that this door was now closed again and this time tightly, and I was safe – safe!

The relief sent the perspiration in a reek from every pore; but the icy revulsion came quickly. As I drew up my knees to get a better purchase on the sill, heaven's torch was suddenly lit up, the closet became a pit of dazzling whiteness amid which I saw the blot of that dead body, with head propped against the wall and eyes –

Remember, I was but fifteen. The legs were hunched up and almost touched mine. I could feel them – though there was no contact – pushing me – forcing me from my frail support. Would it lighten again? Would I have to see – no! any risk first. The window – I no longer thought of it. It was too remote, too difficult. The door – the door – there was my way – the only way which would rid me instantly of any proximity to this hideous object. I flung myself at it – found the knob – turned it and yelled aloud – my foot had brushed against him. I knew the difference and it sent me palpitating over the threshold; but no further. Love of life had returned with my escape from that awful prison-house, and I halted in the semidarkness into which I had plunged, thanking Heaven for the thunder peal which had drowned my loud cry.

For I was not yet safe. He was still there. He had turned out all lights but one, but this was sufficient to show me his tall figure straining up to put out this last jet.

Another instant and darkness enveloped the whole place. He had not seen me and was going. I could hear the sound of his feet as he went stumbling in his zigzag course towards the door. Then every sound both on his part and on mine was lost in a swoop of down-falling rain and I remember nothing more till out of the blankness before me, he started again into view, within the open doorway where in the glare of what he called heaven's candles he stood, poising himself to meet the gale which seemed ready to catch him up and whirl him with other inconsequent things into the void of nothingness. Then darkness settled again and I was left alone with Murder – all the innocence of my youth gone, and my soul a very charnel house.

I had to re-enter that closet; I had to take the only means of escape proffered. But I went through it as we go through the horrors of nightmare. My muscles obeyed my volition, but my sensibilities were no longer active. How I managed to draw myself up to that slippery sill all reeking now with rain, or save myself from falling to my death in the whirling blast that carried everything about me into the ravine below, I do not know.

I simply did it and escaped all – lightning-flash and falling limb, and the lasso of swirling winds – to find myself at last lying my full length along the bridge amid a shock of elements such as nature seldom sports with. Here I clung, for I was breathless, waiting with head buried in my arm for the rain to abate before I attempted a further escape from the place which held such horror for me!

But no abatement came, and feeling the bridge shaking under me almost to cracking, I began to crawl, inch by inch, along its gaping boards till I reached its middle.

There God stopped me.

For, with a clangour as of rending worlds, a bolt, hot from the zenith, sped down upon the bluff behind me, throwing me down again upon my face and engulfing sense and understanding for one wild moment. Then I sprang upright and with a yell of terror sped across the rocking boards beneath me to the road, no longer battling with my desire to look back; no longer asking myself when and how that dead man would be found; no longer even asking my own duty in the case; for Spencer's Folly was on fire and the crime I had just seen perpetrated there would soon be a crime stricken from the sight of men forever.

In the flare of its tremendous burning I found my way up through the forest road to my home and into my father's presence. He like everybody else was up that night, and already alarmed at my continued absence.

'Spencer's Folly is on fire,' I cried, as he cast dismayed eyes at my pallid and dripping figure. 'If you go to the door, you can see it!'

But I told him nothing more.

Perhaps other boys of my age can understand my silence.

I not only did not tell my father, but I told nobody, even after the discovery of Spencer's charred body in the closet so miraculously preserved. With every day that passed, it became harder to part with this baleful secret. I felt it corroding my thoughts and destroying my spirits, and yet I kept still. Only my taste for modelling was gone. I have never touched clay since.

Claymore Tavern did change owners. When I heard that a man by the name of Scoville had bought it, I went over to see Scoville. He was the man. Then I began to ask myself what I ought to do with my knowledge, and the more I asked myself this question, and the more I brooded over the matter, the less did I feel like taking, not the public, but my father, into my confidence.

I had never doubted his love for me, but I had always stood in great awe of his reproof, and I did not know where I was to find courage to tell him all the details of this adventure.

There is one thing I did do, however. I made certain inquiries here and there, and soon satisfied myself as to how Scoville had been able to come into town, commit this horrid deed and escape without anyone but myself being the wiser. Spencer and he had come from the west en route to New York without any intention of stopping off in Shelby. But once involved in play, they got so interested that when within a few miles of the town, Spencer proposed that they should leave the train and finish the game in his own house. Whether circumstances aided them, or Spencer took some extraordinary precautions against being recognised, will never be known. But certain it is that he escaped all observation at the station and even upon the road. When Scoville returned alone, the storm had reached such a height that the roads were deserted, and he, being an entire stranger here at that time, naturally attracted no attention, and so was able to slip away on the next train with just the drawback of buying a new ticket. I, a boy of fifteen, trespassing where I did not belong, was the only living witness of what had happened on this night of dreadful storm, in the house which was now a ruin.

I realised the unpleasantness of the position in which this put me, but not its responsibility. Scoville, ignorant that any other breast than his own held the secret of that hour of fierce temptation and murder, naturally scented no danger and rejoiced without stint in his new acquisition. What evil might I not draw down upon myself by disturbing him in it at this late day. If I were going to do anything, I should have done it at first – so I reasoned, and let the matter slide. I became interested in school and study, and the years passed and I had almost forgotten the occurrence, when suddenly the full remembrance came back upon me with a rush. A man – my father's friend – was found murdered in sight of this spot of old-time horror, and Scoville was accused of the act.

I was older now and saw my fault in all its enormity. I was guilty of that crime – or so I felt in the first heat of my sorrow and despair. I may even have said so – in dreams or in some of my self-absorbed broodings. Though I certainly had not lifted the stick against Mr Etheridge, I had left the hand free which did, and this was a sufficient occasion for remorse – or so I truly felt.

I was so affected by the thought that even my father, with his own weight of troubles, noticed my care-worn face and asked me for an explanation. But I held him off until the verdict was reached, and then I told him. I had not liked his looks for some time; they seemed to convey some doubt of the justice of this man's sentence, and I felt that if he had such doubts, they might be eased by this certainty of Scoville's murderous tendencies and unquestionable greed.

And they were; but as Scoville was already doomed, we decided that it was unnecessary to make public his past offences. However, with an eye upon future contingencies, my father exacted from me in writing this full account of my adventure, which with all the solemnity of an oath I here declare to be the true story of what befell me in the house called Spencer's Folly, on the night of awful storm, September Eleventh, 1895.

OLIVER OSTRANDER.

Witnesses to above signature,

ARCHIBALD OSTRANDER,
BELA JEFFERSON.

Shelby........November 7, 1898.

'What do you think of him now?'

This was the document and these the words which Deborah, widow of the man thus doubly denounced, had been given to read by the father of the writer, in the darkened room which had been and still was to her, an abode of brooding thought and unfathomable mystery.

No wonder that during its reading more than one exclamation of terror and dismay escaped her, as the once rehabilitated form of the dead and gone started into dreadful life again before her eyes. There were so many reasons for believing this record to be an absolute relation of the truth.

Incoherent phrases which had fallen from those long-closed lips took on new meaning with this unveiling of an unknown past. Repugnances for which she could not account in those old days, she now saw explained. He would never, even in passing, give a look at the ruin on the bluff, so attractive to every eye but his own. As for entering its gates – she had never dared so much as to ask him to do so. He had never expressed his antipathy for the place, but he had made her feel it. She doubted now if he would have climbed to it from the ravine even to save his child from falling over its verge. Indeed, she saw the reason now why he could not explain the reason for the apathy he showed in his hunt for Reuther on that fatal day, and his so marked avoidance of the height where she was found.

Then the watch! Deborah knew well that watch. She had often asked him by what stroke of luck he had got so fine a timepiece. But he had never told her. Later, it had been stolen from him; and as he had a mania for watches, that was why, perhaps –

God! was her mind veering back to her old idea as to his responsibility for the crime committed in Dark Hollow? Yes; she could not help it. Denial from a monster like this – a man who with such memories and such spoil, could return home to wife and child, with some gay and confused story of a great stroke in speculation which had brought him in the price of the tavern it had long been his ambition to own – what was denial from such lips worth, though emphasised by the most sacred of oaths, and uttered under the shadow of death. The judge was right. Oliver – whose ingenuous story had restored his image to her mind, with some of its old graces – had been the victim of circumstances and not John Scoville. Henceforth, she would see him as such, and when she had recovered a little from the effect of this sudden insight into the revolting past, she would –

Her thoughts had reached this stage and her hand, in obedience to the new mood, was lightly ruffling up the pages before her, when she felt a light touch on her shoulder and turned with a start.

The judge was at her back. How long he had stood there she did not know, nor did he say. The muttered exclamations which had escaped her, the irrepressible cry of despair she had given when she first recognised the identity of the 'stranger' may have reached him where he sat at the other end of the room, and drawn him insensibly forward till he could overlook her shoulder as she read, and taste with her the horror of these revelations which yet were working so beneficent a result for him and his. It may have been so, and it may have been that he had not made his move till he saw her attitude change and her head droop disconsolately at the reading of the last line. She did not ask, as I have said, nor did he tell her; but when upon feeling his hand upon her shoulder she turned, he was there; and while his lips failed to speak, his eyes were eloquent and their question single and imperative.

'What do you think of him now?' they seemed to ask, and rising to her feet, she met him with a smile, ghastly perhaps with the lividness of the shadows through which she had been groping, but encouraging withal and soothing beyond measure to his anxious and harassed soul.

‘Oliver is innocent,’ she declared, turning once more to lay her hand upon the sheets containing his naive confession. ‘The dastard who could shoot his host for plunder is capable of a second crime holding out a similar inducement. Nothing now will ever make me connect Oliver with the crime at the bridge. As you said, he was simply near enough the hollow to toss into it the stick he had been whittling on his way from the oak tree. I am his advocate from this minute.’

Her eyes were still resting mechanically upon that last page lying spread out before her, and she did not observe in its full glory the first gleam of triumphant joy which, in all probability, Judge Ostrander’s countenance had shown in years. Nor did he see, in the glad confusion of the moment, the quick shudder with which she lifted her trembling hand away from those papers and looked up, squarely at last, into his transfigured visage.

‘Oh, judge!’ she murmured, bursting into a torrent of tears. ‘How you must have suffered to feel so great a relief!’ Then she was still, very still, and waited for him to speak.

‘I suffered,’ he presently proceeded to state, ‘because of the knowledge which had come to me of the scandal with which circumstances threatened us. Oliver had confided to me (after the trial, mind, not before) the unfortunate fact of his having been in possession of the stick during those few odd minutes preceding the murder. He had also told me how he had boasted once, and in a big crowd, too, of his intention to do Etheridge. He had meant nothing by the phrase, beyond what anybody means who mingles boasting with temper, but it was a nasty point of corroborative evidence; and heart-breaking as it was for me to part with him, I felt that his future career would be furthered by a fresh start in another town. You see,’ he continued, a faint blush dyeing his old cheek…old in sorrow not in years… ‘I am revealing mysteries of my past life which I have hitherto kept strictly within my own breast. I cannot do this without shame, because while in the many serious conversations we have had on this subject, I have always insisted upon John Scoville's guilt. I have never allowed myself to admit the least fact which would in any way compromise Oliver. A cowardly attitude for a judge you will say, and you are right; but for a father – Mrs Scoville, I love my boy. I – What's that?'

The front doorbell was ringing.

In a flash Deborah was out of the room. It was as if she had flown with unnecessary eagerness to answer a bidding which, after all, Reuther could easily have attended to. It struck him aghast for the instant, then he began slowly to gather up the papers before him and carry them back into the other room. Had he, instead, made straight for the doorway leading to the front of the house, he would have come upon the figure of Deborah standing alone and with her face pressed in anguish and unspeakable despair against the lintel. Something had struck her heart and darkened her soul since that exalted moment in which she cried:

'Henceforth I will be Oliver's advocate.'

When the judge at last came forth, it was at Reuther's bidding.

A gentleman wished to see him in the parlour.

This was so unprecedented, even of late when the ladies did receive some callers, that he stopped short after his first instinctive step, to ask her if the gentleman had given his name.

She said no; but added that he was not alone; that he had a very strange and not very nice-looking person with him whom mother insisted should remain in the hall. 'Mother requests you to see the gentleman, Judge Ostrander. She said you would wish to, if you once saw the person accompanying him.'

With a dark glance, not directed against her, however, the judge bade her run away to the kitchen and as far from all these troubles as she could, then, locking his door behind him, as he always did, he strode towards the front.

He found Deborah standing guard over an ill-conditioned fellow whose slouching figure slouched still more under his eye, but gave no other acknowledgment of his presence. Passing him without a second look, Judge Ostrander entered the parlour where he found no less a person than Mr Black awaiting him.

There was no bad blood between these two whatever their past relations or present suspicions, and they were soon shaking hands with every appearance of mutual cordiality.

The judge was especially courteous.

'I am glad,' said he, 'of any occasion which brings you again under my roof, though from the appearance of your companion I judge the present one to be of no very agreeable character.'

'He's honest enough,' muttered Black, with a glance towards Deborah, for the understanding of which the judge held no key. Then, changing the subject, 'You had a very unfortunate experience this afternoon. Allow me to express my regret at an outbreak so totally unwarranted.'

A grumble came from the hall without. Evidently his charge, if we may so designate the fellow he had brought there, had his own ideas on this subject.

'Quiet out there!' shouted Mr Black. 'Mrs Scoville, you need not trouble yourself to stand over Mr Flannagan any longer. I'll look after him.'

She bowed and was turning away when the judge intervened.

'Is there any objection,' he asked, 'to Mrs Scoville's remaining present at this interview?'

'None whatever,' answered the lawyer.

'Then, Mrs Scoville, may I request you to come in?'

If she hesitated, it was but natural. Exhaustion is the obvious result of so many excitements, and that she was utterly exhausted was very apparent. Mr Black cast her a commiserating smile, but the judge only noticed that she entered the room at his bidding and sat down by the window. He was keying himself up to sustain a fresh excitement. He was as exhausted as she, possibly more so. He had a greater number of wearing years to his credit.

'Judge, I'm your friend;' thus Mr Black began. 'Thinking you must wish to know who started the riotous procedure which disgraced our town today, I have brought the ringleader here to answer for himself – that is, if you wish to question him.'

Judge Ostrander wheeled about, gave the man a searching look, and failing to recognise him as anyone he had ever seen before, beckoned him in.

'I suppose,' said he, when the lounging and insolent figure was fairly before their eyes, 'that this is not the first time you have been asked to explain your enmity to my long absent son.'

'Naw; I've had my talk wherever and whenever I took the notion. Oliver Ostrander hit me once. I was jest a little chap then and meanin' no harm to anyone. I kept a-pesterin' of 'im and he hit me. He'd a better have hit a feller who hadn't my memory. I've never forgiven that hit, and I never will. That's why I'm hittin' him now. It's just my turn; that's all.'

'Your turn! *Your* turn! And what do you think has given *you* an opportunity to turn on *him*?'

'I'm not in the talkin' mood just now,' the fellow drawled, frankly insolent, not only in his tone but in his bearing to all present. 'Nor can you make it worth my while, you gents. I'll not take money. I'm an honest hard-workin' man who can earn his own livin', and you can't pay me to keep still, or to go away from Shelby a day sooner than I want to. I was goin' away, but I gave it up when they told me that things were beginnin' to look black against Ol Ostrander; that a woman had come into town who was a-stirrin' up things generally about that old murder for which a feller had already been 'lectrocuted, and knowin' somethin' myself about that murder and Ol Ostrander, I – well, I stayed.'

The quiet threat, the suggested possibility, the attack which wraps itself in vague uncertainty, are ever the most effective. As his raucous voice, dry with sinister purpose which no man could shake, died out in an offensive drawl, Mr Black edged a step nearer the judge, before he sprang and caught the young fellow by the coat-collar and gave him a very vigorous shake.

'See here!' he threatened. 'Behave yourself and treat the judge like a gentleman or –'

'Or what?' the bulldog mouth sneered. 'See here yourself,' he now shouted, as the lawyer's hands unloosed and he stood panting; 'I'm not afeard o' you, sir, nor of the jedge, nor of the lady nuther. I *knows* somethin', I do; and when I gets ready to tell it, we'll just see whose coat-collar they'll be handlin'. I came 'cause I wanted to see the inside o' the house Ol Ostrander's father doesn't think him good enough to live in. It's grand; but this part here isn't the whole of it. There's a door somewhere which nobody never opens unless it's the jedge there. I'd like to see what's behind that 'ere door. If it's somethin' to make a good story out of, I might be got to keep quiet about this other thing. I don't know, but I *might*.'

The swagger with which he said this, the confidence in himself which he showed and the reliance he so openly put in the something he knew but could not be induced to tell, acted so strongly upon Mr Black's nerves, that he leaped towards him again, evidently with the intention of dragging him from the house.

But the judge was not ready for this. The judge had gained a new lease of life in the last half-hour and he felt no fear of this sullen bill-poster for all his sly innuendoes. He, therefore, hindered the lawyer from his purpose, by a quick gesture of so much dignity and resolve that even the lout himself was impressed and dropped some of his sullen bravado.

'I have something to say to this fellow,' he announced, looking anywhere but at the drooping figure in the window which ought, above all things in the world, to have engaged his attention. 'Perhaps he does not know his folly. Perhaps he thinks because I was thrown aback today by those public charges against my son and a string of insults for which no father could be prepared, that I am seriously disturbed over the position into which such unthinking men as himself have pushed Mr Oliver Ostrander. I might be if there were truth in these charges or any serious reason for connecting my upright and honourable son with the low crime of a highwayman. *But there is not.* I aver it and so will this lady here whom you have doubtless recognised for the one who has stirred this matter up. You can bring no evidence to show guilt on my son's part,' – these words he directed straight at the discomfited poster of bills – '*because there is no evidence to bring.*'

Mr Black's eyes sparkled with admiration. He could not have used this method with the lad, but he recognised the insight of the man who could. Bribes were a sign of weakness, so were suggested force and counter-attack; but scorn – a calm ignoring of the power of anyone to seriously shake Oliver Ostrander's established position – that might rouse wrath and bring avowal; certainly it had shaken the man; he looked much less aggressive and self-confident than before.

However, though impressed, he was not yet ready to give in. Shuffling about with his feet but not yet shrinking from an encounter few men of his stamp would have cared to subject themselves to, he answered with a remark delivered with a little more civility than any of his previous ones:

'What you call evidence may not be the same as I calls evidence. If you're satisfied at thinkin' my word's no good, that's your business. I know how I should feel if I was Ol Ostrander's father and knew what I know.'

'Let him go,' spoke up a wavering voice. It was Deborah's.

But the judge was deaf to the warning. Deborah's voice had but reminded him of Deborah's presence. Its tone had escaped him. He was too engrossed in the purpose he had in mind to notice shades of inflection.

But Mr Black had, and quick as thought he echoed her request:

'He is forgetting himself. Let him go, Judge Ostrander.'

But that astute magistrate, wise in all other causes but his own, was no more ready now than before to do this.

'In a moment,' he conceded. 'Let me first make sure that this man understands me. I have said that there exists no evidence against my son. I did not mean that there may not be supposed evidence. That is more than probable. No suspicion could have been felt and none of these outrageous charges made, without that. He was unfortunate enough not only to have been in the ravine that night but to have picked up Scoville's stick and carried it towards the bridge, whittling it as he went. But his connection with the crime ends there. He dropped this stick before he came to where the wood path joins Factory Road; and another hand than his raised it against Etheridge. This I aver; and this the lady here will aver. You have probably already recognised her. If not, allow me to tell you that she is the lady whose efforts have brought back this case to the public mind: Mrs Scoville, the wife of John Scoville and the one of all others who has the greatest interest in proving her husband's innocence. If she says, that after the most careful inquiry and a conscientious reconsideration of this case, she has found herself forced to come to the conclusion that justice has already been satisfied in this matter, you will believe her, won't you?'

'I don't know,' drawled the man, a low and cunning expression lighting up his ugly countenance. 'She wants to marry her daughter to your son. Any live dog is better than a dead one; I guess her opinion don't go for much.'

Recoiling before a cynicism that pierced with unerring skill the one joint in his armour he knew to be vulnerable, the judge took a minute in which to control his rage and then addressing the half-averted figure in the window said:

'Mrs Scoville, will you assure this man that you have no expectations of marrying your daughter to Oliver Ostrander?'

With a slow movement more suggestive of despair than any she had been seen to make since the hour of her indecision had first struck, she shifted in her seat and finally faced them, with the assertion:

'Reuther Scoville will never marry Oliver Ostrander. Whatever my wishes or willingness in the matter, she herself is so determined. Not because she does not believe in his integrity, for she does; but because she will not unite herself to one whose prospects in life are more to her than her own happiness.'

The fellow stared, then laughed:

'She's a goodun,' he sneered. 'And you believe that bosh?'

Mr Black could no longer contain himself.

'I believe you to be the biggest rascal in town,' he shouted. 'Get out, or I won't answer for myself. Ladies are not to be treated in this manner.'

Did he remember his own rough handling of the sex on the witness stand?

'I didn't ask to see the ladies,' protested Flannagan, turning with a slinking gait towards the door.

If they only had let him go! If the judge in his new self-confidence had not been so anxious to deepen the effect and make any future repetition of the situation impossible!

'You understand the lady,' he interposed, with the quiet dignity which was so imposing on the bench. 'She has no sympathy with your ideas and no faith in your conclusions. She believes absolutely in my son's innocence.'

'Do you, ma'am?' The man had turned and was surveying her with the dogged impudence of his class. 'I'd like to hear you say it, if you don't mind, ma'am. Perhaps, then, I'll believe it.'

'I –' she began, trembling so, that she failed to reach her feet, although she made one spasmodic effort to do so. 'I believe –

Oh, I feel ill! It's been too much – I –' her head fell forward and she turned herself quite away from them all.

'You see she ain't so eager, jedge, as you thought,' laughed the bill-poster, with a clumsy bow he evidently meant to be sarcastic.

'Oh, what have I done!' moaned Deborah, starting up as though she would fling herself after the retreating figure, now halfway down the hall.

She saw in the look of the judge as he forcibly stopped her, and heard in the lawyer's whisper as he bounded past them both to see the fellow out: 'Useless; nothing will bridle him now'; and finding no support for her despairing spirit either on earth or, as she thought, in heaven, she collapsed where she sat and fell unnoticed to the floor, where she lay prone at the feet of the equally unconscious figure of the judge, fixed in another attack of his peculiar complaint.

And thus the lawyer found them when he returned from closing the gate behind Flannagan.

'I *cannot* say anything, I cannot do anything till I have had a few words with Mrs Scoville. How soon do you think I can speak to her?'

'Not very soon. Her daughter says she is quite worn out. Would it not be better to give her a rest for tonight, judge?'

The judge, now quite recovered, but strangely shrunk and wan, showed no surprise, at this request, odd as it was, on the lips of this honest but somewhat crabbed lawyer, but answered out of the fullness of his own heart and from the depths of his preoccupation:

'My necessity is greater than hers. The change I saw in her is inexplicable. One moment she was all fire and determination, satisfied of Oliver's innocence and eager to proclaim it. The next – but you were with us. You witnessed her hesitation – felt its force and what its effect was upon the damnable scamp who has our honour – the honour of the Ostranders under his tongue. Something must have produced this change. What? good friend, what?'

'I don't know any more than you do, judge. But I think you are mistaken about the previous nature of her feelings. I noticed that she was not at peace with herself when she came into the room.'

'What's that?' The tone was short, and for the first time irritable.

'The change, if there was a change, was not so sudden as you think. She looked troubled, and as I thought, irresolute when she came into the room.'

'You don't know her; you don't know what passed between us. She was all right then, but – go to her, Black. She must have recovered by this time. Ask her to come here for a minute. I won't detain her. I will wait for her warning knock right here.'

Alanson Black was a harsh man, but he had a soft streak in him – a streak which had been much developed of late. Where he loved, he could be extraordinarily kind, and he loved, had loved for years, in his own way which was not a very demonstrative one, this man whom he was now striving to serve. But a counter affection was making difficulties for him just at this minute. Against all probability, many would have said possibility, Deborah Scoville had roused in this hard nature, a feeling which he was not yet ready to name even to himself, but which nevertheless stood very decidedly in his way when the judge made this demand which meant further distress to her.

But the judge had declared his necessity to be greater than hers, and after Mr Black had subjected him to one of his most searching looks he decided that this was so, and quietly departed upon his errand. The judge left alone, sat, a brooding figure in his great chair, with no light in heart or mind to combat the shadows of approaching night settling heavier and heavier upon the room and upon himself with every slow passing and intolerable minute.

At last, when the final ray had departed and darkness reigned supreme, there came a low knock on the door. Then a troubled cry:

'Oh, judge, are you here?'

'I am here.'

'Alone and so dark?'

'I am always alone, and it is always dark. Is there anyone with you?'

'No, sir. Shall I make a light?'

'No light. Is the door quite shut?'

'No, judge.'

'Shut it.'

There came the sound of a hand fumbling over the panels, then a quick snap.

'It is shut,' she said.

'Don't come any nearer; it is not necessary.' A pause, then the quick question ringing hollow from the darkness, 'Why have your doubts returned? Why are you no longer the woman you were when not an hour ago and in this very spot you cried, 'I will be Oliver's advocate!' Then, as no answer came, as minutes passed, and still no answer came, he spoke again and added: 'I know that you are ill and exhausted – broken between duty and sympathy; but you must answer me, Mrs Scoville. My affairs won't wait. I must know the truth and all the truth before this day is over.'

'You shall.' Her voice sounded hollow too and oh, how weary! 'You allowed the document you showed me to remain a little too long before my eyes. That last page – need I say it?'

'Say it.'

'Shows – shows changes, Judge Ostrander. Some words have been erased and new ones written in. They are not many, but –'

'I understand. I do not blame you, Deborah.' The words came after a pause and very softly, almost as softly as her own *but* which had sounded its low knell of doom through the darkness. 'Too many stumbling blocks in your way, Deborah, too much to combat. The most trusting heart must give way under such a strain. That page *was* tampered with. I tampered with it myself. I am not expert at forgery. I had better have left it, as he wrote it.' Then after another silence, he added, with a certain vehemence: 'We will struggle no longer, either you or I. The boy must come home. Prepare Reuther, or, if you think best, provide a place for her where she will be safe from the storm which bids fair to wreck us here. No, don't speak; just ask Mr Black to return, will you?'

'Judge –'

'I understand. Mr Black, Deborah.'

Slowly she moved away and began to grope for the door. As her hand fell on the knob she thought she heard a sob in those impenetrable depths behind her; but when she listened again, all was still; still as if merciful death and not weary life gave its significance to the surrounding gloom.

Shuddering, she turned the knob and paused again for rebuff or command. Neither came; and, realising that having spoken once the judge would not speak again, she slipped softly away, and the door swung to after her.

When Mr Black re-entered the study, it was to find the room lighted and the judge bent over the table, writing.

'You are going to send for Oliver?' he queried.

The judge hesitated, then motioning Black to sit, said abruptly:

'What is Andrews' attitude in this matter?'

Andrews was Shelby's District Attorney.

Black's answer was like the man.

'I saw him for one minute an hour ago. I think, at present, he is inclined to be both deaf and dumb, but if he's driven to action, he will act. And, judge, this man Flannagan isn't going to stop where he is.'

'Black, be merciful to my misery. What does this man know? Have you any idea?'

'No, judge, I haven't. He's as tight as a drum, and as noisy. It is possible – just possible that he's as empty. A few days will tell.'

'I cannot wait for a few days. I hardly feel as if I could wait a few hours. Oliver must come, even if – if the consequences are likely to be fatal. An Ostrander once accused cannot skulk. Oliver has been accused and – Send that!' he quickly cried, pulling forward the telegram he had been writing.

Mr Black took up the telegram and read:

Come at once. Imperative. No delay and no excuse.
ARCHIBALD OSTRANDER.

'Mrs Scoville will supply the address,' continued the poor father. 'You will see that it goes, and that its sending is kept secret. The answer, if any is sent, had better be directed to your office. What do you say, Black?'

'I am your friend, right straight through, judge. Your friend.'

'And my boy's adviser?'

'You wish that?'

'Very much.'

'Then, there's my hand on it, unless he wishes a change when we see him.'

'He will not wish any change.'

'I don't know. I'm a surly fellow, judge. I have known you all these years, yet I've never expressed – never said what I even find it hard to say now, that – that my esteem is something more than esteem; that – that I'll do anything for you, judge.'

'I – we won't talk of that, Black. Tell Mrs Scoville to keep me informed – and bring me any message that may come. The boy, even if he leaves the first thing in the morning, cannot get here before tomorrow night.'

'Not possibly.'

'He will telegraph. I shall hear from him. O God! the hours I must wait; my boy! my boy!'

It was nature's irrepressible cry. Black pressed his hand and went out with the telegram.

Book III

The Door of Mystery

He Must Be Found

Three hours later, an agitated confab took place at the gate, or rather between the two front gates. Mr Black had rung for admittance, and Mrs Scoville had answered the call. In the constrained interview which followed, these words were said:

'One moment, Mrs Scoville. How can I tell the judge! Young Ostrander is gone – flew the city, and I can get no clue to his whereabouts. Some warning of what is happening here may have reached him, or he may be simply following impulses consequent upon his personal disappointments; but the fact is just this – he asked for two weeks' leave to go West upon business, and he's been gone three. Meanwhile, no word has come, nor can his best friends tell the place of his destination. I have been burning the telegraph wires ever since the first despatch, and this is the result.'

'Poor Judge Ostrander!' Then, in lower and still more pathetic tones, 'Poor Reuther!'

'Where is Reuther?'

'At Miss Weeks'. I had to command her to leave me alone with the judge. It's the first time I ever spoke unkindly to her.'

'Shall I tell the judge the result of his telegram, or will you?'

'Have you the messages with you?'

He bundled them into her hand.

'I will hand them in to him. We can do nothing less and nothing more. Then if he wants you, I will telephone.'

'Mrs Scoville?'

She felt his hand laid softly on her shoulder.

'Yes, Mr Black.'

'There is someone else in this matter to consider besides Judge Ostrander.'

'Reuther? Oh, don't I know it! She's not out of my mind a moment.'

'Reuther is young, and has a gallant soul. I mean you, Mrs Scoville, you! You are not to succumb to this trial. You have a future – a bright future – or should have. Do not endanger it by giving up all your strength now. It's precious, that strength, or would be –'

He broke off; she began to move away. Overhead in the narrow space of sky visible to them from where they stood, the stars burned brightly. Some instinct made them look up; as they did so, their hands met. Then a gruff sound broke the silence. It was Alanson Black's voice uttering a grim farewell.

'He must be found! Oliver must be found!' How the words rung in her ears. She had handed in the messages to the waiting father; she had uttered a word or two of explanation, and then, at his request, had left him. But his last cry followed her: 'He must be found!'

When she told it to Mr Black the next morning, he looked serious.

'Pride or hope?' he asked.

'Desperation,' she responded, with a guilty look about her. 'Possibly, some hope is in it, too. Perhaps, he thinks that any charge of this nature must fall before Oliver's manly appearance. Whatever he thinks, there is but one thing to do: find Oliver.'

'Mrs Scoville, the police have started upon that attempt. I got the tip this morning.'

'We must forestall them. To satisfy the judge, Oliver must come of his own accord to face these charges.'

'It's a brave stock. If Oliver gets his father's telegram he will come.'

'But how are we to reach him! We are absolutely in the dark.'

'If I could go to Detroit, I might strike some clue; but I cannot leave the judge. Mr Black, he told me this morning when I carried in his breakfast that he should see no one and go nowhere till I brought him word that Oliver was in the house. The hermit life has begun again. What shall we do? Advise me in this emergency, for I feel as helpless as a child, as a lost child.'

They were standing far apart in the little front parlour, and he gave no evidence of wishing to lessen the space between them, but he gave her a look as she said this, which, as she thought it over afterwards, held in its kindly flame something which had never shone upon her before, whether as maid, wife or widow. But, while she noticed it, she did not dwell upon it now, only upon the words which followed it.

'You say you cannot go to Detroit. Shall I go?'

'Mr Black!'

'Court is adjourned. I know of nothing more important than Judge Ostrander's peace of mind – unless it is yours. I will go if you say so.'

'Will it avail? Let me think. I knew him well, and yet not well enough to know where he would be most likely to go under impulse.'

'There is someone who knows him better than you do.'

'His father?'

'No.'

'Reuther? Oh, she mustn't be told –'

'Yes, she must. She's our one adviser. Go for her – or send me.'

'It won't be necessary. There's her ring at the gate. But oh, Mr Black, think again before you trouble this fragile child of mine with doubts and questions which make her mother tremble.'

'Has she shown the greater weakness yet?'

'No, but –'

'She has sources of strength which you lack. She believes absolutely in Oliver's integrity. It will carry her through.'

'Please let her in, Mr Black. I will wait here while you tell her.'

Mr Black hurried from the room. When his form became visible on the walk without, Deborah watched him from where she stood far back in the room. Why? Was this swelling of her impetuous heart in the midst of such suspense an instinct of thankfulness? A staff had been put in her hand, rough to the touch, but firm under pressure, and she needed such a staff. Yes, it was thankfulness.

But she forgot gratitude and every lesser emotion in watching Reuther's expression as the two came up the path. The child was radiant, and the mother, thus prepared, was not surprised when the young girl, running into her arms, burst out with the glad cry:

'Oliver is no longer in Detroit, but he's wanted here, and Mr Black and I are going to find him. I think I know where to look. Get me ready, mother dear; we are going tonight.'

'You are going tonight?' This was said after the first moment of ebullition had past. 'Where, Reuther? You have not been corresponding with Oliver. How should you know where to look for him?'

Then Reuther told her story.

'Mr Ostrander and I were talking very seriously one day. It was before we became definitely engaged, and he seemed to feel very dispirited and uncertain of the future. There was a treatise he wanted to write, and for this he could get no opportunity in Detroit. 'I need time,' he said, 'and complete seclusion.' And then he made this remark: 'If ever life becomes too much for me, I shall go to one of two places and give myself up to this task.' 'And what are the places?' I asked. 'One is Washington,' he answered, 'where I can have the run of a great library and the influence of the most inspiring surroundings in the world; the other is a little lodge in a mountain top above Lake Placid – Tempest Lodge, they call it; perhaps, in contrast to the peacefulness it dominates.' And he described this last place with so much enthusiasm and weighed so carefully the advantages of the one spot against the other for the absorbing piece of work that he contemplated, that I am sure that if we do not find him in Washington, we certainly shall in the Adirondacks.'

'Let us hope that it will be in Washington,' replied the lawyer, with a keen remembrance of the rigours of an Adirondack fall – rigours of which Reuther in her enthusiasm, if not in her ignorance, appeared to take little count. 'And now,' he went on, 'this is how I hope to proceed. We will go first to Washington, and, if unsuccessful there, to Tempest Lodge. We will take Miss Weeks with us, for I am sure that I could not, without some such assistance, do justice to this young lady's comfort. If you have a picture of Mr Ostrander as he looks now, I hope you will take it, Miss Scoville. With that and the clue to his intentions, which you have given me, I have no doubt that we shall find him within the week.'

'But,' objected Deborah, 'if you know where to look for him, why take the child? Why go yourself? Why not telegraph to these places?'

His answer was a look, quick, sharp and enigmatical enough to require explanation. He could not give it to her then, but later, when Reuther had left them, he said:

'Men who fly their engagements and secrete themselves, with or without a pretext, are not so easily reached. We shall have to surprise Oliver Ostrander, in order to place his father's message in his hands.'

'You may be right. But Reuther? Can she stand the excitement – the physical strain?'

'You have the harder task of the two, Mrs Scoville. Leave the little one to me. She shall not suffer.'

Deborah's response was eloquent. It was only a look, but it made his harsh features glow and his hard eye soften. Alanson Black had waited long, but his day of romance had come – and possibly hers also.

But his thoughts, if not his hopes, received a check when, with every plan made and Miss Weeks, as well as Reuther, in trembling anticipation of the journey, he encountered the triumphant figure of Flannagan coming out of Police Headquarters.

His jaunty air, his complaisant nod, admitted of but one explanation. He had told his story to the chief authorities and been listened to. Proof that he had something of actual moment to tell them; something which the District Attorney's office might feel bound to take up.

Alanson Black felt the shock of this discovery, but was glad of the warning it gave him. Plans which had seemed both simple and natural before, he now saw must be altered to suit the emergency. He could no longer hope to leave town with his little party without attracting unwelcome attention. They might even be followed. For whatever Flannagan may have told the police, there was one thing he had been unable to impart, and that was where to look for Oliver. Only Reuther held that clue, and if they once suspected this fact, she would certainly become the victim of their closest surveillance. Little Reuther, therefore, must not accompany him on his quest, but hold herself quite apart from it; or, better still, be made to act as a diversion to draw off the scent from the chief actor, which was himself. The idea was good, and one to be immediately carried out.

Continuing on to his office, he called up Miss Weeks.

'Are you there?' he asked.

Yes, she was there.

'Alone?'

Yes, Reuther was home packing.

'Nobody around?'

Nobody.

'No one listening on the line?

She was sure not.

'Very well. Listen closely and act quickly. You are not to go to – I will not mention the name; and you are not to wait for me. You are to start at the hour named, but you will buy tickets for Atlantic City, where you must get what accommodations you can. Our little friend needs to be taken out of town – not on business you understand, but to escape the unpleasantness here and to get such change as will distract her mind. Her mother cannot leave her duties, so you have undertaken to accompany the child. The rest leave to me. Have you understood all this?'

'Yes, perfectly; but –'

'Not another word, Miss Weeks. The change will do our little friend good. Trust my judgement, and ask her to do the same. Above all, do not be late for the train. Telephone at once for a cab, and forget everything but the pleasant trip before you. Oh, one minute! There's an article you had better send me. I hope you can guess what it is.'

'I think I can.'

'You know the city I am going to. Mark the package, General Delivery, and let me have it soon. That's all.'

He hung up the receiver.

At midnight he started for Washington. He gave a political reason in excuse for this trip. He did not expect to be believed; but the spy, if such had been sent, had taken the earlier train on which the two ladies had left for Atlantic City. He knew every man who got on board of the same train as himself; and none of them were in league with Police Headquarters.

The First Effort

LEAVES FROM ALANSON BLACK'S NOTEBOOK, FOUND BY REUTHER SOME MONTHS LATER, IN A VERY QUEER PLACE, VIZ.: HER MOTHER'S JEWEL-BOX

At the New Willard. Awaiting two articles – Oliver's picture and a few lines in the judge's writing requesting his son's immediate return. Meanwhile, I have made no secret of my reason for being here. All my inquiries at the desk have shown it to be particularly connected with a certain bill now before Congress, in which Shelby is vitally interested.

Perhaps I can further the interests of this bill in off minutes. I am willing to.

The picture is here, as well as the name of the hotel where the two women are staying. I have spent five minutes studying the face I must be able to recognise at first glance in any crowd. It's not a bad face; I can see his mother's looks in him. But it is not the face I used to know. Trouble develops a man.

There's a fellow here who rouses my suspicions. No one knows him; I don't myself. But he's strangely interested in me. If he's from Shelby – in other words, if he's from the detective bureau there, I've led him a chase today which must have greatly bewildered him. I'm not slow, and I'm not above mixing things. From the Cairo where our present congressman lives, I went to the Treasury, then to the White House, and then to the Smithsonian – with a few newspaper offices thrown in, and some hotels where I took pains that my interviews should not be too brief. When quite satisfied that by these various and somewhat confusing peregrinations I had thrown off any possible shadower, I fetched up at the Library where I lunched. Then, as I thought the time had come for me to enjoy myself, I took a walk about the great building, ending up with the reading room.

Here I asked for a book on a certain abstruse subject. Of course, it was not in my line, but I looked wise and spoke the name glibly. When I sat down to consult it, the man who brought it threw me a short glance which I chose to think peculiar. 'You don't have many readers for this volume?' I ventured. He smiled and answered, 'Just sent it back to the shelves. It's had a steady reader for ten days. Before that, nobody.' 'Is this your steady reader?' I asked, showing him the photograph I drew from my pocket. He stared, but said nothing. He did not have to. In a state of strange satisfaction I opened the book. It was Greek, if not worse, to me, but I meant to read a few paragraphs for the sake of appearances, and was turning over the pages in search of a promising chapter, when – talk of remarkable happenings! – there in the middle of the book was a card – his card! – left as a marker, no doubt, and on this card, an address hastily scribbled in lead pencil. It only remained for me to find that the hotel designated in this address was a Washington one, for me to recognise in this simple but strangely opportune occurrence, a coincidence – or, as *you* would say – an act of Providence as startling as those we read of in books.

The first man I accosted in regard to the location of this hotel said there was none of that name in Washington. The next, that he thought there was, but that he could not tell me where to look for it. The third, that I was within ten blocks of its doors. Did I walk? No, I took a taxi. I thought of your impatience and became impatient too. But when I got there, I stopped hurrying. I waited a full half-hour in the lobby to be sure that I had not been followed before I approached the desk and asked to see Mr Ostrander. No such person was in the hotel or had been. Then I brought out my photograph. The face was recognised, but not as that of a guest. This seemed a puzzle. But after thinking it over for a while, I came to this conclusion: that the address I saw written on the card was not his own, but that of some friend he had casually met.

This put me in a quandary. The house was full of young men; how pick out the friend? Besides, this friend was undoubtedly a transient and gone long ago. My hopes seemed likely to end in smoke – my great coincidence to prove valueless. I was so convinced of this, that I started to go; then I remembered you, and remained. I even took a room, registering myself for the second time that day, which formality over, I sat down in the office to write letters.

Oliver Ostrander is in Washington. That's something.

I cannot sleep. Indeed, I may say that this is the first time in my life when I failed to lose my cares the moment my head struck the pillow.

The cause I will now relate.

I had finished and mailed my letter to you and was just in the act of sealing another, when I heard a loud salutation uttered behind me, and turning, was witness to the meeting of two young men who had run upon each other in the open doorway. The one going out was a stranger to me and I hardly noticed him, but the one coming in was Oliver Ostrander (or his photograph greatly belied him), and in my joy at an encounter so greatly desired but so entirely unhoped for, I was on the point of rising to intercept him, when some instinct of precaution led me to glance about me first for the individual who had shown such a persistent interest in me from the moment of my arrival. There he sat, not a dozen chairs away, ostensibly reading, but with a quick eye ready for me the instant I gave him the slightest chance: a detective, as certainly as I was Black, the lawyer.

What was I to do? The boy was leaving town – was even then on his way to the station as his whole appearance and such words as he let fall amply denoted. If I let him go, would another such chance of delivering his father's message be given me? Should I not lose him altogether; while if I approached him or betrayed in any way my interest in him, the detective would recognise his prey and, if he did not arrest him on the spot, would never allow him to return to Shelby unattended. This would be to defeat the object of my journey, and recalling the judge's expression at parting, I dared not hesitate. My eyes returned with seeming unconcern to the letter I was holding and the detective's to his paper. When we both looked up again the two young men had quit the building and the business which had brought me to Washington was at an end.

But I am far from being discouraged. A fresh start with the prospect of Reuther's companionship, inspires me with more hope for my next venture.

'There is but one thing to do'

A night of stars, seen through swaying tree-tops whose leaves crisping to their fall, murmured gently of vanished hopes and approaching death.

Below, a long, low building with a lighted window here and there, surrounded by a heavy growth of trees which are but the earnest of the illimitable stretch of the Adirondack woods which painted darkness on the encircling horizon.

In the air, one other sound beside the restless murmur I have mentioned – the lap, lap of the lake whose waters bathed the bank which supported this building.

Such the scene without.

Within, Reuther seated in the glow of a hospitable fire of great logs, talking earnestly to Mr Black. As they were placed, he could see her much better than she could see him, his back being to the blaze and she, in its direct glare.

He could, therefore, study her features, without offence, and this he did, steadily and with deep interest, all the while she was talking. He was looking for signs of physical weakness or fatigue; but he found none. The pallor of her features was a natural pallor, and in their expression, new forces were becoming apparent, which give him encouragement, rather than anxiety, for the adventure whose most trying events lay still before them.

Crouching low on the hearth could be seen the diminutive figure of Miss Weeks. She had no time to waste even in a solitude as remote as this, and was crocheting busily by the firelight. Her earnestness gave character to her features which sometimes lacked significance. Reuther loved to glance at her from time to time, as she continued her conversation with Mr Black.

This is what she was saying:

'I cannot point to any one man of the many who have been about us ever since we started north. But that we have been watched and our route followed, I feel quite convinced. So does Miss Weeks. But, as you saw, no one besides ourselves left the cars at this station, and I am beginning to hope that we shall remain unmolested till we can take the trip to Tempest Lodge. How far is it, Mr Black?'

'Twenty-five miles and over a very rough mountain road. Did I not confidently expect to find Oliver there, I should not let you undertake this ride. But the inquiries I have just made lead me to hope for the best results. I was told that yesterday a young man bound for Tempest Lodge, stopped to buy a large basket of supplies at the village below us. I could not learn his name and I saw no one who could describe him; but the fact that anyone not born in these parts should choose to isolate himself so late in the year as this, in a place considered inaccessible after the snow flies, has roused much comment.'

'That looks as if – as if –'

'As if it were Oliver. So it does; and if you feel that you can ride so far, I will see that horses are saddled for us at an early hour tomorrow morning.'

'I can ride, but will Oliver be pleased to see us at Tempest Lodge. Mr Black, I had an experience in Utica which makes it very hard for me to contemplate obtruding myself upon him without some show of permission on his part. We met – that is, I saw him and he saw me; but he gave me no opportunity – that is, he did not do what he might have done, had he felt – had he thought it best to exchange a word with me.'

'Where was this? You were not long in Utica?'

'Only one night. But that was long enough for me to take a walk down one of the principal thoroughfares and it was during this walk I saw him. He was on the same side of the street as myself and rapidly coming my way, but on his eye meeting mine – I could not mistake that unconscious flash of recognition – he wheeled suddenly aside into a cross-street where I dared not follow him. Of course, he did not know what hung on even a momentary interview. That it was not for myself I –' The firelight caught something new to shine upon – a tear on lashes which yet refused to lower themselves.

Mr Black fidgeted, then put out his hand and laid it softly on hers.

'Never mind,' he grumbled; 'men are –' he didn't say what; but it wasn't anything very complimentary. 'You have this comfort,' said he: 'the man at the Lodge is undoubtedly Oliver. Had he gone West, he wouldn't have been seen in Utica three days ago.'

'I have never had any doubt about that. I expect to see him tomorrow, but I shall find it hard to utter my errand quick enough. There will be a minute when he may misunderstand me. I dread that minute.'

'Perhaps, you can avoid it. Perhaps after you have positively identified him I can do the rest. We will arrange it so, if we can.'

Her eyes flashed gratitude, then took on a new expression. She had chanced to glance again at Miss Weeks, and Miss Weeks was not looking quite natural. She was still crocheting, or trying to, but her attitude was constrained and her gaze fixed; and that gaze was not on her work, but directed towards a small object at her side, which Reuther recognised from its open lid to be the little lady's work-box.

'Something is the matter with Miss Weeks,' she confided in a low whisper to Mr Black. 'Don't turn; she's going to speak.'

But Miss Weeks did not speak. She just got up, and, with a careless motion, stood stretching herself for a moment, then sauntered up to the table and began showing her work to Reuther.

'I've made a mistake,' she pettishly complained. 'See if you can find out what's wrong.' And, giving the work into Reuther's hand, she stood watching, but with a face so pale that Mr Black was not astonished when she suddenly muttered in a very low tone:

'Don't move or show surprise. The shade of the window is up, and somebody is looking in from outside. I saw his face reflected in the mirror of my work-box. It isn't anyone I know, but he was looking very fixedly this way and may be looking yet. Now I am going to snatch my work. I don't think you're helping me one bit.'

She suited the action to the word; shook her head at Reuther and went back to her old position on the hearth.

'I was afraid of it,' murmured Reuther. 'If we take the ride tomorrow, it will not be alone. If, on the other hand, we delay our trip, we may be forestalled in the errand upon which so much depends. We are not the only ones who have heard of the strange young man at Tempest Lodge.'

The answer came with quick decision. 'There is but one thing for us to do. I will tell you what it is a little later. Go and sit on the hearth with Miss Weeks, and mind that you laugh and chat as if your minds were quite undisturbed. I am going to have a talk with our host.'

'What's that?'

'That's the cry of a loon.'

'How awful! Do they often cry like that?'

'Not often in the night-time.'

Reuther shuddered.

Mr Black regarded her anxiously. Had he done wrong to let her join him in this strange ride?

'Shall we go back and wait for broad daylight?' he asked.

'No, no. I could not bear the suspense of wondering whether all was going well and the opportunity being given you of seeing and speaking to him. We have taken such precautions – chosen so late (or should I say so early) a start – that I'm sure we have outwitted the man who is so watchful of us. But if we go back, we cannot slip away from him again; and Oliver will have to submit to an humiliation it is our duty to spare him. And the good judge, too. I don't care if the loons do cry; the night is beautiful.'

And it was, had their hearts been in tune to enjoy it. A gibbous moon had risen, and, inefficient as it was to light up the recesses of the forest, it illumined the treetops and brought out the difference between earth and sky. The road, known to the horses, if not to themselves, extended like a black ribbon under their eyes, but the patches of light which fell across it at intervals took from it the uninterrupted gloom it must have otherwise had. Mr Sloan, who was at once their guide and host, promised that dawn would be upon them before they reached the huge gully which was the one dangerous feature of the road. But as yet there were no signs of dawn; and to Reuther, as well as to Mr Black, this ride through the heart of a wilderness in a darkness which might have been that of midnight by any other measure than that of the clock, had the effect of a dream in which one is only sufficiently in touch with past commonplaces to say, 'This is a dream and not reality. I shall soon wake.' A night to remember to the end of one's days; an experience which did not seem real at the time and was never looked back upon as real – and yet, one with which neither of them would have been willing to part.

Their guide had prophesied truly. Heralded by that long cry of the loon, the dawn began to reveal itself in clearness of perspective and a certain indefinable stir in the still, shrouded spaces of the woods. Details began to appear where heretofore all had been mass. Pearl tints proclaimed the east, and presently these were replaced by a flush of delicate colour deepening into rose, and the everyday world of the mighty forest was upon them with its night mystery gone.

But not the romance of their errand, or the anxiety which both felt as to its ultimate fulfilment. This it had been easier to face when they themselves as well as all about them, were but moving shadows in each other's eyes. Full sight brought full realisation. However they might seek to cloak the fact, they could no longer disguise from themselves that the object of their journey might not be acceptable to the man in hiding at Tempest Lodge. Reuther's faith in him was strong, but even her courage faltered as she thought of the disgrace awaiting him whatever the circumstances or however he might look upon his father's imperative command to return.

But she did not draw rein, and the three continued to ride up and on. Suddenly, however, one of them showed disturbance. Mr Sloan was seen to turn his head sharply, and in another moment his two companions heard him say:

'We are followed. Ride on and leave me to take a look.'

Instinctively they also glanced back before obeying. They were just rounding the top of an abrupt hill, and expected to have an uninterrupted view of the road behind. But the masses of foliage were as yet too thick for them to see much but the autumnal red and yellow spread out below them.

'I hear them; I do not see them,' remarked their guide. 'Two horses are approaching.'

'How far are we now from the Lodge?'

'A half-hour's ride. We are just at the opening of the gully.'

'You will join us soon?'

'As quickly as I make out who are on the horses behind us.'

Reuther and the lawyer rode on. Her cheeks had gained a slight flush, but otherwise she looked unmoved. He was less at ease than she; for he had less to sustain him.

The gully, when they came to it, proved to be a formidable one. It was not only deep but precipitous, descending with the sheerness of a wall directly down from the road into a basin of enormous size, where trees stood here and there in solitary majesty, amid an area of rock forbidding to the eye and suggestive of sudden and impassable chasms. It was like circumambulating the sinuous verge of a canyon; and for the two miles they rode along its edge they saw no let-up in the steepness on one side or of the almost equally abrupt rise of towering rock on the other. It was Reuther's first experience of so precipitous a climb, and under other circumstances she might have been timid; but in her present heroic mood, it was all a part of her great adventure, and as such accepted.

The lawyer eyed her with growing admiration. He had not miscalculated her pluck.

As they were making a turn to gain the summit, they heard Mr Sloan's voice behind them. Drawing in their horses, they greeted him eagerly when he appeared.

'Were you right? Are we followed?'

'That's as may be. I didn't hear or see anything more. I waited, but nothing happened, so I came on.'

His words were surly and his looks sour; they, therefore, forebore to question him further, especially as their keenest interest lay ahead, rather than behind them. They were nearing Tempest Lodge. As it broke upon their view, perched like an eagle's eyrie on the crest of a rising peak, they drew rein, and, after a short consultation, Mr Sloan wended his way up alone. He was a well-known man throughout the whole region, and would be likely to gain admittance if anyone could. But all wished the hour had been less early.

However, somebody was up in the picturesque place. A small trail of smoke could be seen hovering above its single chimney, and promptly upon Mr Sloan's approach, a rear door swung back and an old man showed himself, but with no hospitable intent. On the contrary, he motioned the intruder back, and shouting out some very decided words, resolutely banged the door shut.

Mr Sloan turned slowly about.

'Bad luck,' he commented, upon joining his companions. 'That was Deaf Dan. He's got a warm nest here, and he's determined to keep it. 'No visitors wanted,' was what he shouted, and he didn't even hold out his hand when I offered him the letter.'

'Give me the letter,' said Reuther. 'He won't leave a lady standing out in the cold.'

Mr Sloan handed over the judge's message, and helped her down, and she in turn began to approach the place. As she did so, she eyed it with the curiosity of a hungry heart. It was a compact structure of closely cemented stone, built to resist gales and harbour a would-be recluse, even in an Adirondack winter. One end showed stacks of wood through its heavily glazed windows, and between the small stable and the west door there ran a covered way which insured communication, even when the snow lay high about the windows.

The place had a history which she learned later. At present all her thoughts were on its possible occupant and the very serious question of whether she would or would not gain admittance to him.

Mr Sloan had been repulsed from the west door; she would try the east. Oliver (if Oliver it were) was probably asleep; but she would knock, and knock, and knock; and if Deaf Dan did not open, his master soon would.

But when she found herself in face of this simple barrier, her emotion was so strong that she recoiled in spite of herself, and turned her face about as if to seek strength from the magnificence of the outlook.

But though the scene was one of splendour inconceivable, she did not see it. Her visions were all inner ones. But these were not without their strengthening power, as was soon shown. For presently she turned back and was lifting her hand to the door, when it suddenly flew open and a man appeared before her.

It was Oliver. Oliver unkempt and with signs upon him of a night's work of study or writing; but Oliver! – her lover once, but now just a stranger into whose hand she must put this letter.

She tried to stammer out her errand; but the sudden pallor, the starting eyes – the whole shocked, almost terrified appearance of the man she was facing, stopped her. She forgot the surprise, the incredulity of mind with which he would naturally hail her presence at his door in a place so remote and of such inaccessibility. She only saw that his hands had gone up and out at sight of her, and to her sensitive soul, this looked like a rebuff which, while expected, choked back her words and turned her faintly flushing cheek scarlet.

'It is not I,' burst from her lips in incoherent disclaimer of his possible thought. 'I'm just a messenger. Your father –'

'It *is* you!' Quickly his hands passed across his eyes. 'How –' Then his glance, following hers, fell on the letter which she now remembered to hold out.

'It's the copy of a telegram,' she tremblingly explained, as he continued to gaze at it without reaching to take it. 'You could not be found in Detroit and as it was important that you should receive this word from your father, I undertook to deliver it. I remembered your fondness for this place and how you once said that this is where you would like to write your book, and so I came on a venture – but not alone – Mr Black is with me and –'

'Mr Black! Who? What?' He was still staring at his father's letter; and still had made no offer to take it.

'Read this first,' said she.

Then he woke to the situation. He took the letter, and drawing her inside, shut the door while he read it. She, trembling very much, did not dare to lift her eyes to watch its effect, but she was conscious that his back and not his face was turned her way, and that the moment was the stillest one of her whole life.

Then there came a rattling noise as he crushed the letter in his hand.

'Tell me what this means,' said he, but he did not turn his head as he made this request.

'Your father must do that,' was her gentle reply. 'I was only to deliver the letter. I came – we came – thus early, because we thought – we feared we should get no opportunity later to find you here alone. There seem to be people on the road – whom – whom you might feel obliged to entertain and as your father cannot wait –'

He had wheeled about. His face confronted hers. It wore a look she did not understand and which made him seem a stranger to her. Involuntarily she took a step back.

'I must be going now,' said she, and fell – her physical weakness triumphing at last over her willpower.

Escape

'Oliver? Where is Oliver?'

These were Reuther's first words, as, coming to herself, she perceived Mr Black bending helplessly over her.

The answer was brief, almost indifferent. Alanson Black was cursing himself for allowing her to come to this house alone.

'He was here a moment ago. When he saw you begin to give signs of life, he slid out. How do you feel, my – my dear? What will your mother say?'

'But Oliver?' She was on her feet now; she had been lying on some sort of couch. 'He must – oh, I remember now. Mr Black, we must go. I have given him his father's letter.'

'We are not going till you have something to eat. Not a word. I'll –' Why did his eye wander to the nearest window, and his words trail away into silence?

Reuther turned about to see. Oliver was in front, conversing earnestly with Mr Sloan. As they looked, he dashed back into the rear of the house, and they heard his voice rise once or twice in some ineffectual commands to his deaf servant, then there came a clatter and a rush from the direction of the stable, and they saw him flash by on a gaunt but fiery horse, and take with long bounds the road up which they had just laboured. He had stopped to equip himself in some measure for this ride, but not the horse, which was without saddle or any sort of bridle but a halter strung about his neck.

This was flight; or so it appeared to Mr Sloan, as he watched the young man disappear over the brow of the hill. What Mr Black thought was not so apparent. He had no wish to discourage Reuther whose feeling was one of relief as her first word showed.

'Oliver is gone. We shall not have to hurry now and perhaps if I had a few minutes in which to rest –'

She was on the verge of fainting again.

And then Alanson Black showed of what stuff he was made. In ten minutes he had bustled about the half-deserted building, and with the aid of the dazed and uncomprehending deaf-mute, managed to prepare a cup of hot tea and a plate of steaming eggs for the weary girl.

After such an effort, Reuther felt obliged to eat, and she did; seeing which, the lawyer left her for a moment and went out to interview their guide.

'Where's the young lady?'

This from Mr Sloan.

'Eating something. Come in and have a bite; and let the horses eat, too. She must have a rest. The young fellow went off pretty quick, eh?'

'Ya-as.' The drawl was one of doubt. 'But quickness don't count. Fast or slow, he's on his way to capture – if that's what you want to know.'

'What? We are followed then?'

'There are men on the road; two, as I told you before. He can't get by them – *if* that's what he wants to do.'

'But I thought they fell back. We didn't hear them after you joined us.'

'No; they didn't come on. They didn't have to. This is the only road down the mountain, and it's one you've got to follow or go tumbling over the precipice. All they've got to do is to wait for him; and that's what I tried to tell him, but he just shook his arm at me and rode on. He might better have waited – for company.'

Mr Black cast a glance behind him, saw that the door of the house was almost closed and ventured to put another question.

'What did he ask you when he came out here?'

'Why we had chosen such an early hour to bring him his father's message.'

'And what did you say?'

'Wa'al, I said that there was another fellow down my way awful eager to see him, too; and that you were mortal anxious to get to him first. That was about it, wasn't it, sir?'

'Yes. And how did he take that?'

'He turned white, and asked me just what I meant. Then I said that someone wanted him pretty bad, for, early as it was, this stranger was up as soon as you, and had followed us into the mountains and might show up any time on the road. At which he gave me a stare, then plunged back into the house to get his hat and trot out his horse. I never saw quicker work. But it's no use; he can't escape those men. They know it, or they wouldn't have stopped where they did, waiting for him.'

Mr Black recalled the aspect of the gully, and decided that Mr Sloan was right. There could be but one end to this adventure. Oliver would be caught in a manifest effort to escape, and the judge's cup of sorrow and humiliation would be full. He felt the shame of it himself; also the folly of his own methods and of the part he had allowed Reuther to play. Beckoning to his host to follow him, he turned towards the house.

'Don't mention your fears to the young lady,' said he. 'At least, not till we are well past the gully.'

'I shan't mention anything. Don't you be afeared of that.'

And with a simultaneous effort difficult for both, they assumed a more cheerful air, and briskly entered the house.

It was not until they were well upon the road back that Reuther ventured to speak of Oliver. She was riding as far from the edge of the precipice as possible. In descent it looked very formidable to her unaccustomed eye.

'This is a dangerous road for a man to ride bareback,' she remarked. 'I'm terrified when I think of it, Mr Black. Why did he go off quite so suddenly? Is there a train he is anxious to reach? Mr Sloan, is there a train?'

'Yes, Miss, there is a train.'

'Which he can get by riding fast?'

'I've known it done!'

'Then he is excusable.' Yet her anxious glance stole ever and again to the dizzy verge towards which she now unconsciously urged her own horse till Mr Black drew her aside.

'There is nothing to fear in that direction,' said he. 'Oliver's horse is to be trusted, if not himself. Cheer up, little one, we'll soon be on more level ground and then for a quick ride and a speedy end to this suspense.'

He was rewarded by a confiding look, after which they all fell silent.

A half-hour's further descent, then a quick turn and Mr Sloan, who had ridden on before them, came galloping hastily back.

'Wait a minute,' he admonished them, putting up his hand to emphasise the appeal.

'Oh, what now?' cried Reuther, but with a rising head instead of a sinking one.

'We will see,' said Mr Black, hastening to meet their guide. 'What now?' he asked. 'Have they come together? Have the detectives got him?'

'No, not *him*; only his horse. The animal has just trotted up – riderless.'

'Good God! the child's instinct was true. He has been thrown –'

'No.' Mr Sloan's mouth was close to the lawyer's ear. 'There is another explanation. If the fellow is game, and anxious enough to reach the train to risk his neck for it, there's a path he could have taken which would get him there without his coming round this turn. I never thought it a possible thing till I saw his horse trotting on ahead of us without a rider.' Then as Reuther came ambling up, 'Young lady, don't let me scare you, but it looks now as if the young man had taken a shortcut to the station, which, so far as I know, has never been taken but by one man before. If you will draw up closer – here! give me hold of your bridle. Now look back along the edge of the precipice for about half a mile, and you will see shooting up from the gully a solitary tree whose topmost branch reaches within a few feet of the road above.'

She looked. They were at the lower end of the gully which curved up and away from this point like an enormous horseshoe. They could see the face of the precipice for miles.

'Yes,' she suddenly replied, as her glance fell on the one red splash showing against the dull grey of the cliff.

'A leap from the road, if well-timed, would land a man among some very stalwart branches. It's a risk and it takes nerve; but it succeeded once, and I dare say has succeeded again.'

'But – but – if he didn't reach – didn't catch –'

'Young lady, he's a man in a thousand. If you want the proof, look over there.'

He was pointing again, but in a very different direction now. As her anxious eye sought the place he indicated, her face flushed crimson with evanescent joy. Just where the open ground of the gully melted again into the forest, the figure of a man could be seen moving very quickly. In another moment it had disappeared amid the foliage.

'Straight for the station,' announced Mr Sloan; and, taking out his watch, added quickly; 'the train is not due for fifteen minutes. He'll catch it.'

'The train south?'

'Yes, and the train north. They pass here.'

Mr Black turned a startled eye upon the guide. But Reuther's face was still alight. She felt very happy. Their journey had not been for naught. He would have six hours' start of his pursuers; he would be that much sooner in Shelby; he would hear the accusation against him and refute it before she saw him again.

But Mr Black's thoughts were less pleasing than hers. He had never had more than a passing hope of Oliver's innocence, and now he had none at all. The young man had fled, not in response to his father's telegram, but under the impulse of his own fears. They would not find him in Shelby when they returned. They might never find him anywhere again. A pretty story to carry back to the judge.

As he dwelt upon this thought, his reflections grew more and more gloomy, and he had little to say till he reached the turn where the two men still awaited them.

In the encounter which followed no attempt was made by either party to disguise the nature of the business which had brought them thus together. The man whom Mr Black took to be a Shelby detective nodded as they met and remarked, with a quick glance at Reuther:

'So you've come without him! I'm sorry for that. I was in hopes that I might be spared the long ride up the mountain.'

Mr Black limited his answer to one of his sour smiles.

'Whose horse is this?' came in peremptory demand from the other man, with a nod towards the animal which could now be seen idly grazing by the wayside. 'And how came it on the road alone?'

'We can only give you these facts,' rejoined the lawyer. 'It came from Tempest Lodge. It started out ahead of us with the gentleman we had gone to visit on its back. We did not pass the gentleman on the road, and if he has not passed you, he must have left the road somewhere on foot. He did not go back to the Lodge.'

'Mr Black –'

'I am telling you the absolute truth. Make what you will of it. His father desires him home; and sent a message. This message this young lady undertook to deliver, and she did deliver it, with the consequences I have mentioned. If you doubt me, take your ride. It is not an easy one, and the only man remaining at the Lodge is deaf as a post.'

'Mr Black has told the whole story,' averred the guide.

They looked at Reuther.

'I have nothing to add,' said she. 'I have been terrified lest the gentleman you wish to see was thrown from the horse's back over the precipice. But perhaps he found some way of getting down on foot. He is a very strong and daring man.'

'The tree!' ejaculated the detective's companion. He was from a neighbouring locality and remembered this one natural ladder up the side of the gully.

'Yes, the tree,' acknowledged Mr Sloan. 'That, or a fall. Let us hope it was not a fall.'

As he ceased, a long screech from an approaching locomotive woke up the echoes of the forest. It was answered by another from the opposite direction. Both trains were on time. The relief felt by Reuther could not be concealed. The detective noticed it.

'I'm wasting time here,' said he. 'Excuse me, Mr Black, if I push on ahead of you. If we don't meet at the station, we shall meet in Shelby.'

Mr Black's mouth twisted grimly. He had no doubt of the latter fact.

Next minute, they were all cantering in the one direction; the detective very much in the advance.

'Let me go with you to the station,' entreated Reuther, as Mr Black held up his arms to lift her from her horse at the door of the hotel.

But his refusal was peremptory. 'You need Miss Weeks, and Miss Weeks needs you,' said he. 'I'll be back in just five minutes.' And without waiting for a second pleading look, he lifted her gently off and carried her in.

When he returned, as he did in the time specified, he had but one word for her.

'Gone,' said he.

'Thank God!' she murmured and turned to Miss Weeks with a smile.

Not having a smile to add to hers, the lawyer withdrew. Oliver was gone – but gone north.

The Vigil

When Mr Black came into Shelby, he came alone. He was anxious to get back; anxious to face his enemies if he had any; anxious to see Deborah and explain. Miss Weeks and Reuther followed on more slowly; this was better for them and better for him, and better, too, for Deborah, who must hear his story without the distraction of her daughter's presence.

It was dark when he stepped on to the platform, and darker still when he rang the bell of Judge Ostrander's house. But it was not late, and his agitation had but few minutes in which to grow, before the gate swung wide and he felt her hand in his.

She was expecting him. He had telegraphed the hour at which he should arrive, and also when to look for Reuther. Consequently there was no necessity for preliminaries, and he could ask at once for the judge and whether he was strong enough to bear disappointment.

Deborah's answer was certainly disconcerting.

'I've not seen him. He admits nobody. When I enter the library, he retreats to his bedroom. I have not even been allowed to hand him his letters. I put them on his tray when I carry in his meals.'

'He has received letters then?'

'Unimportant ones, yes.'

'None from Oliver?'

'Oh, no.'

A pause.

'Deborah?'

Another pause. The echo of that name so uttered was too sweet in her ear for her to cut it short by too hasty a reply. When she did speak, it was humbly, or should I say, wistfully.

'Yes, Mr Black.'

'I am afraid he never will hear from Oliver. The boy gave us the slip in the most remarkable manner. I will tell you when we get inside.'

She led him up the walk. She moved slowly, and he felt the influence of her discouragement. But once in the lighted parlour, she turned upon him the face he knew best – the mother face.

'Did Reuther see him?' she asked.

Then he told her the whole story.

When she had heard him through, she looked about the room they were in, with a lingering, abstracted gaze he hardly understood till he saw it fall with an indescribable aspect of sorrow upon a picture which had lately been found and rehung upon the wall. It was a portrait of Oliver's mother.

'I am disappointed,' she murmured in bitter reflection to herself. 'I did not expect Oliver to clear himself, but I did expect him to face his accusers if only for his father's sake. What am I to say now to the judge?'

'Nothing tonight. In the morning we will talk the whole subject over. I must first explain myself to Andrews, and, if possible, learn his intentions; then I shall know better what to advise.'

'Did the officer you met on your return from Tempest Lodge follow you to Shelby?'

'I have not seen him.'

'That is bad. He followed Oliver.'

'It was to be expected.'

'Oliver is in Canada?'

'Undoubtedly.'

'Which means –'

'Delay, then extradition. It's that fellow Flannagan who has brought this upon us. The wretch knows something which forbids us to hope.'

'Alas, yes.' And a silence followed, during which such entire stillness rested upon the house that a similar thought rose in both minds. Could it be that under this same roof, and only separated from them by a partition, there brooded another human being helplessly awaiting a message which would never come, and listening, but how vainly, for the step and voice for which he hungered, though they were the prelude to further shame and the signal for coming punishment.

So strong was this thought in both their minds, that the shadow deepened upon both faces, as though a presence had passed between them; and when Mr Black rose, as he very soon did, it was with an evident dread of leaving her alone with this thought.

They were lingering yet in the hall, the goodnight faltering on their lips, when suddenly their eyes flashed together in mutual question, and Deborah bent her ear towards the street.

An automobile was slowing up – stopping – stopping before the gates! Deborah turned and looked at Mr Black. Was it the police? No, for the automobile was starting up again – it was going. Whoever had come had come to stay. With eyes still on those of Mr Black, whose face showed a sudden change, she threw her hand behind her and felt wildly about for the door-knob. She had just grasped it – when the bell rang. Never had it sounded so shrill and penetrating. Never had it rung quite such a summons through this desolate house. Recoiling, she made a motion of entreaty.

'Go,' she whispered. 'Open! I cannot.'

Quickly he obeyed. She heard him pass out and down the walk, and through the first gate. Then there came a silence, followed by the opening of the second gate. Then, a sound like smothered greetings, followed by quickly advancing steps and a voice she knew:

'How is my father? Is he well? I cannot enter till I know.'

It was Oliver! – come from some distant station, or from some other line which he had believed unwatched. Tumultuous as her thoughts were, she dared not indulge in them for a moment, or give way to gratitude or any other emotion. There were words to be said – words which must be uttered on the instant and with as much imperiousness as his own.

Throwing the door wide, she called down the steps:

'Yes, he is well. Come in, Mr Ostrander, and you, too, Mr Black. Instructions have been given me by the judge, which I must deliver at once. He expects you, Oliver,' she went on, as the two men stepped in. 'But not knowing when, he bade me say to you immediately upon your entrance (and I am happy to be able to do this in Mr Black's presence), that much as he would like to be on hand to greet you, he cannot see you tonight. You may wish to go to him – but you must restrain this wish. Nor are you to talk, though he does not forbid you to listen. If you do not know what has happened here, Mr Black will tell you, but for tonight at least, and up to a certain hour tomorrow, you are to keep your own counsel. When certain persons whose names he has given me can be gotten together in this house, he will join you, giving you your first meeting in the presence of others. Afterwards he will see you alone. If these plans distress you, if you find the delay hard, I am to say that it is even harder for him than it can be for you. But circumstances compel him to act thus, and he expects you to understand and be patient. Mr Black, assure Mr Ostrander that I am not likely to overstate the judge's commands, or to add to or detract from them in the least particular – that I am simply the judge's mouthpiece.'

'You may believe that, Mr Ostrander.' Young Ostrander bowed.

'I have no doubt of the fact,' he assured her, with an unsuccessful effort to keep his trouble out of his voice. 'But as my father allows me some explanation, I shall be very glad to hear what has happened here to occasion my imperative recall.'

'Do you not read the papers, Mr Ostrander?'

'I have not looked at one since I started upon my return.'

Mr Black glanced at Deborah, who was slipping away. Then he made a move towards the parlour.

'If you will come in and sit down, Mr Ostrander, I'll tell you what you have every right to know.'

But when they found themselves alone together, Oliver's manner altered.

'One moment,' said he, before Mr Black could speak. 'I should like to ask you first of all, if Miss Scoville is better. When I left you both so suddenly at Tempest Lodge, she was not well. I –'

'She is quite recovered, Mr Ostrander.'

'And is here?'

'Not yet. I came back quickly – like yourself.'

Involuntarily their glances met in a question which perhaps neither desired to have answered. Then Oliver remarked quite simply:

'My haste seemed warranted by my father's message. Five minutes, one minute even is of great importance when you have but fifteen in which to catch a train.'

'And by such a route!'

'You know my route.' A short laugh escaped him. 'I feared the delay – possibly the interference – But why discuss these unimportant matters! I succeeded in my efforts. I am here, at my father's command, unattended and, as I believe, without the knowledge of anyone but yourself and Mrs Scoville. But your reason for these hasty summons – that is what I am ready now to hear.' And he sat down, but in such a way as to throw his face very much into the shadow.

This was a welcome circumstance to the lawyer. His task promised to be hard enough at the best. Black night had not offered too dark a screen between him and the man thus suddenly called upon to face suspicions the very shadow of which is enough to destroy a life. The hardy lawyer shrunk from uttering the words which would make the gulf imaginatively opening between them a real, if not impassable, one. Something about the young man appealed to him – something apart from his relationship to the judge – something inherent in himself. Perhaps it was the misery he betrayed. Perhaps it was the memory of Reuther's faith in him and how that faith must suffer when she saw him next. Instantaneous reflections; but epoch-making in a mind like his. Alanson Black had never hesitated before in the face of any duty, and it robbed him of confidence. But he gave no proof of this in voice or manner, as pacing the floor in alternate approach and retreat, he finally addressed the motionless figure he could no longer ignore.

'You want to know what has happened here? If you mean lately, I shall have to explain that anything which has lately occurred to distress your father or make your presence here desirable, has its birth in events which date back to days when this was your home and the bond between yourself and father the usual and natural one.'

Silence in that shadowy corner! But this the speaker had expected, and must have exacted even if Oliver had shown the least intention of speaking.

'A man was killed here in those old days – pardon me if I am too abrupt – and another man was executed for this crime. You were a boy – but you must remember.'

Again he paused; but no more in expectation of or desire for an answer than before. One must breathe between the blows he inflicts, even if one is a lawyer.

'That was twelve years ago. Not so long a time as has elapsed since you met a waif of the streets and chastised him for some petty annoyance. But both events, the great and the little, have been well remembered here in Shelby; and when Mrs Scoville came amongst us a month or so ago, with her late but substantial proofs of her husband's innocence in the matter of Etheridge's death, there came to her aid a man, who not only remembered the beating he had received as a child, but certain facts which led him to denounce by name, the party destined to bear at this late day the onus of the crime heretofore ascribed to Scoville. That name he wrote on bridges and walls; and one day, when your father left the courthouse, a mob followed him, shouting loud words which I will not repeat, but which you must understand were such as must be met and answered when the man so assailed is Judge Ostrander. Have I said enough? If so, raise your hand and I will desist for tonight.'

But no movement took place in the shadow cast by Oliver's figure on the wall before which Mr Black had paused, and presently, a voice was heard from where he sat, saying:

'You are too merciful. I do not want generalities but the naked truth. What did the men shout?'

'You have asked for a fact, and that I feel free to give you. They shouted, 'Where is Oliver, your guilty son, Oliver? You saved him at a poor man's expense, but we'll have him yet.' You asked me for the words, Mr Ostrander.'

'Yes.' The pause was long, but the 'Yes' came at last. Then another silence, and then this peremptory demand: 'But we cannot stop here, Mr Black. If I am to meet my father's wishes tomorrow, I must know the ground upon which I stand. What evidence lies back of these shouts? If you are my friend – and you have shown yourself to be such – you will tell me the whole story. I shall say nothing more.'

Mr Black was not walking now; he was standing stock-still and in the shadow also. And with this space and the double shadow between them, Alanson Black told Oliver Ostrander why the people had shouted: 'We will have him yet.'

When he had quite finished, he came into the light. He did not look in the direction he had avoided from the first, but his voice had a different note as he remarked:

'I am your father's friend, and I have promised to be yours. You may expect me here in the morning, as I am one of the few persons your father has asked to be present at your first interview. If after this interview you wish anything more from me, you have only to signify it. I am blunt, but not unfeeling, Mr Ostrander.'

A slight lift of the hand, visible now in the shadow, answered him; and with a silent bow he left the room.

In the passageway he met Deborah.

'Leave him to himself,' said he. 'Later, perhaps, you can do something for him.'

But she found this quite impossible. Oliver would neither eat nor sleep. When the early morning light came, he was sitting there still. Was his father keeping vigil also? We shall never know.

The Curtain Lifted

Ten o'clock! and one of the five listed to be present had arrived – the rector of the church which the Ostranders had formerly attended.

He was ushered into the parlour by Deborah, where he found himself received not by the judge in whose name he had been invited, but by Mr Black, the lawyer, who tendered him a simple good morning and pointed out a chair.

There was another person in the room – a young man who stood in one of the windows, gazing abstractedly out at the line of gloomy fence rising between him and the street. He had not turned at the rector's approach, and the latter had failed to recognise him.

And so with each new arrival. He neither turned nor moved at anyone's entrance, but left it to Mr Black to do the honours and make the best of a situation, difficult, if not inexplicable to all of them. Nor could it be seen that any of these men – city officials, prominent citizens and old friends, recognised his figure or suspected his identity. Beyond a passing glance his way, they betrayed neither curiosity nor interest, being probably sufficiently occupied in accounting for their own presence in the home of their once revered and now greatly maligned compeer. Judge Ostrander, attacked through his son, was about to say or do something which each and every one of them secretly thought had better be left unsaid or undone. Yet none showed any disposition to leave the place; and when, after a short, uneasy pause during which all attempts at conversation failed, they heard a slow and weighty step approaching through the hall, the suspense was such that no one but Mr Black noticed the quick whirl with which Oliver turned himself about, nor the look of mortal anguish with which he awaited the opening of the door and his father's entrance among them. No one noticed, I say, until, simultaneously with the appearance of Judge Ostrander on the threshold, a loud cry swept through the room of 'Don't! don't!' and the man they had barely noticed, flashed by them all, and fell at the judge's feet with a smothered repetition of his appeal: 'Don't, father, don't!'

Then, each man knew why he had been summoned there, and knowing, gazed earnestly at these two faces. Twelve years of unappeased longing, of smothered love, rising above doubts, persisting in spite of doubts, were concentrated into that one instant of mutual recognition. The eye of the father was upon that of the son and that of the son upon that of the father and for them, at least in this first instant of reunion, the years were forgotten and sin, sorrow and on-coming doom effaced from their mutual consciousness.

Then the tide of life flowed back into the present, and the judge, motioning to his son to rise, observed very distinctly:

'*Don't* is an ambiguous word, my son, and on your lips, at this juncture, may mislead those whom I have called here to hear the truth from us and the truth only. You have heard what happened here a few days ago. How a long-guarded, long-suppressed suspicion – so guarded and so suppressed that I had no intimation of its existence even, found vent at a moment of public indignation, and I heard you, you, Oliver Ostrander, accused to my face of having in some boyish fit of rage struck down the man for whose death another has long since paid the penalty. This you have already been told.'

'Yes.' The word cut sharply through the silence; but the fire with which the young man rose and faced them all showed him at his best. 'But surely, no person present believes it. No one can who knows you and the principles in which I have been raised. This fellow whom I beat as a boy has waited long to start this damnable report. Surely he will get no hearing from unprejudiced and intelligent men.'

'The police have listened to him. Mr Andrews, who is one of the gentlemen present, has heard his story and you see that he stands here silent, my son. And that is not all. Mrs Scoville, who has loved you like a mother, longs to believe in your innocence, and cannot.'

A low cry from the hall.

It died away unheeded.

'And Mr Black, her husband's counsel,' continued the father, in the firm, low tones of one who for many long days and nights had schooled himself for the duty of this hour, 'shares her feeling. He has tried not to; but he does. They have found evidences – you know them; proofs which might not have amounted to much had it not been for the one mischievous fact which has undermined public confidence and given point to these attacks. I refer to the life we have led and the barriers we have ourselves raised against our mutual intercourse. These have undone us. To the question, 'Why these barriers?' I can find no answer but the one which ends this struggle. Succumbing myself, I ask you to do so also. Out of the past comes a voice – the voice of Algernon Etheridge, demanding vengeance for his untimely end. It will not be gainsaid. Not satisfied with the toll we have both paid in these years of suffering and repression, unmindful of the hermit's life I have led and of the heart disappointments you have borne, its cry for punishment remains insistent. Gentlemen – hush! Oliver, it is for me to cry *don't* now – John Scoville was a guilty man – a murderer and a thief – but he did not wield the stick which killed Algernon Etheridge. Another hand raised that. No, do not look at the boy. He is innocent! Look here! look here!' And with one awful gesture, he stood still – while horror rose like a wave and engulfed the room – choking back breath and speech from every living soul there, and making a silence more awful than any sound – or so they all felt, till his voice rose again and they heard – 'You have trusted to appearances; you must trust now to my word. I am the guilty man, not Scoville, and not Oliver, though Oliver may have been in the ravine that night and even handled the bludgeon I found at my feet in the recesses of Dark Hollow.'

Then consternation spoke, and muttered cries were heard of 'Madness! It is not we who are needed here but a physician!' and dominating all, the ringing shout:

'You cannot save me so, father. I hated Etheridge and I slew him. Gentlemen,' he prayed in his agony, coming close into their midst, 'do not be misled for a moment by a father's devotion.'

His lifted head, his flashing eye, drew every look. Honour confronted them in a countenance from which all reserve had melted away. No guilt showed there; he stood among them, a heroic figure.

Slowly, and with a dread which no man might measure, the glances which had just devoured his young but virile countenance passed to that of the father. They did not leave it again. 'Son?' With what tenderness he spoke, but with what a ring of desolation. 'I understand your effort and appreciate it; but it is a useless one. You cannot deceive these friends of ours – men who have known my life. If you were in the ravine that night, so was I. If you handled John Scoville's stick, so did I, *and after you*! Let us not struggle for the execration of mankind; let it fall where it rightfully belongs. It can bring no sting keener than that to which my breast has long been subject. Or –' and here his tones sank, in a last recognition of all he was losing forever, 'if there is suffering in a once proud man flinging from him the last rag of respect with which he sought to cover the hideous nakedness of an unsuspected crime, it is lost in the joy of doing justice to the son who would take advantage of circumstances to assume his father's guilt.'

But Oliver, with a fire which nothing could damp, spoke up again:

'Gentlemen, will you see my father so degrade himself? He has dwelt so continually upon the knowledge which separated us a dozen years ago that he no longer can discriminate between the guilty and the innocent. Would he have sat in court; would he have uttered sentences; would he have kept his seat upon the bench for all these years, if he had borne within his breast this secret of personal guilt? No. It is not in human nature to play such a part. I was guilty – and I fled. Let the act speak for itself. The respect due my father must not be taken from him.'

Confession and counter-confession! What were they to think! Alanson Black, aghast at this dread dilemma, ran over in his mind all that had led him to accept Oliver's guilt as proven, and then, in immediate opposition to it, the details of that old trial and the judge's consequent life; and, voicing the helpless confusion of the others, observed with forced firmness:

'We have heard much of Oliver's wanderings in the ravine on that fatal night, but nothing of yours, Judge Ostrander. It is not enough for you to say that you were there; you must prove it.'

'The proof is in my succumbing to the shock of hearing Oliver's name associated with this crime. Had he been guilty – had our separation come through his crime and not through my own, I should have been prepared for such a contingency, and not overwhelmed by it.'

'And were you not prepared?'

'No, before God!'

The gesture accompanying this oath was a grand one, convincing in its fervour, its majesty and power.

But facts are stubborn things, and while most of those present were still thrilling under the effect of this oath, the dry voice of District Attorney Andrews was heard for the first time, in these words:

'Why, then, did you, on the night of Bela's death, stop on your way across the bridge to look back upon Dark Hollow and cry in the bitterest tones which escape human lips, "Oliver! Oliver! Oliver!" You were heard to speak this name, Judge

Ostrander,' he hastily put in, as the miserable father raised his hand in ineffectual protest. 'A man was lurking in the darkness behind you, who both saw and heard you. He may not be the most prepossessing of witnesses, but we cannot discredit his story.'

'Mr Andrews, you have no children. To the man who has, I make my last appeal. Mr Renfrew, you know the human heart both as a father and a pastor. Do you find anything unnatural in a guilty soul bemoaning its loss rather than its sin, in the spot which recalled both to his overburdened spirit?'

'No.'

The word came sharply, and it sounded decisive; but the ones which followed from Mr Andrews were no less so.

'That is not enough. We want evidence, actual evidence that you are not playing the part your son ascribes to you.'

The judge's eyes glared, then suddenly and incomprehensively softened till the quick fear that his mind as well as his memory had gone astray, vanished in a feeling none of them could have characterised, but which gave to them all an expression of awe.

'I have such evidence,' announced the judge. 'Come.'

Turning, he stepped into the hall. Oliver, with bended head and a discouraged mien, quickly followed. Alanson Black and the others, casting startled and inquiring looks at each other, brought up the rear. Deborah Scoville was nowhere to be seen.

At the door of his own room, the judge paused, and with his hand on the curtain, remarked with unexpected composure: 'You have all wondered, and others with you why for the last ten years I have kept the gates of my house shut against every comer. I am going to show you.'

And with no further word or look, scarcely even giving attention to Oliver's anguished presence, he led them into the study and from there on to that inner door known and talked of through the town as the door of mystery. This he slowly opened with the key he took from his pocket; then, pausing with the knob in his hand, he said:

'In the years which are past, but two persons beside myself have crossed this threshold, and these only under my eye. Its secret was for my own breast. Judge what my remorse has been; judge the power of my own secret self-condemnation, by what you see here.'

And, entering, he reached up, and pulled aside the carpet he had strung up over one end of the room, disclosing amid a number of loosened boards, the barred cell of a condemned convict.

'This was my bed, gentlemen, till a stranger coming into my home, made such an acknowledgment of my sin impossible!'

Dark Hollow

Later, when the boards he had loosened in anticipation of this hour were all removed, they came upon a packet of closely written words hidden in the framework of the bed.

It read as follows:

Whosoever lays hands on this MS will already be acquainted with my crime. If he would also know its cause and the full story of my hypocrisy, let him read these lines written, as it were, with my heart's blood.

I loved Algernon Etheridge; I shall never have a dearer friend. His odd ways, his lank, possibly ungainly figure crowned by a head of scholarly refinement, his amiability when pleased, his irascibility when crossed, formed a character attractive to me from its very contradictions; and after my wife's death and before my son Oliver reached a companionable age, it was in my intercourse with this man I found my most solid satisfaction.

Yet we often quarrelled. His dogmatism frequently ran counter to my views, and, being myself a man of quick and violent temper, hard words sometimes passed between us, to be forgotten the next minute in a handshake, or some other token of mutual esteem. These dissensions – if such they could be called – never took place except in the privacy of his study or mine. We thought too much of each other to display our differences of opinion abroad or even in the presence of Oliver; and however heated our arguments or whatever our topic we invariably parted friends, till one fateful night.

O God! that years of repentance, self-hatred and secret immolation can never undo the deed of an infuriated moment. Eternity may console, but it can never make me innocent of the blood of my heart's brother.

We had had our usual wordy disagreement over some petty subject in which he was no nearer wrong nor I any nearer right than we had been many times before; but for some reason I found it harder to pardon him. Perhaps some purely physical cause lay back of this; perhaps the nervous irritation incident upon a decision then pending in regard to Oliver's future, heightened my feelings and made me less reasonable than usual. The cause does not matter, the result does. For the first time in our long acquaintance, I let Algernon Etheridge leave me, without any attempt at conciliation.

If only I had halted there! If, at sight of my empty study, I had not conceived the mad notion of waylaying him at the bridge for the handshake I missed, I might have been a happy man now, and Oliver – but why dwell upon these might-have-beens! What happened was this:

Disturbed in mind, and finding myself alone in the house, Oliver having evidently gone out while we two were disputing, I decided to follow out the impulse I have mentioned. Leaving by the rear, I went down the lane to the path which serves as a shortcut to the bridge. That I did this unseen by anybody is not so strange when you consider the hour, and how the only person then living in the lane was, in all probability, in her kitchen. It would have been better for me, little as I might have recognised it at the time, had she been where she could have witnessed both my going and coming and faced me with the fact.

John Scoville, in his statement, says that after giving up his search for his little girl, he wandered up the ravine before taking the path back which led him through Dark Hollow. This was false, as well as the story he told of leaving his stick by the chestnut tree in the gully at foot of Ostrander Lane. For I was on the spot, and I know the route by which he reached Dark Hollow and also through whose agency the stick came to be there.

Read, and learn with what tricks the devil beguiles us men.

I was descending this path, heavily shadowed, as you know, by a skirting of closely growing trees and bushes, when just where it dips into the hollow, I heard the sound of a hasty foot come crashing up through the underbrush from the ravine and cross the path ahead of me. A turn in the path prevented me from seeing the man himself, but as you will perceive and as I perceived later when circumstances recalled it to my mind, I had no need to see him to know who it was or with what intent he took this method of escape from the ravine into the fields leading to the highway. Scoville's stick spoke for him, the stick which I presently tripped over and mechanically picked up, without a thought of the desperate use to which I was destined to put it.

Etheridge was coming. I could hear his whistle on Factory Road. There was no mistaking it. It was an unusually shrill one and had always been a cause of irritation to me, but at this moment it was more; it roused every antagonistic impulse within me. He whistling like a galliard, after a parting which had dissatisfied me to such an extent that I had come all this distance to ask his pardon and see his old smile again! Afterwards, long afterwards, I was able to give another interpretation to his show of apparent self-satisfaction, but then I saw nothing but the contrast it offered to my own tender regrets, and my blood began to boil and my temper rise to such a point that recrimination took the place of apology when in another moment we came together in the open space between the end of the bridge and Dark Hollow.

He was in no better mood than myself to encounter insult, and what had been a simple difference between us flamed into a quarrel which reached its culmination when he mentioned Oliver's name with a taunt, which the boy, for all his obstinate clinging to his journalistic idea, did not deserve.

Knowing my own temper, I drew back into the Hollow.

He followed me.

I tried to speak.

He took the word out of my mouth. This may have been with the intent of quelling my anger, but the tone was rasping, and noting this and not his words, my hand tightened insensibly about the stick which the devil (or John Scoville) had put in my hand. Did he see this, or was he prompted by some old memory of boyish quarrels that he should give utterance to that quick, sharp laugh of scorn! I shall never know, but ere the sound had ceased, the stick was whirling over my head – there came a crash and he fell. My friend! My friend!

Next moment the earth seemed too narrow, the heavens too contracted for my misery. That he was dead – that my blow had killed him, I never doubted for an instant. I knew it, as we know the face of Doom when once it has risen upon us. Never, never again would this lump of clay, which a few minutes before had filled the Hollow with shrillest whistling, breathe or think or speak. He was dead, dead, dead! *– and I? What was I?*

The name which no man hears unmoved, no amount of repetition makes easy to the tongue or welcome to the ear!... the name which I had heard launched in full forensic eloquence so many times in accusation against the wretches I had hardly regarded as being in the same human class as myself, rang in my ear as though intoned from the very mouth of hell. I could not escape it. I should never be able to escape it again. Though I was standing in a familiar scene – a scene I had known and frequented from childhood, I felt myself as isolated from my past and as completely set apart from my fellows as the shipwrecked mariner tossed to precarious foothold on his wave-dashed rock. I forgot that other criminals existed. In that one awful moment I was in my own eyes the only blot upon the universe – the sole inhabitant of the new world into which I had plunged – the world of crime – the world upon which I had sat in judgement before I knew –

What broke the spell? A noise? No, I heard no noise. The sense of some presence near, if not intrusive? God knows; all I can say is that, drawn, by some other will than my own, I found my glance travelling up the opposing bluff till at its top, framed between the ragged wall and towering chimney of Spencer's Folly, I saw the presence I had dreaded, the witness who was to undo me.

It was a woman – a woman with a little child in hand. I did not see her face, for she was just on the point of turning away from the dizzy verge, but nothing could have been plainer than the silhouette which these two made against the flush of that early evening sky. I see it yet in troubled dreams and desperate musings. I shall see it always; for hard upon its view, fear entered my soul, horrible, belittling fear, torturing me not with a sense of guilt but of its consequences. I had slain a man to my hurt, I a judge, just off the bench; and soon...possibly before I should see Oliver again...I should be branded from end to end of the town with that name which had made such havoc in my mind when I first saw Algernon Etheridge lying stark before me.

I longed to cry out – to voice my despair in the spot where my sin had found me out; but my throat had closed, and the blood in my veins ceased flowing. As long as I could catch a glimpse of this woman's fluttering skirt as she retreated through the ruins, I stood there, self-convicted, above the man I had slain, staring up at that blotch of shining sky which was as the gate of hell to me. Not till their two figures had disappeared and it was quite clear again did the instinct of self-preservation return, and with it the thought of flight.

But where could I fly? No spot in the wide world was secret enough to conceal me now. I was a marked man.

Better to stand my ground, and take the consequences, than to act the coward's part and slink away like those other men of blood I had so often sat in judgement upon.

Had I but followed this impulse! Had I but gone among my fellows, shown them the mark of Cain upon my forehead, and prayed, not for indulgence, but punishment, what days of gnawing misery I should have been spared!

But the horror of what lay at my feet drove me from the Hollow and drove me the wrong way. As my steps fell mechanically into the trail down which I had come in innocence and kindly purpose only a few minutes before, a startling thought shot through my benumbed mind. The woman had shown no haste in her turning! There had been a naturalness in her movement, a dignity and a grace which spoke of ease, not shock. What if she had not seen! What if my deed was as yet unknown! Might I not have time for – for what? I did not stop to think; I just pressed on, saying to myself, 'Let Providence decide. If I meet anyone before I reach my own door, my doom is settled. If I do not –'

And I did not. As I turned into the lane from the ravine I heard a sound far down the slope, but it was too distant to create apprehension, and I went calmly on, forcing myself into my usual leisurely gait, if only to gain some control over my own emotions before coming under Oliver's eye.

That sound I have never understood. It could not have been Scoville since in the short time which had passed, he could not have fled from the point where I heard him last into the ravine below Ostrander Lane. But if not he, who was it? Or if it was he, and some other hand threw his stick across my path, whose was this hand and why have we never heard anything about it? It is a question which sometimes floats through my mind, but I did not give it a thought then. I was within sight of home and Oliver's possible presence; and all other dread was as nothing in comparison to what I felt at the prospect of meeting my boy's eye. My boy's eye! my greatest dread then, and my greatest dread still! In my terror of it I walked as to my doom.

The house which I had left empty, I found empty; Oliver had not yet returned. The absolute stillness of the rooms seemed appalling. Instinctively, I looked up at the clock. It had stopped. Not at the minute – I do not say it was at the minute – but near, very near the time when from an innocent man I became a guilty one. Appalled at the discovery, I fled to the front. Opening the door, I looked out. Not a creature in sight, and not a sound to be heard. The road was as lonely and seemingly as forsaken as the house. Had time stopped here too? Were the world and its interests at a pause in horror of my deed? For a moment I believed it; then more natural sensations intervened and, rejoicing at this lack of disturbance where disturbance meant discovery, I stepped inside again and went and sat down in my own room.

My own room! Was it mine any longer? Its walls looked strange; the petty objects of my daily handling, unfamiliar. The change in myself infected everything I saw. I might have been in another man's house for all connection these things seemed to have with me or my life. Like one set apart on an unapproachable shore, I stretched hands in vain towards all that I had known and all that had been of value to me.

But as the minutes passed, as the hands of the clock I had hastily rewound moved slowly round the dial, I began to lose this feeling. Hope which I thought quite dead slowly revived. Nothing had happened, and perhaps nothing would. Men had been killed before, and the slayer passed unrecognised. Why might it not be so in my case? If the woman continued to remain silent; if for any reason she had not witnessed the blow or the striker, who else was there to connect me with an assault committed a quarter of a mile away? No one knew of the quarrel; and if they did, who could be so daring as to associate one of my name with an action so brutal? A judge slay his friend! It would take evidence of a very marked character to make even my political enemies believe that.

As the twilight deepened I rose from my seat and lit the gas. I must not be found skulking in the dark. Then I began to count the ticks measuring off the hour. If thirty minutes more passed without a rush from without, I might hope. If twenty? – if ten? – then it was five! then it was – ah, at last! The gate had clanged to. They were coming. I could hear steps – voices – a loud ring at the bell. Laying down the pen I had taken up mechanically, I moved slowly towards the front. Should I light the hall gas as I went by? It was a natural action, and, being natural, would show unconcern. But I feared the betrayal which my ashy face and trembling hands might make. Agitation after the news was to be expected, but not before! So I left the hall dark when I opened the door.

And thus decided my future.

For in the faces of the small crowd which blocked the doorway, I detected nothing but commiseration; and when a voice spoke and I heard Oliver's accents surcharged with nothing more grievous than pity, I realised that my secret was as yet unshared, and seeing that no man suspected me, I forebore to declare my guilt to anyone.

This sudden restoration from soundless depths into the pure air of respect and sympathy confused me; and beyond the words killed! struck down by the bridge! *I heard little, till slowly, dully like the call of a bell issuing from a smothering mist, I caught the sound of a name and then the words, 'He did it just for the watch'; which hardly conveyed meaning to me, so full was I of Oliver's look and Oliver's tone and the way his arm supported me as he chided them for their abruptness and endeavoured to lead me away.*

But the name! It stuck in my ear and gradually it dawned upon my consciousness that another man had been arrested for my crime and that the safety, the reverence and the commiseration that were so dear to me had been bought at a price no man of honour might pay.

But I was no longer a man of honour. I was a wretched criminal swaying above a gulf of infamy in which I had seen others swallowed but had never dreamed of being engulfed myself. I never thought of letting myself go – not at this crisis – not while my heart was warm with its resurgence into the old life.

And so I let pass this second opportunity for confession. Afterwards, it was too late – or seemed too late to my demoralised judgement.

My first real awakening to the extraordinary horrors of my position was when I realised that circumstances were likely to force me into presiding over the trial of the man Scoville. This I felt to be beyond even my rapidly hardening conscience. I made great efforts to evade it, but they all failed. Then I feigned sickness, only to realise that my place would be taken by Judge Grosvenor, a notoriously prejudiced man. If he sat, it would go hard with the prisoner, and I wanted the prisoner acquitted. I had no grudge against John Scoville. I was grateful to him. By his own confession he was a thief, but he was no murderer, and his bad repute had stood me in good stead. Attention had been so drawn to him by the circumstances in which the devil had entangled him, that it had never even glanced my way and now never would. Of course, I wanted to save him, and if the only help I could now give him was to sit as judge upon his case, then would I sit as judge whatever mental torture it involved.

Sending for Mr Black, I asked him point-blank whether in face of the circumstance that the victim of this murder was my best friend, he would not prefer to plead his case before Judge Grosvenor. He answered no: that he had more confidence in my equity even under these circumstances than in that of my able, but headstrong, colleague; and prayed me to get well. He did not say that he expected me on this very account to show even more favour towards his client than I might otherwise have done, but I am sure that he meant it; and, taking his attitude as an omen, I obeyed his injunction and was soon well enough to take my seat upon the bench.

No one will expect me to enlarge upon the sufferings of that time. By some I was thought stoical; by others, a prey to such grief that only my duty as judge kept me to my task. Neither opinion was true. What men saw facing them from the bench was an automaton wound up to do so much work each day. The real Ostrander was not there, but stood, an unseen presence at the bar, undergoing trial side by side with John Scoville, for a crime to make angels weep and humanity hide its head: hypocrisy!

But the days went by and the inexorable hour drew nigh for the accused man's release or condemnation. Circumstances were against him – so was his bearing which I alone understood. If, as all felt, it was that of a guilty man, it was so because he had been guilty in intent if not in fact. He had meant to attack Etheridge. He had run down the ravine for that purpose, knowing my old friend's whistle and envying him his watch. Or why his foolish story of having left his stick behind him at the chestnut? But the sound of my approaching steps higher up on the path had stopped him in mid-career and sent him rushing up the slope ahead of me. When he came back after a short circuit of the fields beyond, it was to find his crime forestalled and by the very weapon he had thrown into the Hollow as he went scurrying by. It was the shock of this discovery, heightened by the use he made of it to secure the booty thus thrown in his way without crime, which gave him the hangdog look we all noted. That there were other reasons – that the place recalled another scene of brutality in which intention had been followed by act, I did not then know. It was sufficient to me then that my safety was secured by his own guilty consciousness and the prevarications into which it led him. Instead of owning up to the encounter he had so barely escaped, he confined himself to the simple declaration of having heard voices somewhere near the bridge, which to all who know the ravine appeared impossible under the conditions named.

Yet, for all these incongruities and the failure of his counsel to produce any definite impression by the prisoner's persistent denial of having whittled the stick or even of having carried it into Dark Hollow, I expected a verdict in his favour. Indeed, I was so confident of it that I suffered less during the absence of the jury than at any other time, and when they returned, with that air of solemn decision which proclaims unanimity of mind and a ready verdict, I was so prepared for his acquittal that for the first time since the opening of the trial, I felt myself a being of flesh and blood, with human sentiments and hopes. And it was:

'Guilty!'

When I woke to a full realisation of what this entailed (for I must have lost consciousness for a minute, though no one seemed to notice), the one fact staring me in the face – staring as a live thing stares – was that it would devolve upon me to pronounce his sentence; upon me, Archibald Ostrander, an automaton no longer, but a man realising to the full his part in this miscarriage of justice.

Somehow, strange as it may appear, I had thought little of this possibility previous to this moment. I found myself upon the brink of this new gulf before the dizziness of my escape from the other had fully passed. Do you wonder that I recoiled, sought to gain time, put off delivering the sentence from day to day? I had sinned – sinned irredeemably – but there are depths of infamy beyond which a man cannot go. I had reached that point. Chaos confronted me, and in contemplation of it, I fell ill.

What saved me? A new discovery, and the loving sympathy of my son Oliver. One night – a momentous one to me – he came to my room and, closing the door behind him, stood with his back to it, contemplating me in a way that startled me.

What had happened? What lay behind this new and penetrating look, this anxious and yet persistent manner? I dared not think. I dared not yield to the terror which must follow thought. Terror blanches the cheek and my cheek must never blanch under anybody's scrutiny. Never, never, so long as I lived.

'Father,' – the tone quieted me, for I knew from its gentleness that he was hesitating to speak more on his own account than on mine – 'you are not looking well; this thing worries you. I hate to see you like this. Is it just the loss of your old friend, or – or –'

He faltered, not knowing how to proceed. There was nothing strange in this. There could not have been much encouragement in my expression. I was holding on to myself with much too convulsive a grasp.

'Sometimes I think,' he recommenced, 'that you don't feel quite sure of this man Scoville's guilt. Is that so? Tell me, father.'

I did not know what to make of him. There was no shrinking from me; no conscious or unconscious accusation in voice or look, but there was a desire to know, and a certain latent resolve behind it all that marked the line between obedient boyhood and thinking, determining man.

With all my dread – a dread so great I felt the first grasp of age upon my heartstrings at that moment – I recognised no other course than to meet this inquiry of his with the truth – that is, with just so much of the truth as was needed. No more, not one jot more. I, therefore, answered, and with a show of self-possession at which I now wonder:

'You are not far from right, Oliver. I have had moments of doubt. The evidence, as you must have noticed, is purely circumstantial.'

'But a jury has convicted him.'

'Yes.'

'On the evidence you mention?'

'Yes.'

'What evidence would satisfy you? *What would* you *consider a conclusive proof of guilt?'*

I told him in the set phrases of my profession.

'Then,' he declared as I finished, 'you may rest easy as to this man's right to receive a sentence of death.'

I could not trust my ears.

'I know from personal observation,' he proceeded, approaching me with a firm step, 'that he is not only capable of the crime for which he has been convicted, but that he has actually committed one under similar circumstances, and possibly for the same end.'

And he told me the story of that night of storm and bloodshed, a story which will be found lying near this, in my alcove of shame and contrition.

It had an overwhelming effect upon me. I had been very near death. Suicide must have ended the struggle in which I was engaged, had not this knowledge of actual and unpunished crime come to ease my conscience. John Scoville was worthy of death, and, being so, should receive the full reward of his deed. I need hesitate no longer.

That night I slept.

But there came a night when I did not. After the penalty had been paid and to most men's eyes that episode was over, I turned the first page of that volume of slow retribution which is the doom of the man who sins from impulse, and has the recoil of his own nature to face relentlessly to the end of his days.

Scoville was in his grave.

I was alive.

Scoville had shot a man for his money.

I had struck a man down in my wrath.

Scoville's widow and little child must face a cold and unsympathetic world, with small means and disgrace rising, like a wall, between them and social sympathy, if not between them and the actual means of living.

Oliver's future faced him untouched. No shadow lay across his path to hinder his happiness or to mar his chances.

The results were unequal. I began to see them so, and feel the gnawing of that deathless worm whose ravages lay waste the breast, while hand and brain fulfil their routine of work, as though all were well and the foundations of life unshaken.

I suffered as only cowards suffer. I held on to honour; I held on to home; I held on to Oliver, but with misery for my companion and a self-contempt which nothing could abate. Each time I mounted the bench, I felt a tug at my arm as of a visible, restraining presence. Each time I returned to my home and met the clear eye of Oliver beaming upon me with its ever growing promise of future comradeship, I experienced a rebellion against my own happiness which opened my eyes to my own nature and its inevitable demand. I must give up Oliver; or yield my honours, make a full confession and accept whatever consequences it might bring. I am a proud man, and the latter alternative was beyond me. With each passing day, the certainty of this became more absolute and more fixed. In every man's nature there lurk possibilities of action which he only recognises under stress, also impossibilities which stretch like an iron barrier between him and the excellence he craves. I had come up against such an impossibility. I could forego pleasure, travel, social intercourse, and even the companionship of the one being in whom all my hopes centred, but I could not, of my own volition, pass from the judge's bench to the felon's cell. There I struck the immovable, the impassable.

I decided in one awful night of renunciation that I would send Oliver out of my life.

The next day I told him abruptly...hurting him to spare myself...that I had decided after long and mature thought to yield to his desire for journalism, and that I would start him in his career and maintain him in it for three years if he would subscribe to the following conditions:

They were the hardest a loving father ever imposed upon a dutiful and loving son.

First: he was to leave home immediately...within a few hours, in fact.

Secondly: he was to regard all relations between us as finished; we were to be strangers henceforth in every particular save that of the money obligation already mentioned.

Thirdly: he was never to acknowledge this compact, or to cast any slur upon the father whose reasons for this apparently unnatural conduct were quite disconnected with any fault of his or any desire to punish or reprove.

Fourthly: he was to pray for his father every night of his life before he slept.

Was this last a confession? Had I meant it to be such? If so, it missed its point. It awed but did not enlighten him. I had to contend with his compunctions, as well as with his grief and dismay. It was an hour of struggle on his part and of implacable resolution on mine. Nothing but such hardness on my part would have served me. Had I faltered once he would have won me over, and the tale of my sleepless nights been repeated. I did not falter; and when the midnight stroke rang through the house that night, it separated by its peal, a sin-beclouded but human past from a future arid with solitude and bereft of the one possession to retain which my sin had been hidden.

I was a father without a son – as lonely and as desolate as though the separation between us were that of the grave I had merited and so weakly shunned.

And thus I lived for a year.

But I was not yet satisfied.

The toll I had paid to Grief did not seem to me a sufficient punishment for a crime which entailed imprisonment if not death. How could I insure for myself the extreme punishment which my peace demanded, without bringing down upon me the full consequences I refused to accept.

You have seen today how I ultimately answered this question. A convict's bed! a convict's isolation.

Bela served me in this; Bela who knew my secret and knowing continued to love me. He gathered up these rods singly and in distant places and set them up across the alcove in my room. He had been a convict once himself.

Being now in my rightful place, I could sleep again.

But after some weeks of this, fresh fears arose. An accident was possible. For all Bela's precautions, someone might gain access to this room. This would mean the discovery of my secret. Some new method must be devised for securing me absolutely against intrusion. Entrance into my simple, almost unguarded cottage must be made impossible. A close fence should replace the pickets now surrounding it – a fence with a gate having its own lock.

And this fence was built.

This should have been enough. But guilt has terrors unknown to innocence. One day I caught a small boy peering through an infinitesimal crack in the fence, and, remembering the window grilled with iron with which Bela had replaced the cheerful casement in my den of punishment, I realised how easily an opening might be made between the boards for the convenience of a curious eye anxious to penetrate the mystery of my seclusion.

And so it came about that the inner fence was put up.

This settled my position in the town. No more visits. All social life was over.

It was meet. I was satisfied at last. I could now give my whole mind to my one remaining duty. I lived only while on the bench.

March Fifth, 1898.
There is a dream which comes to me often: a vision which I often see.

It is that of two broken and irregular walls standing apart against a background of roseate sky. Between these walls the figures of a woman and child, turning about to go.

The bridge I never see, nor the face of the man who died for my sin; but this I see always: the gaunt ruins of Spencer's Folly and the figure of a woman leading away a little child.

That woman lives. I know now who she is. Her testimony was uttered before me in court, and was not one to rouse my apprehensions. My crime was unwitnessed by her, and for years she has been a stranger to this town. But I have a superstitious horror of seeing her again, while believing that the day will come when I shall do so. When this occurs, when I look up and find her in my path, I shall know that my sin has found me out and that the end is near.

1909
O shade of Algernon Etheridge, unforgetting and unforgiving! The woman has appeared! She stood in this room today. Verily, years are nothing with God.

Added later.
I thought I knew what awaited me if my hour ever came. But who can understand the ways of Providence or where the finger of retributive Justice will point. It is Oliver's name and not mine which has become the sport of calumny. Oliver's! Could the irony of life go further! Oliver's!

There is nothing against him, and such folly must soon die out; but to see doubt in Mrs Scoville's eyes is horrible in itself and to eliminate it I may have to show her Oliver's account of that long-forgotten night of crime in Spencer's Folly. It is naively written and reveals a clean, if reticent, nature; but that its effect may be unquestionable I will insert a few lines to cover any possible misinterpretation of his manner or conduct. There is an open space, and our handwritings were always strangely alike. Only our e's differed, and I will be careful with the e's.

Her *confidence must be restored at all hazards.*

My last foolish attempt has undone me. Nothing remains now but that sacrifice of self which should have been made twelve years ago.

Sunset

'I do not wish to seem selfish, Oliver, but sit a little nearer the window where I can see you whenever I open my eyes. Twelve years is a long time to make up, and I have such a little while in which to do it.'

Oliver moved. The moisture sprang to his eyes as he did so. He had caught a glimpse of the face on the pillow and the changes made in a week were very apparent. Always erect, his father had towered above them then even in his self-abasement, but he looked now as though twenty years, instead of a few days, had passed over his stately head and bowed his incomparable figure. And not that alone. His expression was different. Had Oliver not seen him in his old likeness for that one terrible half-hour, he would not know these features, so sunken, yet so eloquent with the peace of one for whom all struggle is over, and the haven of his long rest near.

The heart, which had held unflinchingly to its task through every stress of self-torture, succumbed under the relief of confession, and as he himself had said, there was but little time left him to fill his eyes and heart with the sight of this strong man who had replaced his boy Oliver.

He had hungered so for his presence even in those days of final shrinking and dismay. And now, the doubts, the dread, the inexpressible humiliation are all in the past and there remains only this – to feast his eyes where his heart has so long feasted, and to thank God for the blessedness of a speedy going, which has taken the sword from the hand of Justice and saved Oliver the anguished sight of a father's public humiliation.

Had he been able at this moment to look beyond the fences which his fear had reared, he would have seen at either gate a silent figure guarding the walk, and recalled, perhaps, the horror of other days when at the contemplation of such a prospect, his spirit recoiled upon itself in unimaginable horror and revolt. And yet, who knows! Life's passions fade when the heart is at peace. And Archibald Ostrander's heart was at peace. Why, his next words will show.

'Oliver' – his voice was low but very distinct, 'never have a secret; never hide within your bosom a thought you fear the world to know. If you've done wrong – if you have disobeyed the law either of God or man – seek not to hide what can never be hidden so long as God reigns or men make laws. I have suffered, as few men have suffered and kept their reason intact. Now that my wickedness is known, the whole page of my life defaced, content has come again. I am no longer a deceiver, my very worst is known.'

'Oliver?' – This some minutes later. 'Are we alone?'

'Quite alone, father. Mrs Scoville is busy and Reuther – Reuther is in the room above. I can hear her light step overhead.'

The judge was silent. He was gazing wistfully at the wall where hung the portrait of his young wife. He was no longer in his own room, but in the cheery front parlour. This Deborah had insisted upon. There was, therefore, nothing to distract him from the contemplation I have mentioned.

'There are things I want to say to you. Not many; you already know my story. But I do not know yours, and I cannot die till I do. What took you into the ravine that evening, Oliver, and why, having picked up the stick, did you fling it from you and fly back to the highway? For the reason I ascribed to Scoville? Tell me, that no cloud may remain between us. Let me know your heart as well as you now know mine.'

The reply brought the blood back into his fading cheek.

'Father, I have already explained all this to Mr Andrews, and now I will explain it to you. I never liked Mr Etheridge as well as you did, and I brooded incessantly in those days over the influence which he seemed to exert over you in regard to my future career. But I never dreamed of doing him a harm, and never supposed that I could so much as attempt any argument with him on my own behalf till that very night of infernal complications and coincidences. The cause of this change was as follows: I had gone upstairs, you remember, leaving you alone with him as I knew you desired. How I came to be in the room above I don't remember, but I was there and leaning out of the window directly over the porch when you and Mr Etheridge came out and stood in some final debate on the steps below. He was talking and you were listening, and never shall I forget the effect his words and tones had upon me. I had supposed him devoted to you, and here he was addressing you tartly and in an ungracious manner which bespoke a man very different from the one I had been taught to look upon as superior. The awe of years yielded before this display, and finding him just human like the rest of us, the courage which I had always lacked in approaching him took instant possession of me, and I determined with a boy's unreasoning impulse to subject him to a personal appeal not to add his influence to the distaste you at present felt for the career upon which I had set my heart. Nothing could have been more foolish and nothing more natural, perhaps, than the act which followed. I ran down into the ravine with the wild intention, so strangely duplicated in yourself a few minutes later, of meeting and pleading my cause with him at the bridge, but unlike you, I took the middle of the ravine for my road and not the secluded path at the side. It was this which determined our fate, father, for here I ran up against the chestnut tree, saw the stick and, catching it up without further thought than of the facility it offered for whittling, started with it down the ravine. Scoville was not in sight. The moment was the one when he had quit looking for Reuther and wandered away up the ravine. I have thought since that perhaps the glimpse he had got of his little one peering from the scene of his crime may have stirred even his guilty conscience and sent him off on this purposeless ramble; but, however this was, I did not see him or anybody else as I took my way leisurely down towards the bridge, whittling at the stick and thinking of what I should say to Mr Etheridge when I met him. And now for Fate's final and most fatal touch! Nothing which came into my mind struck me quite favourably. The encounter which seemed such a very simple matter when I first contemplated it, began to assume quite a different aspect as the moment for it approached. By the time I had come abreast of the hollow, I was tired of the whole business, and hearing his whistle and knowing by it that he was very near, I plunged up the slope to avoid him, and hurried straight away into town. That is my story, father. If I heard your steps approaching as I plunged across the path into which I had thrown the stick in my anger at having broken the point of my knife-blade upon it, I thought nothing of them then. Afterwards I believed them to be Scoville's, which may account to you for my silence about this whole matter both before and during the trial. I was afraid of the witness stand and of what might be elicited from me if I once got into the hands of the lawyers. My abominable reticence in regard to his former crime would be brought up against me, and I was yet too young, too shy and uninformed to face such an ordeal of my own volition. Unhappily, I was not forced into it, and – but we will not talk of that, father.'

'Son,' – a long silence had intervened, – 'there is one thing more. When – how – did you first learn my real reason for sending you from home? I saw that my position was understood by you when our eyes first met in this room. But twelve years had passed since you left this house in ignorance of all but my unnatural attitude towards you. When, Oliver, when?'

'That I cannot answer, father; it was just a conviction which dawned gradually upon me. Now, it seems as if I had known it always; but that isn't so. A boy doesn't reason; and it took reasoning for me to – to accept –'

'Yes, I understand. And that was your secret! Oh, Oliver, I shall never ask for your forgiveness. I am not worthy it. I only ask that you will not let pride or any other evil passion stand in the way of the happiness I see in the future for you. I cannot take from you the shame of my crime and long deception, but spare me this final sorrow! There is nothing to part you from Reuther now. Alike unhappy in your parentage, you can start on equal terms, and love will do the rest. Say that you will marry her, Oliver, and let me see her smile before I die.'

'Marry her? Oh, father, will such an angel marry me?'

'No, but such a woman might.'

Oliver came near, and stooped over his father's bed.

'Father, if love and attention to my profession can make a success of the life you prize, they shall have their opportunity.'

The father smiled. If it fell to others to remember him as he appeared in his mysterious prime, to Oliver it was given to recall him as he looked then with the light on his face and the last tear he was ever to shed glittering in his fading eye.

'God is good,' came from the bed; then the solemnity of death settled over the room.

The soft footfalls overhead ceased. The long hush had brought the two women to the door where they stood sobbing. Oliver was on his knees beside the bed, his head buried in his arms. On the face so near him there rested a ray from the westering sun; but the glitter was gone from the eye and the unrest from the heart. No more weary vigils in a room dedicated to remorse and self-punishment. No more weary circling of the house in the dark lane whose fences barred out the hurrying figure within from every eye but that of Heaven. Peace for him; and for Reuther and Oliver, hope!

Biographical note

Born in New York in 1846, Anna Katharine Green was the daughter of a prominent criminal lawyer. Her father remarried following the death of her mother and the family moved from Brooklyn to Buffalo.

Poetry was Green's first love, but when her verse failed to sell, she soon turned her hand to detective fiction. Her first novel, *The Leavenworth Case* (1878), was an instant best-seller, spawning numerous imitations and drawing praise from all quarters. Her debut even caused a debate in the Pennsylvania State over whether the book could 'really have been written by a woman'.

Green went on to write more than forty detective novels over the course of her career. Featuring young amateur detectives, she is said to have created the first female detectives in American fiction. Agatha Christie paid tribute to Green in her autobiography and indeed in one Agatha Christie novel, Hercule Poirot praises a Green novel saying 'It is admirable... One savours its period atmosphere, its studied and deliberate melodrama... An excellent psychological study.' President Wilson praised her books for giving him the 'most authentic thrills'. And before he attained the fame he enjoys today, a young Arthur Conan Doyle even sought Green out while touring America as he wanted to meet the writer he so admired.

Anna Katharine Green's novels, with their combination of mystery and romance, and their use of women detectives in domestic settings and modern scientific methods, changed the face of modern detective fiction for ever. Her pioneering work eventually earned her the epithet 'the mother of the detective novel'. She died in Buffalo, New York in 1935.

Under our three imprints, Hesperus Press publishes over 300 books by many of the greatest figures in worldwide literary history, as well as contemporary and debut authors well worth discovering.

Hesperus Classics handpicks the best of worldwide and translated literature, introducing forgotten and neglected books to new generations.

Hesperus Nova showcases quality contemporary fiction and non-fiction designed to entertain and inspire.

Hesperus Minor rediscovers well-loved children's books from the past – these are books which will bring back fond memories for adults, which they will want to share with their children and loved ones.

SELECTED TITLES FROM HESPERUS PRESS

Author	*Title*	Foreword writer
Pietro Aretino	*The School of Whoredom*	Paul Bailey
Pietro Aretino	*The Secret Life of Nuns*	
Jane Austen	*Lesley Castle*	Zoë Heller
Jane Austen	*Love and Friendship*	Fay Weldon
Honoré de Balzac	*Colonel Chabert*	A.N. Wilson
Charles Baudelaire	*On Wine and Hashish*	Margaret Drabble
Giovanni Boccaccio	*Life of Dante*	A.N. Wilson
Charlotte Brontë	*The Spell*	
Emily Brontë	*Poems of Solitude*	Helen Dunmore
Mikhail Bulgakov	*Fatal Eggs*	Doris Lessing
Mikhail Bulgakov	*The Heart of a Dog*	A.S. Byatt
Giacomo Casanova	*The Duel*	Tim Parks
Miguel de Cervantes	*The Dialogue of the Dogs*	Ben Okri
Geoffrey Chaucer	*The Parliament of Birds*	
Anton Chekhov	*The Story of a Nobody*	Louis de Bernières
Anton Chekhov	*Three Years*	William Fiennes
Wilkie Collins	*The Frozen Deep*	
Joseph Conrad	*Heart of Darkness*	A.N. Wilson
Joseph Conrad	*The Return*	Colm Tóibín
Gabriele D'Annunzio	*The Book of the Virgins*	Tim Parks
Dante Alighieri	*The Divine Comedy: Inferno*	
Dante Alighieri	*New Life*	Louis de Bernières
Daniel Defoe	*The King of Pirates*	Peter Ackroyd
Marquis de Sade	*Incest*	Janet Street-Porter
Charles Dickens	*The Haunted House*	Peter Ackroyd
Charles Dickens	*A House to Let*	
Fyodor Dostoevsky	The Double	Jeremy Dyson
Fyodor Dostoevsky	Poor People	Charlotte Hobson
Alexandre Dumas	*One Thousand and One Ghosts*	

George Eliot	*Amos Barton*	Matthew Sweet
Henry Fielding	*Jonathan Wild the Great*	Peter Ackroyd
F. Scott Fitzgerald	*The Popular Girl*	Helen Dunmore
Gustave Flaubert	Memoirs of a Madman	Germaine Greer
Ugo Foscolo	*Last Letters of Jacopo Ortis*	Valerio Massimo Manfredi
Elizabeth Gaskell	*Lois the Witch*	Jenny Uglow
Théophile Gautier	*The Jinx*	Gilbert Adair
André Gide	*Theseus*	
Johann Wolfgang von Goethe	*The Man of Fifty*	A.S. Byatt
Nikolai Gogol	*The Squabble*	Patrick McCabe
E.T.A. Hoffmann	*Mademoiselle de Scudéri*	Gilbert Adair
Victor Hugo	*The Last Day of a Condemned Man*	Libby Purves
Joris-Karl Huysmans	*With the Flow*	Simon Callow
Henry James	*In the Cage*	Libby Purves
Franz Kafka	*Metamorphosis*	Martin Jarvis
Franz Kafka	*The Trial*	Zadie Smith
John Keats	*Fugitive Poems*	Andrew Motion
Heinrich von Kleist	*The Marquise of O–*	Andrew Miller
Mikhail Lermontov	*A Hero of Our Time*	Doris Lessing
Nikolai Leskov	*Lady Macbeth of Mtsensk*	Gilbert Adair
Carlo Levi	*Words are Stones*	Anita Desai
Xavier de Maistre	*A Journey Around my Room*	Alain de Botton
André Malraux	*The Way of the Kings*	Rachel Seiffert
Katherine Mansfield	*Prelude*	William Boyd
Edgar Lee Masters	*Spoon River Anthology*	Shena Mackay
Guy de Maupassant	*Butterball*	Germaine Greer
Prosper Mérimée	*Carmen*	Philip Pullman
Sir Thomas More	*The History of King Richard III*	Sister Wendy Beckett
Sándor Petőfi	*John the Valiant*	George Szirtes
Francis Petrarch	*My Secret Book*	Germaine Greer